A midnight vis

"Alex?" Nicki sat up ... d beneath her sheet. ... n here scaring me ha... ...e night? Who do you think you are?"

"Your first lover?" He sat down on the bed, much too close to her. She could feel the heat of him against her hip right through the sheet. "Talk to me, Nicki. Tell me what you saw last night."

"Why don't you tell me why you're here? Why now, when you've been in town for months?"

"You knew that?"

"That you were back?" She hoped he didn't hear the pain she tried to bury deep in her heart. "Have you been gone so long you've forgotten what it's like to live in a small town?"

His hand stroked her cheek. The caress made her shiver. "You're still soft as midnight."

She didn't want to respond to his touch, but it would have been easier to stop breathing. She stared into his eyes and tried not to want him anymore. "We aren't the same people, Alex."

His mouth descended, covering hers. Firm lips demanded a response. This wasn't the kiss of her dreams, or her memories. This was an assault of raw passion.

He broke away. "Yes, we are."

Dear Reader,

I've been fascinated by Alex Coughlin since he appeared in *For His Daughter*. The man just can't seem to stay out of trouble. Since he insists on popping up, I decided he'd better explain why he walks so close to the edge with his dangerous, dark good looks and his collection of less-than-savory friends.

And as soon as I started writing, I discovered I wasn't the only one who couldn't forget him. Nicki Michaels is about to watch her peaceful, uneventful life blow sky-high when she tries to help a friend and finds herself on the wrong side of a two-way mirror, staring at the one man she's never been able to forget.

Nothing is ever what it seems in Fools Point. I hope you'll enjoy *The Silent Witness*.

Happy Reading!

Dani Sinclair

The Silent Witness
Dani Sinclair

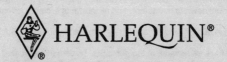

TORONTO • NEW YORK • LONDON
AMSTERDAM • PARIS • SYDNEY • HAMBURG
STOCKHOLM • ATHENS • TOKYO • MILAN • MADRID
PRAGUE • WARSAW • BUDAPEST • AUCKLAND

For Mary McGowan and Karin and Rita Shaughnessy
with thanks. A special thanks to Kelsey Roberts.
And always for Roger, Chip, Dan and Barb.

ISBN 0-373-22565-2

THE SILENT WITNESS

Copyright © 2000 by Patricia A. Gagne

This edition published by arrangement with Harlequin Books S.A.

® and TM are trademarks of the publisher. Trademarks indicated with
® are registered in the United States Patent and Trademark Office, the
Canadian Trade Marks Office and in other countries.

Visit us at www.eHarlequin.com

Printed in U.S.A.

ABOUT THE AUTHOR

With the premiere of *Mystery Baby* for Harlequin Intrigue in 1996, Dani Sinclair launched her dream career. An avid reader, she never took her own writing seriously until her only sister caught her between career moves and asked her to write a romance novel. Dani quickly discovered she could combine her love of action/adventure with a dash of humor while creating characters who find love together despite the odds. Dani lives in a Maryland suburb outside of Washington, D.C., a place she's found to be a great source for both intrigue and humor!

Books by Dani Sinclair

Don't miss any of our special offers. Write to us at the following address for information on our newest releases.

Harlequin Reader Service
U.S.: 3010 Walden Ave., P.O. Box 1325, Buffalo, NY 14269
Canadian: P.O. Box 609, Fort Erie, Ont. L2A 5X3

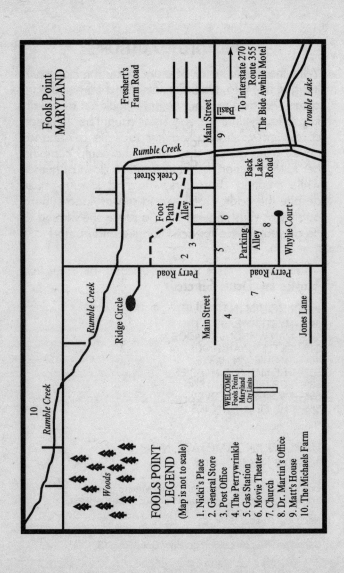

Fools Point
MARYLAND

Fresherr's
Farm Road

Rumble Creek

Creek Street

Foot Path

Alley

Main Street

Basil

9

To Interstate 270
Route 355
The Bide Awhile Motel

Trouble Lake

Back
Lake
Road

1

6

5

Parking

Alley

8

Whylie Court

2   3

7

Perry Road

Perry Road

Rumble Creek

Rumble Creek

Ridge Circle

Main Street

4

Jones Lane

10

Woods

WELCOME
Fools Point
Maryland
City Limits

FOOLS POINT
LEGEND
(Map is not to scale)

1. Nicki's Place
2. General Store
3. Post Office
4. The Perrywrinkle
5. Gas Station
6. Movie Theater
7. Church
8. Dr. Martin's Office
9. Matt's House
10. The Michaels Farm

CAST OF CHARACTERS

Nicki Michaels —Her favor to a friend made her a target for murder. Now she must put her trust in the man who loved her and left her.

Alex Coughlin —The town bad boy is back—but this time, his reputation hides a bigger secret.

Thorton Biggs —His death was premeditated— was it also a setup?

Bernie Michaels —Nicki's father knows more about Alex than he's ever admitted.

Hope Michaels —Is Nicki's sister a pawn, or a player?

Thad Osher —He has a bad attitude, but does that make him a crooked cop?

Ilona Toskov —What did she see in the alley, and who is she trying to protect?

Pavel Toskov —Ilona's brother is handy with his fists.

Vic Unsdorf —Will silence cost him his life?

Matt Williams —The precocious teen knows more than he's saying.

Prologue

"He *knows* where you are!"

The five words on the other end of the phone caused her stomach muscles to contort violently. She continued peering out the window at the street below straining to see. Was someone lurking in the doorway of the small appliance store across the street? His words made it more than likely. The darkened shop made it impossible to tell for sure.

"He can't *know.*"

"I'm telling you, he knows. It's all coming unraveled. We have to talk, right away!"

Her mind twisted, looking for a way out. A movement caught her attention. Someone *was* watching from the shadows across the street. She was pretty sure she knew who that someone was. She turned from the window, bumping her already bruised arm and nearly stepping on Nicki's cat. She ignored the pain and the animal. If he was right, she was no longer safe. Not here. Not anywhere.

"How soon can you meet me behind the craft store on Main Street?"

"Two minutes," he said, sounding surprised. "I'm at the restaurant."

"Hurry."

She disconnected but continued to clutch the phone's portable handset like a lifeline. Reaching for her purse, she almost knocked the bowl of fresh flowers off the coffee table. The heavy weight of the gun inside the soft leather bag reassured her. She pulled out the weapon, staring at the dull, ugly metal. No matter. Ugly, but deadly. No one would add new bruises to her body with this in her hand.

She blocked the cat when it tried to escape into the night. Shutting the door, she hurried as she descended the back stairs over the shop as quietly as possible. It was nearly nine o'clock. Nicki would be closing the craft store any minute now. She must be gone before Nicki headed upstairs to the apartment for the night.

She reached the darkness of the alley and the parking lot behind the shops and stopped. Her lips formed a curse. She held Nicki's telephone. Her own cell phone sat on the hall table by the door. She'd have to go back for it.

A car engine shattered the silence of the moonless night. The vehicle swung around the corner and entered the alley. There was no time to go back for her telephone now. Yet, even as she hurried forward, instinct screamed that she wasn't alone. Someone else shared the darkness of the alley.

The car stopped in front of her only a few feet away. Now or never. It was too late for second thoughts. She really had no options left at all.

She stepped from the deep shadows.

The explosive sound of the barrage of gunshots seemed to echo off the walls of the old brick buildings. She turned to run. Her fingers punched 911 into the phone she still held.

"Emergency operator. Do you need police, fire or medical assistance?"

She reached the stairs. A figure rose from between two parked cars. She fired the gun in her hand at the shape, and knew she had missed. He ducked, but she had seen him—just as he had seen her. She fled up the stairs and back inside the apartment. The handset dropped from her fingers, bouncing across the carpeting. She grabbed her cell phone and plunged through the front door. Her heart hammered in her throat as her fingers pressed the now familiar number.

Chapter One

"Nicki? What's the matter? You sound funny."

Nicki locked the front door and turned off the main light. There were no customers inside the craft shop so it didn't matter if she closed early. What did matter was the man leaning almost negligently against the brick wall near the mouth of the alley across the street.

"Nothing's wrong." She told herself he wasn't staring at her windows, he was just waiting for someone. The second feature at the movie theater started at nine. He was probably waiting to meet someone and go inside. He could even be waiting for someone to come out from the last show. It was silly to feel so uneasy. "Everything's fine. What's up?"

"I was wondering if you could go out and check your car after you close tonight. I can't find my gold bracelet and I think I might have lost it in your car the other day."

Nicki called on patience. Her much younger half-sister wasn't generally careless, but the request didn't surprise Nicki. If it didn't involve a horse, Hope seldom paid a lot of attention to details.

Nicki's gaze flicked to the street. The man was in deep shadows, but he was still there.

"Uh, Hope, I'll let you know if I find it."

"Okay. Did Ilona find you okay the other day?"

Shocked, Nicki forgot about the man and focused on her sister. Ilona Toskov had been her roommate at the University of Maryland more than eight years ago. Nicki had run into her at a Frederick shopping center a few weeks ago and they'd decided to meet for lunch the following month. Two days ago, Ilona arrived on Nicki's doorstep, scared, bruised, and seeking a haven.

"What are you talking about?"

Hope hesitated. "Is something wrong, Nicki? She called here trying to find you and I gave her your number and told her where you lived. That was okay, wasn't it?"

"Yes. Of course. It's just that Ilona is having some, uh…personal problems. I didn't know she'd spoken with you."

"Oh. She didn't say anything about that to me."

Nicki wasn't surprised. Ilona had seemed horribly embarrassed. An abusive boyfriend who turned out to be married wasn't something most women would want to discuss with anyone.

"Look, Hope, I'd rather you wouldn't mention her name to anyone else right now, all right?" Especially not with Ilona hiding in Nicki's apartment over the store at this very moment.

"No problem. So you'll go out back right after you close and check for my bracelet?"

"I'll check."

"Thanks, Nicki. Talk to you later."

Nicki replaced the receiver and stared out the window of her shop. The man was still there.

Nervously, she checked the lock on the front door, flipped the sign to Closed, removed the cash drawer and headed for her minuscule office. A car barreled down the alley leading to the parking area behind the building. Nicki tensed.

Good grief. If she kept jumping at every sound she'd need tranquilizers. Someone probably wanted to reach one of the stores before it closed. Despite her own slow evening, she hoped the store they wanted to reach wasn't hers.

Nicki sighed as she opened the safe. Fools Point didn't have much crime as a rule, but lately, things had been changing. There was that unsolved car bombing several months ago in which a man had died a terrible death. The police believed it was gang related. That struck a nerve locally, occurring so close to town. Then the rash of car thefts in the area was increasing, and Fay Garvey's murder and the destruction of the Bide Awhile Motel had shocked everyone. Only a month later Jerome Inglewood had been killed in a bank robbery in D.C. Local men had been involved. They'd gone after Jerome's pregnant wife because she was a witness to the murder.

Nicki sighed again. There was no such thing as a safe place anymore. Ilona had brought that home when she sought refuge in Nicki's apartment two nights ago.

Ilona refused to go to the police. The bruises and threats her boyfriend had made had given both women good reason to be nervous.

Nicki closed the safe and spun the lock. She hefted the awkwardly shaped box of new supplies and tried to plan the next window display in her mind. But her mind wouldn't cooperate. She was far too edgy.

A car engine idled behind the store. She needed to get a grip. There was nothing sinister in that. Three days ago, she wouldn't have thought a thing of it.

Three days ago, her life had been a whole lot simpler.

Telling herself to stop acting so jumpy, she carried the box out front. The car suddenly backfired several times. The noise reminded her of firecrackers going off.

Nicki hesitated. She set the box down and listened hard. Gunshots could sound like firecrackers.

Heart in her throat, Nicki ran to check the lock on the rear entrance. That lock was the only thing that stood between her and whoever was in the alley outside. Thankfully, the dead bolt was in place. The rear door was secure and there were no windows back here to worry about. She was safe.

So was Ilona, as long as she didn't unbolt the apartment door upstairs.

Nicki peered through the peephole. All she could see in the darkness was the hood of the running car. Nicki hesitated, unwilling to telephone the police until she was sure of what she'd heard. She strained to listen over the sound of blood pounding through her veins. The car continued to idle harmlessly.

Shots? Or backfires like she'd first thought? Ilona wouldn't thank her for calling the police and drawing attention to the shop needlessly.

Nicki practically jumped three feet in the air when the telephone sliced through the silence. She hurried to the office, shutting down lights as she went. She didn't want to draw attention to the store from the outside. Everything was okay, she told herself. Ilona's boyfriend could not have found her. Ilona was safe.

But she had to be terrified.

As Nicki reached for the receiver, she saw both phone lines were lit. The business line flashed with the incoming call. Ilona? Calling from the apartment phone? Nicki lifted the receiver. A click filled her ear. She frowned, her pulses racing.

The house line was no longer lit. But why would Ilona hang up? She wouldn't have.

Unless she didn't have a choice.

Nicki snatched her purse from the bottom desk drawer. In her rush to get upstairs, she tripped over the edge of the large box she'd left sitting out. Stumbling sideways, she knocked into a cardboard display and nearly fell. With an oath, she shoved the box to one side.

She wasn't usually clumsy, but a sense of urgency practically overwhelmed her. Nicki couldn't explain why, but she needed to get to Ilona. She had to be certain her friend was all right.

Nicki fumbled for her keys, dropping them, then stepping on them in her frantic hurry. As she locked the shop door, a figure dashed out of the alley and raced across the street. For a second, her breath caught in her throat.

Was it the same man who'd been watching her shop? Though she'd never had a clear view of his face, there was something hauntingly familiar about the form that sprinted out of sight.

With an impatient shake of her head, she opened the communal door leading up to her apartment and the one across the landing.

Her apartment door gaped open, showering the steep staircase with light. She scooped up her cat, who'd taken the opportunity to try to sneak outside, and rushed up the stairs.

"Ilona!"

Silence met her call.

Nicki set Ginger down inside and closed the door. She didn't have to search her small apartment to know Ilona was gone. The emptiness struck her immediately.

She nearly tripped over the handset of her portable telephone that lay on the carpet. Had Ilona dropped it as she fled? But why had she run? Nicki picked it up, trying to stem the apprehension hammering in her throat. There were no signs of struggle.

The telephone in her hand shattered the silence. Jolted by surprise, Nicki answered cautiously as if the instrument itself presented some danger.

"Hello?"

"Nicki!" Ilona's usually sultry voice came over the line as if she was out of breath.

"Ilona! Where are you?"

"He found me!"

Fear welded the handset to Nicki's fingers.

"I tried to go out the back but a man started shooting!"

"Your boyfriend shot at you?" The bruises and threats made that a frightening possibility.

"No! The other man."

"What other man?" Ilona's rush of words weren't making any sense. "Slow down, Ilona."

"Oh, God, Nicki, I just saw a man get killed. Right in front of me!"

For a second, fear nearly made Nicki deaf. "What?"

"A man walked up to the car and shot the driver. I saw the whole thing."

Gunshots. Not backfires.

"Are you okay?"

"Of course not! I'm terrified! Don't you understand? A car pulled up and a man walked up to it and opened fire. I was standing right there! I've never been so scared."

"But you aren't hurt?"

Ilona didn't seem to hear her. "I can't believe it! It was so incredible! Then I did something really stupid, Nicki. I called the police!"

"That's not stupid. You—"

"No! It is stupid! They'll have a record of the call! They'll know there was a witness!"

Nicki tried to stay calm. "It's okay."

"No! It's *not* okay! I can't be a witness!"

"Take it easy, Ilona. Who was the man?"

"Which man? Never mind. It doesn't matter. I've never seen either of those men before."

"But you said your boyfriend found you."

"I'm rattled, Nicki. Will you just listen a minute?" Almost calmly, Ilona began to describe the man in the car. Nicki thought about the man she'd seen run across the street.

"Nicki, I can't tell the police what I saw!" Ilona concluded.

"Of course you can. You have to. A man is dead. You have to tell them—"

"No! *You'll* have to tell them."

Nicki stared at the flowers on her coffee table. The cut crystal bowl rested precariously near the edge of the table. "Ilona, I didn't see the murder, you did."

"I know that, but the police don't. You have to pretend to be me. You can tell the police what I saw. I'll describe everything to you."

Nicki sank down on the couch and shoved the flowers back into place. "You can't be serious."

"You have to! Please, Nicki! They're going to think the caller was you anyhow. I didn't give them my name."

"But—"

"Is that sirens in the background?"

Only then did Nicki process the sound of the siren turning down the alley. The police were here already.

"Promise me, Nicki! You have to promise me!"

"Ilona, this is crazy. Just come back and tell them what you saw."

"I won't. I can't! If you don't give them the description then the murderer will get away free. Is that what you want? Because I'm not coming back, Nicki."

Nicki gripped the telephone even more tightly. Ginger jumped up beside her on the couch, her feline eyes staring with unwinking intelligence. Nicki reached out to stroke the comforting fur.

"Look, Ilona, I know you're scared, but be reasonable. All you have to do is tell the police what you saw. They'll protect you. I keep telling you they'll protect you from the man who hurt you too."

Silence.

Finally, in a stilted voice Ilona said, ''The man who hurt me *is* a policeman, Nicki.''

The words filled her ear like a tidal wave of destruction. No wonder Ilona had refused to discuss going to the police. No wonder she was so frightened. Who do you turn to when the protectors turn on you?

''I didn't want to tell you,'' Ilona continued. ''I was afraid you wouldn't let me stay if you knew.''

''Of course I would have let you stay,'' Nicki said automatically. But she realized she would have been even more nervous if she had known the truth. ''Look, Ilona—''

''Don't tell me I should report him. I'm not going to and that's all there is to it. Now, are you going to cover for me or not?''

''But I can't be a witness when I wasn't even there.''

''All you have to do is describe what I saw. No one will know it wasn't you in the alley. Please, Nicki. I'm so scared. I don't want that man's murderer to walk free just because I'm afraid.''

''Then come back and—''

''Nicki!''

Nicki realized her options were down to two. She could refuse, but then she'd have to explain the phone call. And that might put Ilona in harm's way if her boyfriend found out. Only, to agree to this preposterous plan...Nicki envisioned the figure running across the street and hesitated. Maybe she had seen the killer after all.

''Tell me exactly what you saw.''

Nicki listened closely this time. The general description could fit a dozen men right here in Fools Point. The dark jeans, T-shirt and wavy black hair also fit the man Nicki had seen standing across the street. The man who had looked so hauntingly familiar.

But it couldn't be Alex. He'd been in town for months now and he hadn't once come to see her. She shelved the tiny seed of hurt. Rumor had it that he'd taken up with Vic Unsdorf and some other unsavory friends. The men were nothing but trouble. In fact, Alex had already been questioned in several incidents lately. Her stomach clenched.

"Give me that description again," she demanded.

Jeans, dark shirt, dark wavy hair, six feet, muscular.

Alex.

"Ilona, I can't!"

She heard Ilona sigh. "Then you can't. Take care of yourself, Nicki."

"Wait! What about you? Where are you going to go?"

"Don't worry. I'll find another place to stay."

Nicki gripped the portable phone more tightly. "Are you absolutely sure about what you saw?"

"I was standing right there!"

She couldn't do this. She couldn't.

"I've got to go before he finds me. Thanks for everything, Nicki."

"Wait!"

Ilona hung up before Nicki's common sense could offer more of a protest. She shut her eyes trying desperately to think. An authoritative pounding sounded on her back door. Nicki quivered in reaction. Time was up. She had a choice—betray her old friend or her first lover.

Taking a deep breath, Nicki slowly stood and went to admit the police.

"ON YOUR FEET, Coughlin."

Alex stared at Sergeant Thad Osher's boyishly round face and thought about how good it would feel to plant his fist in that smugly satisfied expression. Keys jingled in the lock. The cell door parted. Alex came off the cot in one unhurried motion. The fast movement was enough to make Osher take a quick step back. His hand automatically went to the weapon at his side.

"Planning to shoot me, Thaddie?"

Red-faced, Osher glared at him. "Just give me a reason. Turn around."

"Restraints?" He tried not to let the other man see how angry he was. "You really are afraid of me, aren't you? My lawyer's going to have a field day with this one. I don't imagine Chief Hepplewhite's going to be any too pleased either. He cares about things like a prisoner's rights."

"Shut up."

Osher clamped the handcuffs around his wrists tight enough to pinch. Alex didn't make a sound, not even when he was given a shove forward that caused him to crash against the far wall.

Down the hall, a cluster of men waited outside a room. Alex recognized Jake Collins right away. Collins had recently converted the old Perry place into a local bar and restaurant. There were a lot of wild rumors circulating about the newcomer and where he'd earned the money to pull off such a feat. But Alex knew that was mostly because Collins tended to keep to himself.

Alex's gaze shifted. Another man was Officer Derek Jackstone, dressed in jeans and a T-shirt. He almost hadn't recognized the man. Jackstone would do well if he ever tried undercover work. Put him in different clothing and he tended to blend in.

One of the other two men also looked vaguely familiar, but Alex couldn't place him or the fourth man immediately.

The room they waited outside of served as the interrogation room. Alex had graced the insides before. He didn't have to wonder why they were all being herded in there now.

"I'm going to take these cuffs off in a minute for the lineup, Coughlin, but just remember, one false move—"

"What lineup?"

"Shut up."

Osher gave him another shove. All four men looked up. Jackstone took a quick step in their direction. He was a good cop. "Problem, Thad?"

"No problem. Right, Coughlin?"

Alex met Jackstone's eyes. "Osher arrested me, but he won't tell me the specific charge. He also won't let me call my lawyer."

Derek's frown deepened. Osher scowled. "Plenty of time for that after the lineup."

Alex spun around fast enough to make Osher back up again. "What lineup? I want to know why I'm being held."

"You read him his rights, Thad?"

"Of course I did."

"Osher's never heard of illegal harassment," Alex told Jackstone. "I think my lawyer is going to have to instruct him."

"Take the cuffs off, Thad," Derek said. "Mr. Coughlin isn't going to cause us any trouble. Isn't that right?"

"Not at all," Alex told him pleasantly. "I plan to cause Osher here a great deal of trouble, but all of it will be legal, I promise."

When Osher would have shoved him again, Jackstone quickly stepped between them.

"Back off, Derek," Osher demanded.

"You're letting him bait you, Thad. Let him go."

"No way. I'm personally going to see this smart-mouthed punk is put away until he's too old to hold a fork."

Alex stared hard at Osher's ruddy complexion. "Even if it means you have to manufacture evidence?"

Osher shoved Jackstone aside. He gripped Alex's shirt-front. Coffee foully laced his breath. "I don't have to manufacture anything, Coughlin. We've got an eyewitness to that shooting last night. That should put you away for a very long time."

"That's enough, Thad," Jackstone said quickly. "Let him go and get those cuffs off him. We've got an audience, in case you forgot. The chief isn't going to like this."

Osher muttered a vicious oath, but he released the cuffs. Alex rubbed his chafed wrists openly, while trying to think back to the events of the night before. Eyewitnesses were notoriously unreliable, but what if this one *did* pick him out?

"Come on, Coughlin," Jackstone said quietly. "Let's get this over with." He opened the door to the interrogation room.

"This is your idea of an official lineup?"

"We aren't equipped with all the bells and whistles, but this will do," the young officer replied.

"My lawyer's going to be rubbing his hands with glee."

Osher cursed again, but allowed Jackstone to lead Alex into the room. Alex heard the lock click on the door behind them. The room was empty except for a table and three chairs. One wall had a two-way mirror. Alex resisted the urge to make a childishly rude gesture in that direction. Instead, he sauntered over to perch on the edge of the tabletop.

He stared directly into his own face, careful to keep his features as expressionless as possible, while mentally reviewing his actions the night before. Who was their witness? And exactly what had the person seen?

The witness could be one of the shop owners who'd stepped out back, or a customer in the parking lot, or even someone in one of the apartments over the shops. None of the stores had rear-facing windows. Fortunately, that meant the witness couldn't be Nicki. She'd been inside her shop all night, right up until the gunshots had sounded.

Alex frowned. Once he'd learned about her craft shop, he'd deliberately stayed away from that part of town. The last thing he could afford was the complication of running into Nicki Michaels again after all this time. But everything had changed last night with a single phone call. All his good intentions dissolved. He'd stood across the street and watched her move around inside her store while he remembered things that were better left forgotten.

"Stand up, Coughlin." Osher's voice came from a speaker on the wall in the corner. "Everyone needs to stand against the rear wall and face the mirror."

Jake Collins frowned. So did one of the other two men Alex didn't know. In fact, that man looked decidedly nervous. Alex paid him a little more attention, especially when he found himself sandwiched between Collins and the stranger. The man's jeans were crusted with dirt and greasy stains. He smelled of motor oil and sweat and stale cigarettes. He had a working man's hands. Dirt was caked under the split and broken fingernails. Alex wondered who he was and what he was doing here in Fools Point. A drifter? They didn't get many of those here in town.

One at a time, Osher had the men take a step forward and stand in profile. Despite the fact that all of them had dark hair and were of a similar build, if someone *had* seen Alex in the alley last night, they weren't going to be fooled by this charade. Most police forces didn't bother with lineups any more. They showed victims or witnesses pictures instead, but Osher was making it blatantly clear who he wanted this witness to point out. Chief Hepplewhite had picked a bad week to take his wife into D.C. for medical evaluation.

Hepplewhite was a good cop. Smart, thorough, with no axes to grind. Osher, on the other hand, couldn't find a clue if he was stepping on one. Alex stepped back and waited to be denounced. Minutes later, Osher's voice filled the room again. This time, he sounded disgusted.

"Okay, let's do it one more time."

Alex breathed a sigh of relief. The witness hadn't picked

him out. But then, what *had* the witness seen last night? He was going to have to find the person and have a little talk.

"TAKE ANOTHER LOOK, Ms. Michaels. A good look this time."

Nicki couldn't do anything else. Her insides had twisted the moment the four men had walked into the room. Alex Coughlin, big as life and twice as sexy, had strolled over to perch on the edge of the table. He stared straight into her eyes. Suddenly, she was sixteen again and desperately in love.

He had to be almost thirty-four by now. And he still needed a haircut and a shave. She almost smiled. Then she realized her fingers were half-raised as if to stroke that cheek. She clutched her hands together as Sergeant Osher spoke to the men.

Nicki shook her head to rid it of the wash of bittersweet memories. This was hardly the time or the place.

"Ms. Michaels, you aren't even trying," Osher protested. "You don't have to be afraid. We'll protect you."

She pulled her arm away from his annoying touch. "I'm not the least bit afraid, Sergeant Osher. But, like I told you, it all happened fast. It was very dark outside. I've complained to city hall about that broken streetlight behind the store several times. No one does anything."

"Ms. Michaels, I know it was dark, but you were right there. You saw the murder."

Stubbornly, she shook her head. "I can't point a finger at anyone, I told you that. I never got a clear look at his face."

At least she could say that and speak the truth. She had never seen the murder let alone the murderer's face. In her heart, she knew it was Alex she'd seen running across the street. But that didn't mean he'd pulled the trigger, despite what Ilona had said.

Nicki would go to jail herself before she'd make a positive identification of anyone. She'd given the police the description Ilona had passed on to her. That was as far as she was willing to go. Her mind refused to reconcile the Alex she had known with a man who could walk up to a car and kill someone in cold blood.

Her Alex had been tough. Ready to defend himself—or anyone weaker if it came to that. But he had never sought trouble. Of course, he hadn't needed to. It always came looking for him.

She shrugged off that memory. She was now certain Alex had been across the street right before the shooting. If she was right, he would have had to run across the street the minute she started back to her office with the cash drawer in order to be in position to fire those shots.

Okay, it was possible. Barely. She didn't want to believe it. Nicki chewed on her bottom lip. Anyone witnessing a murder would run away. That didn't make Alex a killer.

Did it?

"Try, Ms. Michaels. Try real hard."

She glared at the policeman and decided even if she had seen the murder with her own eyes, she wouldn't have said so to this bully. Thad Osher made her skin crawl. She didn't like the way he *almost* leered whenever their paths crossed. He seemed to think he was irresistible to women, but he made *her* feel dirty and undressed.

"I'm sorry. I just can't say for sure."

She stared at Alex. A pang of loss held her transfixed. She'd thought him unbearably sexy at nineteen. Cocky. Sure of himself. Running all over town on that secondhand motorcycle he'd bought. Refusing to let the scandal surrounding his father's death touch him, despite all the whispers and pointed fingers. Alex had been bitter and angry as a teenager, but he'd never been anything but kind to her.

She'd never forgotten the day he'd picked wildflowers for her down by Trouble Lake. He'd talked about his dreams for the future. A future that hadn't included a sixteen-year-old girlfriend, she'd finally realized. Back then, she'd been so sure he'd return for her one day. But he never had.

Osher brought his fist down on his thigh in a gesture of frustration. "Did you see the guy or not?"

She looked into his glittering eyes and wanted to run. Instead she squared her shoulders defiantly. "Badgering me isn't going to change a thing, Sergeant. I told you what I saw. I've looked at your suspects. Now, I need to open my shop."

He stood too close. Nicki decided he had mean eyes. She fought down an instinctive need to back away and held her ground. Sergeant Osher was the type to take advantage of any perceived weakness.

"You know, Ms. Michaels, once the word gets out there was a witness, that shop might not be a safe place for a woman like you."

A trace of fear mixed with her loathing. "Are you threatening me, Sergeant?"

His eyes flickered. "Not at all. Call it a friendly warning. You'll be a lot safer once the murderer is behind bars."

"Then I suggest you find him."

She half expected him to grab her arm as she stalked from the room, but he didn't. She could feel twin spots of color on her cheeks as she strode quickly past Carolyn. The pretty receptionist, who also served as the police dispatcher, watched with a frowning expression of concern. Another time Nicki would have stopped to chat. Now, she just wanted to escape.

Nicki hung on to her haughty pose as she left the building and stepped into the wilting heat and humidity of the August sunshine. She was trembling with reaction, so furious she couldn't think straight.

How dare he threaten her? Because no matter what he said, Osher's words had been a threat. He was supposed to be a police officer. One of the men who protected the people. But he was the kind of man who gave policemen a bad reputation. How could his wife stand to be around him?

Nicki clung to her anger as she crossed the street and walked briskly past the General Store. Bianca Tooley waved to her from inside the post office a minute later. Nicki didn't pause to talk with the lonely woman as she often did. All she wanted was the sanctuary of her safe little store.

Seeing Alex again had brought back all sorts of memories. Hot nights and even hotter kisses. He'd been the town's bad boy and her first lover. And she'd cried enough tears to overflow Trouble Lake when he left. But Alex had never once looked back, just as he'd sworn. As far as she knew, this was the first time in all those years that he'd ever returned to town. He hadn't even come home for his mother's funeral. Was he here now because of his sister?

Ironically, Kayla was engaged to marry a D.C. police officer. And according to Mildred Kitteridge over at the General Store, the town council had approved Chief Hepplewhite's request to hire more help. Alex's soon-to-be brother-in-law was about to become the second in command of the Fools Point police force.

Could Alex really have killed a man in cold blood?

The question plagued her all day long as she taught a decoupage class, a knitting class, and two ceramic classes between waiting on customers. By the time the last brush had been cleaned, the last jar of glaze put away, and the large kiln loaded and turned on, Nicki was more than ready for an early night.

She ate dinner without tasting a bite. She was too edgy to settle down with her needlepoint project. Her cat stropped her leg in sympathy.

"Thanks, Ginger. If only Ilona would call so I could be sure she's okay." But the telephone remained obstinately silent.

Ginger parrumphed and butted her lightly. Nicki scratched behind the cat's ears, then went to check the locks. She drew a tub of steamy water and added the new bath oil she'd been meaning to try. The scent really did remind her of gardenias.

Lighting several fat candles, she piled her hair on top of her head, selected a bottle of wine from the refrigerator and picked up her novel. She would read and soak and dispel these useless memories that had haunted her all day.

Less than twenty minutes later, she knew it was no use. She simply couldn't keep her mind on the printed pages. The story deserved her attention, but thoughts of Alex kept intruding. He was a mature man now. Still cocky and full of swaggering confidence, and still irresistibly attractive.

Maybe Hope was right. Nicki *was* turning into a spinster. She'd even started talking to her cat. Smiling, she patted herself dry and pulled on her long satin robe.

"I wonder if other single women like satin lingerie and sleep in the nude, Ginger." The cat raised her head inquiringly from the rug. Seeing no food in the offing, she curled again and closed her eyes. Cats had their priorities straight.

Nicki refilled her glass and settled down to watch the news. When she found herself almost nodding off, she turned off the TV and the light. Going to the front window that looked out over Main Street, she paused. Her heart began to pound. Was there someone standing in the shadows beside the appliance store once again?

Nicki stared so hard her eyes began to burn, but no one

and nothing moved. It must have been her imagination. There wasn't anyone there. Still, she remained standing for several more minutes just watching to be certain.

Feeling a bit foolish, she rechecked her door locks and headed for the bedroom. Maybe she and Ginger should get a dog. A large dog, like Spider, the Labrador retriever Bianca Tooley always kept at her side.

Good grief. Hope was more right than she knew. Nicki was turning into Miss Tooley.

Nicki tossed her robe over the nightstand and climbed into bed. Was Ilona safe? Had Alex Coughlin really walked up to a car in the alley and shot a man in cold blood?

Her last thought was that she hoped not.

The dream began with a memory. Alex's soft kisses slowly awakened her passion. His arms held her, the way only his arms ever had. But now they were a man's arms. Hard. Protective.

She was dreaming and she knew it, but she clung to the dream, not wanting to wake. She was on the brink of something wonderful. She tried to ignore the sense of wrongness that disturbed the dream and tugged at her half-conscious brain.

The creak of the floorboard next to her bed snapped her eyes open. Too late, she felt the presence inside the room. A hand came out of the darkness to clamp over her mouth.

"Don't scream."

Chapter Two

Terror gripped her. Nicki struggled, but she was pinned beneath the weight of her attacker, tangled in her sheet.

"Nicki, stop it!"

The low growl brought an instant halt to her struggles. Though she tried to make out his features in the darkness, she couldn't. But never in a million years would she forget that voice. She stopped moving. Stopped breathing.

"Alex?"

"I think you broke my nose."

The adrenaline seeped from her body. Badly shaken, she lay beneath him while a myriad of remembered emotions assaulted her. She selected anger and drew it on like a cloak.

How dare he scare her like this?

"Get off me!"

She shoved as hard as she could. Alex rolled away from her in the darkness. When she would have reached for the light switch, he stopped her, gripping her hand firmly.

"No lights."

"Why not? What do you mean coming in here scaring me half to death in the middle of the night? Who do you think you are?"

"Your first lover?"

The words charged the silence with an arc of electricity that should have been visible to the naked eye.

"You bastard," she said quietly.

"Not technically." He stood up and sighed. "I'm sorry, Nicki. That was uncalled for."

"Yes. It was." She braced herself on her hands, halfway to a sitting position. "What are you doing here, Alex?"

In the darkness of the room, she sensed him rocking back on his heels. "Tonight? I need to know why Osher thinks you are an eyewitness to the murder last night."

Hurt primed her anger, pushing aside all the other emotions. Even though it was too dark to make out more than shapes and shadows in the room, she covered her bare breasts with the sheet and sat up, suddenly all too aware that she was naked beneath the thin bit of linen.

"Why don't you go ask him? He has my statement."

The whistle of Alex's pent-up breath was loud in the silent room.

"I've done all the talking with Osher that I plan to do. Talk to me, Nicki," he coaxed. "Tell me what you saw last night."

There had been a time when she would have told him anything. Everything. A time when she would have cheerfully lied for him or worse. But she wasn't sixteen any more and he wasn't the brash young Alex Coughlin she'd loved so desperately.

No. Now he was the brash *mature* Alex Coughlin. And that made him twice as dangerous.

"Get out of my house, Alex."

"I can't do that, Nicki. You were in your shop last night. You would have had to break speed records to get upstairs to your apartment before those shots were fired. That means you didn't see the crime. Unless you opened the back door. Is that what you did, Nicki?"

"How do you know what I was doing last night?"

"You know the answer to that," he said after a moment.

"I want to hear your version."

He sat down on the bed, much too close to her. She could feel the heat of him against her hip right through the sheet. A heat she would have welcomed with open arms once upon a time.

"No games, Nic. This is too important."

"I'd say so. A man died last night."

"Yes. Now exactly what did you see?"

Nervously, she tugged on the sheet, aware that his eyes tracked the movement despite the darkness of the room.

"Why don't you tell me what *you* were doing here last night. Tell me why you were watching my shop. Why last night when you've been in town for months?"

"You knew that?"

"That you were back?" She hoped he didn't hear the pain she tried to bury deep in her heart. "Have you been gone so long you've forgotten what it's like to live in a small town, Alex? I knew you were back an hour after you breezed in on that motorcycle, acting like the world owed you big time. I can't believe you're still thumbing your nose at the police. I would have thought you'd have outgrown that phase years ago. Think your father would be proud?"

The carefully chosen barb struck its target. She heard his indrawn hiss. He reached forward suddenly and grabbed her forearms in a grip she couldn't break.

The moment his rough palms touched her skin, her body seemed to go wild. The rush of sensual memories mixed with an undercurrent of new fear. Why had she pushed him? Ilona had described the murderer clearly. Alex fit the killer's description right down to the clothes he'd been wearing.

"You always did have more guts than brains," he said

softly. "Let's leave my father out of this. I haven't got a lot of time right now. Tell me what you saw."

Fear raised the hair on her forearms. Alex could kill her right here and no one would know. There wasn't a thing she could do to stop him. The implacable hardness she sensed in him went deeper than she would have thought. Where was the young man she had loved so desperately? Didn't any of him remain?

"I'm not telling you anything." She refused to be cowed by Alex. Part of her didn't believe he would harm her no matter how much he'd changed. But there was another part that wasn't quite so certain.

"Stubborn. My God, you're stubborn." His hand stroked her cheek. The caress made her shiver. "But you're still as soft as midnight."

"Don't."

"Why not? It's true."

She didn't want to respond to his touch, but it would have been easier to stop breathing. She stared into the darkness of his eyes and tried not to want him anymore.

"We aren't the same people, Alex." But the remembered feel of his hands on her was erasing time and stirring forgotten yearnings to life.

"Yes we are."

His mouth descended, covering hers. Firm, hard lips demanded a response. For an instant, she yielded. Only, this wasn't the kiss of her dreams, or even the kiss of her memory. This was an assault of raw, hard passion.

Nicki went still, even though her body clamored in instant recognition.

Alex broke away the moment he realized she wasn't reciprocating. Rife with self-loathing, he leaned back, running a hand through hair that was already tangled and windblown from his ride over here.

What was he doing? For one crazed second, the exotic

scent of her had driven him over some edge. He'd lost control in a way he hadn't done since that summer all those years ago. One taste. One incredible taste, and it was fifteen years ago all over again. He wanted her with a longing that stunned him.

Alex stood and stepped away from the bed. Now he was the one who was shaking. He slicked his hands down his jeans, trying to still the crazy waves of desire that demanded more.

He'd always had excellent night vision, so despite the darkness, he saw how wide her eyes were. Wide and accusing. The sheet had slipped to reveal most of one rounded breast. She'd wrapped her arms tightly around her middle. She was still shaking as well, he realized.

"What do you want, Alex?"

The soft question lashed him with the barbs of her fear. He'd scared her.

Alex cursed. He felt dirty—like he'd never be clean again. The months of rough living were taking their toll. He was so tired of it all. Staring at her, he couldn't help but feel he'd just soiled something important. The thought wouldn't go away. He couldn't afford to care, but he did.

"Thad Osher wants my neck in a noose, Nicki," he said quietly. "He doesn't care what he has to do to put it there."

"Was it something you said?"

A tremor lay beneath her sweetly mocking voice. He hated knowing he had put it there. But he was secretly relieved that she wasn't backing down. She had spunk. He should have remembered that about her. She never had backed away from anything. Not even when running with "that Coughlin boy" was the sort of reputation a nice girl didn't want.

"Nicki, I'm sorry. I know you won't believe this, but I've stayed away for good reason. In fact, I wouldn't have come to see you at all if—"

"Gee thanks, that's just what a woman wants to hear."

"—you hadn't begged me."

He'd hurt her again, and he hadn't meant to.

"What did you say?!" she demanded.

She yanked on the sheet, holding it beneath her chin as she sat up straighter. The action only drew his attention to the womanly shape of her. He'd wanted her when she was jailbait. Pure poison for a boy whose father was labeled a thief and a murderer. And he wanted her now when he was perilously close to being branded himself.

"Why did you call, Nicki? What do you want from me?"

"I don't know what you're talking about. I wouldn't call you in a million years."

He wished he dared turn on a light. Her words sounded so sincere. What was she trying to pull?

A possibility exploded in his mind. He hated the very idea. *But.* Was there the slightest chance Nicki had been trying to set him up?

His Nicki? No. She'd never do that. But she wasn't his anymore. Hadn't been his for a very long time. She'd been in love with him once. And what did they say about a woman scorned?

For crying out loud! Nicki wasn't like that. Was he going to start seeing bogeymen around every corner?

But what did he really know about her anymore?

He couldn't turn loose of that thought. Maybe she'd known Thorton Biggs. They could even have been lovers for all he knew. Hadn't he wondered why the man had driven into that alley last night? So much would be explained if Biggs had come there to see her.

The truth was, for all Alex knew, she'd killed Biggs herself and set Alex in place to take the fall. He might not like the idea, but he couldn't dismiss it on the basis of what had happened between them fifteen years ago.

"So you wouldn't call me in a million years, huh?" Her taunt rankled. "Well, I'm sure the feeling is mutual, but the fact is, you *did* call, Nicki. You said we had to talk, and like a fool, I agreed."

Tired from too little sleep and the stress of the last few months, he was suddenly angry. Nicki had been the only good thing he could remember about Fools Point, and she'd used their relationship to set him up.

"You asked me to meet you at five minutes after nine behind your shop," he snapped. "In fact, you pleaded—quite fetchingly. Ring any bells?"

"No!"

He ignored her protest, warming to his theme. The memory of that phone call was sharp and clear. She *had* called him.

"I came early. Don't pretend you didn't see me standing across the street."

He'd known the moment that she saw him. He'd leaned back against the rough bricks and simply watched her. Anticipation had brought him there early. Caution had kept him waiting. He should have paid more attention to the caution.

"The way you kept watching me, I figured you couldn't wait for a trip down memory lane," he said, waiting to see how she'd react.

"In your dreams!"

"Fantasies." He lowered his voice. "You were always part of my fantasies, remember, Nic? I never forgot. I almost walked across the street early, but you said to meet outside. I figured it was shades of yesterday. You wanted to see me, but you didn't want anyone in town to know it was me you were seeing." And that still stung.

"I don't know what you're talking about. I never called you. And if you'll recall, it was *you* who insisted we keep our relationship quiet fifteen years ago. I didn't care who knew about us.''

Her voice sounded wounded, but he knew she was lying about the phone call. What he needed to discover was why.

''Except your father.''

Nicki winced.

''You've really perfected that innocent act, Nic. Only it won't work. We both know just how innocent you aren't.''

Her fist bunched on the sheet. ''Yes, we do.''

Were those tears in her eyes? Anger drained away. What was he doing? This was all wrong. They shouldn't be wounding each other like this.

''Get out of here, Alex,'' she said with quiet dignity. ''I never want to see you again.''

The calm words nicked his heart with another barb of guilt. He clenched his jaw and unballed his own fists. This was no good. They were dicing each other to ribbons. What if things weren't what they seemed? Come to that, what in his world was what it seemed anymore?

''Don't lie to me, Nicki.''

She stared at him in silence.

Alex ran a hand through his hair again. He wasn't sure when he'd started hating his life, but he was damn sure things had to change soon.

''Did you know Thorton Biggs?''

She didn't respond.

''Did *you* kill him, Nic?'' That at least provoked a reaction.

''How dare you! I covered for you today. I was such a fool that I told them I couldn't identify anyone. I should have told them the truth. I should have told them how you came running out of that alley. But I didn't. I'm so stupid, I didn't.''

Tears were thick in her voice. He reached for her, but she drew back against the headboard. With an oath, he walked over to her bedroom window, disgusted with himself. He pushed the hair back from his face and stared out at the night.

"I didn't kill Thorton, Nicki. We were…acquaintances."

"Fellow gang members?"

He didn't look toward her. "Call it what you like. I ran behind your shop when I heard the shots. Someone had climbed over the fence right before I got there. He was disappearing into the trees when I saw him. I tried to go after him, but I got caught on the fence and he had too much of a head start, so I went to check Thorton. It was obvious he was beyond help. I knew what would happen if they caught me there, so I ran in the opposite direction."

"Why tell me? Tell Sergeant Osher."

Alex snorted. "Think he'd listen, let alone believe? Look, I'm sorry Nicki." For so many things. "I don't want to believe you set me up—"

"How nice of you."

"—but you asked me to come or I never would have set foot anywhere near you."

"You mentioned that fact."

He cursed under his breath. She didn't understand, and he was in no position to explain.

"Look, are you going tell me why you called me or not?"

"I did *not* call you."

Nicki crossed her arms over her chest defiantly. The sheet slipped dangerously low. Distracted, he stared at her in the darkness.

"What the devil are you wearing?" he growled. He knew quite well that the large expanse of skin was angel soft to the touch. There was nothing wrong with his memory—or his imagination.

"Nothing."

Alex cursed again. She knew just how to bait him. Her

virginal body had been so softly lush, rounded in gentle curves that made a young man's hands itch to explore. The last vestiges of baby fat had been starting to disappear. Those vestiges were completely gone now, but the curves were still there, honed and slimmed to a more mature, but no less desirable look. He had watched her figure last night, even when he told himself he was being a fool. Watched and wanted, when it was the last thing he should have been doing.

But any man would look at Nicki. The smart ones would go back for a second look.

"Go away Alex. I don't want you here."

Her words snapped his mind back to business. This was no time to let the past intrude. "Thank you for not telling Osher you saw me. If you had, I'd still be in jail."

"He arrested you?" She snapped her mouth shut as if regretting that he'd provoked a response.

"Maybe you haven't noticed, Nicki, but Thad Osher isn't a real nice guy. He's got a chip on his shoulder a mile wide. And that chip has my name on it."

"Why?"

Alex paused. "Now, that's a real good question."

He hadn't really considered it before. He and Osher had clashed from day one, but it hadn't really occurred to Alex to wonder why. Now he thought about that. He was going to have to take a much closer look at Thad Osher.

Obviously, Nicki wasn't going to tell him why she'd called. Maybe he was a fool, but he couldn't believe that her purpose had been to set him up. She wasn't that good an actress, and there'd be no reason. Just lousy timing all around. He'd better find Vic Unsdorf and see if Thorton's murder was rumored to be a gang hit for some infraction.

Something brushed his leg in the darkness. Alex kicked out and spun, his hand going for a weapon.

"Don't you dare hurt my cat!"

The small animal had sidestepped quickly. Alex was instantly relieved that he hadn't injured the little thing. Undaunted, the cat came forward and stropped his legs a second time. He bent and lifted the animal, whose white furred areas stood out even in the dark. Eyes glowed from some reflected light source.

"Sorry, kitty. You startled me." He scratched its head and it began to purr in his arms. "You always did want a cat. What's its name?"

"Ginger." Nicki said it as if she was reluctant to tell him even that much.

"Hello, Ginger." He stroked its silky fur, reminded of Nicki's soft hair. That thought sent him walking over to set the animal on Nicki's bed.

Time to get out of here.

"I'm sorry, Nic. I never wanted to hurt you, but it seems that's all I've ever done. Your dad was right about us all those years ago. We were way too young. And now it's much too late. Have a good life."

He strode from the room without waiting for a response. Funny how much regret was eating at his soul. The past should never be allowed to haunt a man like this.

Nicki bit her lip to keep from calling him back. She'd never felt more confused in all her life. Why did Alex insist she'd called him? And what did he mean about her father? The two of them had never even met.

What difference did any of it make now? Alex wasn't the boy of her dreams or the man she'd hoped he'd turn into. He was a bitter, angry man who probably regretted ever giving her a second look.

Ginger butted her hand, mewing softly in a bid for attention. Nicki stroked her absently while she wondered how Alex had gotten inside her apartment. The question nagged her out of bed. She reached for her robe and went from room to room checking doors and even the small windows.

All were still locked, yet Alex was gone. Had he materialized from her dream?

She lay down again, but it was a long time before she fell asleep. Her dreams had turned to nightmares.

IN THE EARLY morning hours, Nicki drove out to her father's horse farm. The property lay just beyond the much larger, wealthier Huntington Horse Farm. For years, the Huntingtons had been trying to get her father to sell out to them, but Bernie Michaels had a streak of stubborn that ran all the way to the core of his being. Despite the heart ailment that had caused him to cut way back on his activities, he still managed the farm and his family with a will of iron.

Nicki found her sister, Hope, in the kitchen clearing away the remains of breakfast.

"Hey!" Hope greeted. "Did you find my bracelet?"

"Good morning to you, too. I forgot to look. The car's out front if you want to check."

"You forgot to look?" Hope's eyes danced merrily.

"In case you haven't heard, a man was shot and killed behind my store. The police had the area sealed off until yesterday afternoon."

Hope gaped at her. "What man?"

"Someone named Thorton Biggs." Nicki walked over and closed the forgotten dishwasher.

"I haven't heard a newscast in days, Nicki. Do they know who killed him?"

"Thad Osher thinks it was Alex Coughlin. Osher arrested him for questioning."

Her sister gripped the edge of the table. "Oh, no! He couldn't have! Osher's wrong. Alex wouldn't kill anyone."

Nicki eyed her sister. "Funny, that's what Alex says. But why would *you* say that? You don't even know Alex."

"No, but you used to like him." Hope wouldn't meet her eyes. "So you did get to talk to him?"

"Briefly." She wasn't about to tell her sister about her discussion with Alex. While puzzled by Hope's initial reaction, she didn't have a lot of time this morning for prying answers from her sister. Hope took after her father when it came to sheer cussed stubbornness.

"Where's Dad?"

"Getting Big Man ready to take over to the Huntingtons. He's going to cover one of their mares. What about Alex?"

"What *about* Alex?"

Her sister shifted, looking uncomfortable.

"Why all the concern about Alex?"

Her sister wouldn't meet her eyes. "You used to be in love with him. Remember when you'd sneak out and meet him?"

"Some things are best forgotten," Nicki said firmly. "Alex is one of them."

"You don't mean that."

"Yes. I do."

Hope started to say something else, but ended up staring at her with a bewildered expression.

"You want to tell me what's going on, Hope?"

"Nothing! Nothing's going on."

Her sister was lying, but why? "You didn't try to set me up the other night by any chance, did you?"

"I don't know what you're talking about."

Nicki recognized the stubborn set to her sister's lips. She wouldn't get anywhere with the direct approach.

"Hope, we need to discuss this."

"I told you, I don't know what you're talking about and I've got to get going."

She'd get nothing further out of her sister right now, Nicki realized, so she changed tactics before her sister could escape. "Hold on a minute. Why is Dad working with the Huntingtons?"

"You know Dad," Hope said vacantly. "He doesn't let personal issues get in the way of business."

"But working with the Huntingtons?"

"Jeff Huntington wanted to buy Big Man. Dad and I argued for days, but he finally agreed not to sell. Big Man is going to turn this place around, Nicki. I told Dad he was a winner. Since Jeff couldn't buy him, Mr. Huntington offered us a lot of stud money to cover some of his mares."

"Oh."

"Look, I've got to get outside and bring the rig around."

"Dad lets you do that now?"

Hope nodded. They shared a look of sad understanding. "He's letting me do a lot of the stuff now."

"Are you okay with that?"

"Sure. I love this place and the business. It's what I've always wanted. You know that."

Nicki did. "I'm glad Dad's finally accepted your abilities. What about your bracelet?"

"Huh? Oh. I'll look for it later."

"While you're at it, how about returning those earrings of mine you borrowed a couple of weeks ago."

"Huh? Oh. Right. I'll give them back. Here comes Dad. I need to use the bathroom before I go to the barn."

Nicki watched her sister skitter away. Hope was acting weird even for her, but Nicki would have to investigate the cause later. She wanted to know what Alex had meant last night when he said her father had been right about them. It had been her first thought on waking this morning.

"Thought that was your car I heard," Bernie greeted her. "You in trouble?"

Nicki sighed. Some things never changed. "No, Dad. I'm not in trouble."

Her father strode to the sink and washed his hands. He'd lost more weight that he couldn't afford to lose and his surly expression was more pinched than usual. Was it just the light, or did his skin have a gray cast to it this morning? He didn't like questions about his health, especially since he'd been diagnosed with that heart condition last year. If he'd just go and have the recommended surgery they could all breathe easier.

"Thought maybe that murder out back of your store was a problem for you. Heard they arrested that Coughlin boy."

Nicki seized on the unexpected opening. "They let him go. But Alex said something that made me wonder. Did you know I was…sort of seeing him in high school?"

Her father studied her, his expression unreadable. "You and I have never been close, Nicki. My fault, I guess. We're too much alike, you and me. Besides, you always reminded me of your mother."

Nicki fought a sudden lump of emotion. Her father never spoke of his emotions. And he never spoke of her mother, who'd died in a car crash shortly after Nicki's birth.

"But you're my daughter and I've always done the best I could for you."

"I know that Dad. I love you too. I—"

"You were barely sixteen. Alex Coughlin would have ruined your life. I told him as much. Knew you wouldn't see it, but I made him promise to leave you alone. I'd do the same thing all over again if I had to and that's all I'm going to say on the matter. Where's your sister?"

"But Dad—"

"Here I am." Hope came around the corner a little too conveniently. No doubt she'd been standing out of sight in the dining room listening. "Ready to go?"

"Yeah. Move the rig and we'll get him loaded. It would have been easier just to sell him."

"Maybe so, but we'll make more money this way, trust me, Dad."

Their father harrumphed and stomped toward the door.

"Hold it, Dad," Nicki demanded. "Our conversation

isn't over. You can't tell me you had a hand in an event that affected my entire life and just walk away.''

''Nothing more to say. It's over and done, girl.''

''Well I have plenty more to say!''

''Naturally, but I don't have time right now. We'll talk later.'' He opened the door and stepped outside.

''You're darn right we will,'' she called after him. ''This conversation isn't over.''

''We really do have to go, Nicki,'' Hope said. ''If you're going to stick around, Brent's coming out here today.''

''Why?''

''He didn't say. Are you going to wait for him?''

''If he comes before I have to get back and open the shop.'' Three years older than Hope, Brent's MBA had landed him a prestigious job at a firm in D.C. that kept him constantly busy. Both of Nicki's younger brothers had turned into fine young men with solid careers.

She waited as long as she dared for Brent, occupying her time by preparing a casserole for supper and running a mop over the kitchen floor. Hope never complained, but Nicki knew taking care of the horses and their father left her younger sister little free time. There were times when Nicki felt guilty for finally walking away, even though she knew she had nothing to feel guilty about. Her father had basically forced her out once Hope was old enough not to need her constant support. He'd wanted Nicki to resume her own life and she suspected he'd felt guilty himself for needing her all those years.

She drove back through town, her thoughts more muddled than when she'd left. She hated that she couldn't stop thinking about Alex. Or the past. Her lips still tingled from his kiss this morning. Why had he been so angry? If anyone should have been upset, it was her.

What had her father done?

As she drove through the sleepy little town of Fools

Point, she tried to eye it from a stranger's viewpoint. Small, quaint, almost picturesque with Sugarloaf Mountain for a backdrop. Still, this wasn't exactly a tourist mecca. What would have drawn a stranger behind her store? Why her place? And why last night in particular?

Could the man have had something to do with Ilona?

No, Ilona said she'd never seen him before. But it suddenly occurred to Nicki to wonder what Ilona had been doing outside in the first place. She'd been too scared to venture out of Nicki's apartment since she'd arrived. Had she tried to leave because she'd seen Alex loitering across the street? That could be why she'd described him so well. Maybe in the trauma of seeing the shooting, her mind had become confused. Her memory might have substituted Alex for the real killer.

Okay it was a stretch. Nicki was still trying to make excuses for Alex.

If only Ilona would call her again. She needed to know her friend was all right.

Nicki decided to concentrate on Hope's skittish behavior. She and her sister sounded a lot alike. Alex could easily have mistaken Hope's voice for her own. And Hope had been insistent about Nicki going out to look for that bracelet right away. But why would her sister try to set them up?

Nicki pulled into the alley to park in her usual spot behind her store. The lot was mostly empty. The only cars around at this hour belonged to the people living over the stores. She knew everyone, of course, but this was the first time she'd ever paid attention to the cars parked around her. Strangely uneasy, she decided the lot had a deserted, spooky feel to it this morning.

Small wonder. A man had died here. The knowledge seemed unreal. Everything looked so normal. The tall chain-link fence separated the parking spaces from the woods behind the alley that ran the length of the block. She'd always known this area was isolated, but it had never been scary before.

Her imagination was running wild, that was all. There was nothing to feel nervous about today. Now if she could just convince her heart to stop fluttering so wildly.

As she started toward the store, a sudden movement caught the corner of her eye. Nicki whirled. A figure stepped from behind the large trash bin.

"Ms. Michaels!"

The fear-charged adrenaline dissipated quickly, leaving her feeling spent and foolish. Matt Williams, a local boy, ran up to her.

"You scared me, Matt. What are you doing out here at this hour?"

The youth gazed around nervously. He was rumpled and dirty. In fact, he looked like he'd spent the night in the dumpster. There were circles under his young eyes and she saw several old and not-so-old scratches on his arms.

"Are you okay, Matt?"

His head bobbed agreement. Only then did she realize how tall he'd grown. He had to be close to six feet already, though he hadn't yet grown into that gangly body. His features belonged to a youth. A trace of hair was barely visible across his upper lip. He was going to be a big, good-looking man one day. In fact, he reminded her of her oldest brother, Gavin.

"Can I talk to you, Ms. Michaels?"

"Of course, Matt. You want to come in and have something to eat?"

"No. Thank you." His eyes slid back and forth, scanning the area. The very alertness of his stance was making her edgy all over again. Matt had a hunted look about him.

"Is something wrong, Matt?"

"It's all over town that you saw the shooting."

Nicki grimaced. Why had she let Ilona talk her into that foolish admission? She wasn't surprised that gossip was all over town, but hearing a reference to it made her feel increasingly guilty. She should have stuck to her instincts and refused to let Ilona put her in such a vulnerable position.

"Is it true? Did you see what happened too?"

Her heart jumped into her throat. "Too? You mean you saw the shooting, Matt?"

The youth looked poised for flight. Fear lit eyes that were much too old for his fifteen years. "Yeah."

"Why didn't you tell the police?"

"No way! I'm not gonna end up like him."

"Him who? You mean Thorton Biggs?"

Matt didn't seem to hear her questions. "You were smart not to tell them everything. The cops can't protect us, you know."

She thought of Thad Osher and understood immediately. The man was a cop, but he was also a jerk. She laid a hand on Matt's arm and he jumped like a startled deer.

"It's okay, Matt."

"No. That's why I came to warn you. We aren't safe anymore. You have to go away. Someplace safe."

"Matt, it's okay." But his fear had communicated itself just fine. She felt suddenly exposed, standing in the middle of the alley like this. "Let's go inside and—"

The crack of the gun was shockingly loud. The shot must have passed between her head and Matt's because it shattered the corner brick right behind them.

"Run!"

The boy was already taking his own advice. He sprinted to the dumpster with impressive speed.

Nicki heard the second and third shots ricochet before she followed his example and ran. She headed for the steps leading up to her apartment. Her fingers fumbled with the keys in her hand, searching for the one that would open the door. Another shot. Louder. Closer.

She reached the steps. Running footsteps pounded toward her. Too scared to scream, she started to climb. The keys slipped through her fingers.

"Nicki!"

She whirled.

Alex stood behind her, a gun in his right hand. It was pointed directly at her chest.

Chapter Three

Her gaze riveted on the gun in his hand. Without taking time to explain, Alex spun around sweeping the alley with his eyes. Nothing and no one moved.

"Are you okay?" he asked.

"That depends. Are you planning to shoot me?"

Her voice was tremulous and her face was pale, but Nicki stared at him without flinching. The alley was deathly quiet.

He bent to retrieve her keys. "Come down from there and let's get inside."

"Why?"

"Because someone is shooting out here!"

"I noticed."

Still, she hesitated. Alex realized he'd scared her. Did she think he'd been the one doing the shooting?

"For crying out loud, Nic. Will you come down here and get inside? You're a sitting duck on those steps. He may still be out here."

"You're just full of compliments these days, aren't you?" But she wasted no more time coming down the steps. Her gaze swept the parking lot and worry lined her forehead. He handed her the keys and waited while she unlocked the back door to her shop. For an instant, he sensed her mental debate, but she didn't slam the door in his face. He entered behind her and shoved the gun in his waistband.

"Tell me what happened."

"Don't you know?"

She flicked on an overhead light. The room was neatly organized with worktables and shelves. A bank of kilns stood against the outside wall.

"Did you think I was the one firing at you?" he asked.

She turned to regard him. "Were you?"

Alex sighed. "If I wanted you dead, you'd be dead, Nicki."

"Gee, thanks."

"Nicki!"

"You're the only one around here I've seen holding a gun, Alex."

"What about the person you saw the other night?"

Her eyes darted away.

"Tell me what's going on, Nicki."

"You tell me. You're the one with the gun."

"Forget the gun, will you?" Exasperated, he glared at her.

The scream of an approaching siren halted her response. Alex swore softly. If Osher caught him in here with a weapon, he wouldn't be given a chance to explain.

"Here." He pulled the gun from his waistband and tried to hand it to Nicki. She backed right into a shelving unit filled with bisque. One piece fell to the ground and shattered.

"I don't want it!"

"Hide it for me. If Osher catches me with it, he'll throw me in jail and toss away the key. I don't have time for that right now."

"Of course not. How inconvenient. But as it happens, I don't want to go to jail either."

"Nic…"

The police car came to a stop out back.

"Are you going to help me or not?"

For a second, he thought she was going to refuse. Then she took the gun gingerly, holding it by the barrel. With a glance around, she walked over to a kiln and lifted the lid. Without ceremony, set the gun inside.

"Try to remember to pull it out before you fire that kiln," he warned. "It'll make a heck of an explosion otherwise."

A loud rap on the door made them both jump.

Nicki stared in consternation.

"Take it easy. Answer it," he whispered, "but don't mention me, okay?"

"No. It is *not* okay."

He kissed her forehead. "Thanks, Nic. I owe you." He moved past her office and into the large bathroom. Leaving the door mostly open.

"Officer Jackstone!" she greeted.

Alex relaxed. He liked Derek Jackstone. The man was a good cop.

"We got a report of more gunshots here in the alley."

"Oh no!"

"You didn't hear anything?"

"I just came down. I must have been in the *bathroom*."

Why did he keep forgetting how spunky she was, Alex mused.

"So you didn't see anything?" Jackstone asked.

"I'm sorry. No."

"Okay. Stay inside, Ms. Michaels. Away from the windows. I'm going to check around. Hold off opening the store for a few minutes, all right?"

"Yes, of course."

"Lock the door behind me."

"I will."

Alex heard the sound of the deadbolt being turned in

place. He stepped out to meet her. "Thanks, Nicki. You okay?"

"No!" She glared at him. "What are you doing here, Alex? Why are you carrying a gun? Who was firing at me? And why?"

"I wish I knew, Nicki."

"That's not an answer."

"It's the best I can do right now. I heard the shots, but I didn't see who was doing the shooting."

He rubbed his eyes, more tired than he could remember being in a long time. He was getting too old to stay up all night.

"Officer Jackstone wants me to wait before I open the store."

"I heard."

"That means he'll be coming back."

"Are you worried about me, Nicki?" He took a step closer, liking the sudden nervous awareness in her eyes.

"Take your gun and go, Alex."

He reached out to stroke a tendril of hair. Her lashes fluttered closed in reaction. Such long, pretty lashes.

"I can't do that, Nicki. They'll arrest me."

She stared at him, her concern palpable. She moistened her lips, reminding him of how sweet they could taste. He could smell the faintest hint of gardenias on her skin and he took another step closer, wanting to inhale the scent of her.

Remembered passion shimmered in her eyes, stirring to life each exciting memory of how it felt to hold her, to kiss her, to touch all those hidden—

"What sort of trouble are you in, Alex?"

She stepped to one side, opening the distance between them. A distance that should be a chasm, he thought ruefully.

"Nothing that concerns you. Go ahead and get your store ready to open. Pretend I'm not here."

"My pleasure."

He realized his curt answer had hurt her again. He didn't want her hurt.

Nicki swallowed hard and managed a glare. How dare he send out such mixed signals? One minute he was devouring her with his eyes and the next he acted like she didn't mean a thing to him and never had.

"I must have been really stupid at sixteen." It would have made a terrific exit line. Too bad she couldn't fade to black. Instead, she walked up front where he couldn't follow without the risk of being seen by someone outside.

Alex made a sound of frustration. Good. Did he think she'd stand by and let him toy with her emotions? She hadn't been pining all these years for Alex Coughlin.

"Why a craft store, Nicki?" he called softly from the shadows of the hall.

"Why not a craft store?" She picked up a duster and pretended to be busy. She did not want him to know how badly she'd wanted to taste his kiss again.

"I thought you wanted to go to college and become a teacher."

"Yeah, well, we don't always get what we want in life, do we, Alex."

"What happened?"

She thought about telling him it was none of his business, but decided that was childish.

"My stepmother died in a car crash. I had to leave school and come home and help Dad. Hope was only fourteen and Brent and Gavin were still in high school. Someone had to run the house while Dad ran the business."

"I'm sorry."

"So was I, at the time. But things worked out okay. There was a financial settlement from the accident and Dad gave each of us a share. Mine was enough to buy into Millie's Craft Shop before Millie retired. Millie taught me what I needed to know about running the store and eventually I bought her out. So I teach crafts instead of reading. How come you didn't go to college like you planned?''

''Who says I didn't?''

She turned and regarded him, letting her slow perusal express what she wanted to say. Nicki would have sworn he blushed.

He crossed his legs at the ankles and leaned against the wall. It bothered her that he could look so sexy and so at ease when she was so desperately aware of him on every level.

''Life may not have turned out like either of us thought it would,'' he said, ''but you could still go to school now.''

''So could you.''

''Nicki...'' he sighed and ran a hand through his hair.

Alex had great hair. She remembered how much she'd liked running her fingers through his thick waves.

''You're still very beautiful,'' he told her.

The unexpected compliment left her speechless. Especially since he sounded so sincere. His eyes watched her with a hooded expression as he tucked a thumb into the waistband of his jeans.

''Do you ever think about us?''

The slow drawl of his voice sent remembered shivers of awareness skittering along her nerves.

''No.'' The lie tripped off her tongue. He tipped his head to the side in an expression that clearly said he didn't believe her.

''I have. More than once. You were the only good memory I took with me when I left Fools Point.''

Before she could reply, someone hammered on the rear door. Alex slipped inside the bathroom without a word.

Nicki opened the back door, expecting Officer Jackstone, and came face to face with Thad Osher.

"Ms. Michaels."

Nicki squelched a shudder of distaste.

"Are you going to let me come in?"

If only she could say no. She stepped aside and Osher entered, sweeping the room with a hard look. The look he gave her was just short of a leer.

"Nice."

Nicki swallowed a retort. She wouldn't achieve anything by baiting him. Sergeant Osher lived for conflict. She gave him silence.

Osher scowled. "Tell me what happened out back."

"I have no idea."

"You telling me you didn't hear the shots?" His eyes narrowed.

"I am if you're asking."

"Ms. Michaels, someone fired several rounds into your building. Be hard not to hear the shots when one of 'em struck right outside your door."

"Not if I was in the bathroom with the water running and the door closed."

"Is that right?"

He moved closer, deliberately violating her space. His eyes dared her to move away. Though he repelled her, she lifted her chin defiantly. "Yes, that's right. And if you put that hand on me, you'd better be preparing to take me to jail."

Osher hesitated, his hand raised in midreach.

"Because I guarantee you, I'm going to scream bloody murder."

He dropped his hand to his side. "Now why would you want to go and do a thing like that, Ms. Michaels?"

"Because I don't like being touched, *Sergeant.*"

He squinted at her. Anger added tight lines around his

mouth and eyes. He wasn't going to take this rebuke any better than the others she'd given him on those rare occasions when their paths had crossed. Nicki only prayed that Officer Jackstone was still outside and near enough to hear her if she had to make good on her threat.

"Really? You don't like being touched, huh?"

"I don't like her being touched either."

Alex's low drawl sent her spinning around. He leaned against the wall in another negligent pose, but Nicki knew him well enough to know that Alex seethed with controlled tension.

"I especially don't like her being touched by you," Alex added.

"Well, well, well. Isn't this cozy?" Osher gave her an evil glare and then turned his entire focus on Alex. "We've been looking for you, Coughlin."

"Looks like you found me."

"Yeah." Osher drew his weapon.

Nicki's mouth dropped open in stunned shock. "What are you doing?"

Osher didn't look at her. "You're under arrest, Coughlin."

"What for?" Nicki demanded. "He didn't do anything."

"Suspicion of murder." He spared Nicki another glare. "I knew there was a reason you didn't pick him out of the lineup."

"There was. I couldn't identify him."

Osher sneered. "Right. We've got hard evidence this time."

"That's not possible," Alex said calmly.

"You shoulda' been more careful, Coughlin. You tore your shirt on the fence the other night. We matched the fibers."

"Even if you matched fibers, which I doubt, I could have torn my shirt at any time." But he had started to go over the fence after the figure running away and his shirt had snagged.

"Tell it to your lawyer. That gave us enough to get a warrant to search your place today." Osher smiled triumphantly. "And your car, which has been impounded along with your motorcycle. Bet you'll never guess what we found."

"Dust bunnies?"

"A gun, smart guy. One with several rounds fired. One that is the same caliber as the one used to kill Thorton Biggs. Want to take bets this will turn out to be the murder weapon?"

Alex straightened. "Not unless you planted it yourself."

"Turn around and put your hands on the wall," Osher snapped, suddenly all business. "You know the drill by now, Coughlin."

Slowly, Alex turned around. Nicki watched in horror as Thad Osher walked toward him. "But, Alex didn't do anything!" she protested.

Osher shot her a look of scorn. "I'll deal with you later, Ms. Michaels. Aiding and abetting is—"

In that moment, Alex erupted in a blur of action. He spun around so fast, Nicki barely saw the foot that caught Osher in the chest. She flattened herself against a shelving unit as the two men grappled. It was quickly apparent that Thad Osher was outmatched. Alex brought his hand down in a blow that sent the gun spinning across the floor, almost at Nicki's feet. Without hesitation, she kicked the weapon under the shelving unit.

The fight was over in seconds. Osher lay doubled on her floor dry-heaving while Alex ran out the front door.

Nicki hesitated. Osher groaned. A trickle of blood ran from his nose. She ran to the back door and flung it open. Officer Jackstone was talking to the woman who ran the beauty shop two doors down. Nicki motioned him urgently.

"Ms. Michaels?"

"Alex just decked Sergeant Osher."

"What?" He pushed past her. She followed more slowly, trying to get her emotions under control. She needed to be calm while she decided what to tell them.

Osher was pushing himself to his feet and cursing loudly when she got inside.

"The bastard took my gun," he told Derek Jackstone.

"He did not!" Immediate anger pushed caution aside. "Your gun went under that shelf over there after you dropped it. And Alex wouldn't have touched you in the first place if you hadn't been threatening me."

Officer Jackstone whipped around. "Thad threatened you?"

"He was leering at me. I warned him if he touched me I'd scream. That's when Alex came to my rescue."

"Why you lyin' little—"

"Shut up, Thad," Jackstone told him.

"He pulled out his gun and said Alex was under arrest. Then he threatened me so Alex hit him."

"He threatened you?"

"I did not!"

She glared at Osher. "You said you'd take care of me later. I took that as a threat. So did Alex." She turned to Jackstone. "I want to press charges of illegal harassment against Sergeant Osher. I've had enough of his threats and sexual innuendos."

Osher swore and took a step in her direction. Derek Jackstone stepped between them. "Cool it, Thad."

"She's lying!"

"Ms. Michaels, what was Alex Coughlin doing here?"

"He came to ask me if I saw or heard anything the night of the murder. He was under the correct impression that Sergeant Osher was trying to pin the crime on him. I think Alex planned to talk to all the shopkeepers along here."

"Probably to find out who else saw him commit the murder," Osher said.

Nicki scowled at him. "You appear to have some sort of grudge against Alex. Alex told me he was afraid of being railroaded into jail. The way you act, I can believe it."

"Why you little tramp."

"Be quiet, Thad."

"You kept pushing me to identify him in that farce of a lineup. Don't you dare deny it," she insisted.

Derek looked like he wanted to curse. Osher did. Volubly. "Knock it off, Thad. This is a mess."

"She's lying. We'll take her in and get her to tell the truth."

"No. We won't."

Osher turned on him. "In case you forgot, I outrank you."

"I haven't forgotten anything, but I think you have. Let's go outside and discuss this. Now!" Jackstone bent and fished Osher's gun out from under the shelving unit.

"What about her?"

"Ms. Michaels, I have to ask that you remain here in town."

"I have a business to run. I'm not going anywhere. But I meant what I said about pressing charges. I'm tired of being harassed by this man."

Osher started to say something nasty, but Jackstone held up both hands. "Okay. Both of you calm down. I'll return and take your statement later, Ms. Michaels. Let's go outside, Thad."

Thad did, cursing all the way. The glower he cast her way sent alarm racing through her. She'd just made a deadly enemy.

Nicki locked the door behind them, then collapsed in a chair, suddenly so cold she shivered. Maybe she'd made matters worse for herself, but at least she'd given Alex time to get away.

Was it the past, raging hormones, or sheer stupidity that made her want to believe Alex had nothing to do with the murder? Maybe it was just that she disliked Thad Osher so much she found it easy to believe the opposite of anything he said.

Osher could have planted the murder weapon in Alex's car as Alex alleged, but that would make Osher the murderer. While Nicki could well believe the hotheaded officer might shoot someone, it seemed to her that if he did, he'd pretend it happened in the line of duty.

Still, there was a curious kind of logic if she assumed Thad Osher had killed Thorton Biggs for some reason known only to the two of them. Did she dare suggest this to Officer Jackstone?

No. She couldn't. She'd told them that she'd seen the murder. Thad Osher was blond, not dark haired. To tell the truth now, she'd have to admit she lied earlier about witnessing the crime. That meant she'd have to tell Officer Jackstone about Ilona.

Oh, why had she agreed to cover for her friend? Stupid. Look where it had gotten her. Ilona was someplace hiding from her boyfriend and as a result, a murderer might go free.

Nicki suddenly sat up straighter. Ilona had said her boyfriend was a cop. A married cop. Thad Osher was married. And even though Nicki thought he was a creep, he wasn't a bad-looking creep. What if he was Ilona's cop? And what if Ilona had seen Thad Osher kill Thorton Biggs? That would explain her fear and her refusal to come forward with what she'd seen.

The more Nicki thought about the idea, the more she liked it. But that still left her with a major problem. How could she tell anyone what she suspected?

If only she could talk to Ilona.

ALEX KNEW HE wouldn't get far so he didn't even try. He went out the shop door and in through the doorway leading upstairs to the overhead apartments. In minutes, he was inside Nicki's place.

He stared around curiously. The furniture was second-hand, but cheerfully, boldly restored. Samples of her crafts were everywhere without giving the rooms a cluttered look. Alex began a systematic search of her apartment, moving quietly. Nicki and the police were right below him. Despite the solid construction of the building, he didn't want to alert anyone to his presence. He hoped whoever lived across the hall wasn't the nosy type.

He felt guilty as he looked through her belongings, but he needed to know why Nicki was keeping secrets. By the time he reached her bedroom, he was fairly certain he wouldn't find anything at all. Nicki was who and what she'd always been. A friendly, loving, open person. So why was she behaving so oddly?

He opened a dresser drawer and came face to face with her underwear. When he'd known her, she'd worn plain cotton, not these erotic, bold materials. He certainly would like to see her in some of this. He lifted a vibrantly sexy red garment, picturing her curves filling the provocative satin and lace. This was made for a man's seduction.

What man did she wear it for?

The question stayed in the back of his mind as he went through her closet. There, he discovered more changes from the girl he'd known to the woman who intrigued him now. Everything from the jeans he remembered, to softer, more feminine items. Those were the garments that stirred his imagination.

He pulled aside a hanger with a slinky red dress. The red teddy made perfect sense now. Nicki would be a knockout in the dress, but any man who suspected what she was wearing beneath it would go nuts waiting to peel the dress from her body.

Alex moved on, wondering what was wrong with him today, and very much afraid he knew the answer. He had a job to do, but all he wanted to concentrate on was Nicki.

A box on her closet shelf held mementos. He pawed through the contents without finding anything out of the ordinary until he came to the photo album. Wildflowers had been pressed on the first page. His own features stared back at him from a series of snapshots on the next page. Young. Surly. Angry at the world.

At everyone except Nicki, that is.

He'd picked those wildflowers for her that day. And in return, under a blazing summer sun, she'd given him the priceless gift of herself.

Alex closed the book and returned the box to its shelf. He only wished he could set aside his own memories as easily. He proceeded to search the rest of the room with detached determination. There was nothing other than what he would expect to find.

He nearly fell over her small cat as he went to check the spare bedroom. Ginger brushed against him in a bid for attention. "Not now, cat."

He fished a bra and a toy mouse out from under the daybed. The black nylon and lace was in keeping with the other intimate apparel he'd found in Nicki's bedroom, except this bra was three sizes larger than anything Nicki could wear.

"So all that says is she had company," he told the calico cat, who gleefully threw the mouse in the air and chased after it as it bounced across the carpeting.

"Too bad you can't tell me who this belongs to, Ginger. Not one sign of a lover. No pictures, no extravagant gifts, not one thing out of place. Nicki always did like the quiet life.''

And according to the checkbook he'd found, the quiet life was all Nicki could afford. The shop apparently eked out a living as long as she was frugal. She deserved better.

He hated that he was going to add to her problems. If he had a choice, he'd leave right now. But it was too late to keep her out of the trouble surrounding Fools Point.

He picked up her telephone and made a couple of quick calls. As he finished the second one, the front door burst open without warning.

"Ilona?" Nicki called out breathlessly.

"Sorry," he said. "Only me."

"You? What are you doing here? The entire police force is out looking for you."

"Yeah, I noticed. I was hoping they wouldn't think to look for me here."

She sagged against the door frame. "I don't believe this."

"Well, actually, I'm not too happy about the situation either."

"Why did you come up here?"

Alex spread his hands. "I didn't have any place else to go."

"You're going to get me arrested."

"No. I promise. I won't drag you any further into this mess."

"We both know what your promises are worth, don't we?"

The words settled in the air between them.

"I'm sorry, Nic."

"Sorry doesn't cut it anymore, Alex."

"Do you want me to go?"

"Yes."

Anger flashed in her eyes. Anger and pain. It was the pain that started him walking.

"No. Darn it, wait. You can't go. They'll be watching the shop."

He paused. They were close enough that he could touch her with very little effort. He tucked his thumbs into his belt and rocked back on his heels. "I never meant to hurt you, Nicki."

"Don't you dare turn that lost puppy charm on me, Alex Coughlin. I won't stand for it anymore. You can stay here until it's dark. Then you have to go. I've got to get back downstairs. I have a class starting in five minutes."

She turned away without meeting his eyes.

"Thank you."

"Don't thank me, Alex. I'm doing it for me, not you. I have no intention of giving Thad Osher a reason to arrest me."

He set his jaw at the cop's name, but swallowed his comment. Instead he asked the question that he'd wanted to ask since she burst into the apartment. "Who's Ilona?"

Nicki paused, halfway down the steps. "She was my college roommate. I've got to go. Don't make any noise or they'll hear you downstairs."

She fled, closing the street door behind her. Alex went slowly down the steps and retrieved Ginger who'd seized the opportunity to explore.

Why didn't Nicki want to talk to him about Ilona? And where had he heard the name before? It was an unusual name. Perhaps he'd better have another, more detailed look around Nicki's apartment. An evasive Nicki was a guilty Nicki. But guilty of what?

Fifteen minutes later, he was mulling over the battered box he'd found inside her jewelry box. All these years she'd kept the tiny heart pendant with the ruby chip he'd given her. He didn't like the disturbing way it made him feel. Nicki had always been a romantic, but surely she hadn't been pining for him all these years.

He'd found nothing to tie her to Thorton Biggs or any of the other names on his mental list. The location of Thorton's death could have been coincidence. As for the call, he wondered how much nerve it had taken her to swallow her pride and call him. He refused to feel guilty. Seeing her again had never been an option and all the wishing in the world wouldn't change that fact.

Alex lay down on her bed and closed his eyes. It would be hours before Nicki would come upstairs again and the strain of the past few days was taking its toll. He yawned and let his conscious mind drift.

The telephone jarred him out of a deep, dreamless sleep hours later. He stared at the phone, waiting for the answering machine to kick in.

"Ms. Michaels, it's me. Matt. Look, Ms. Michaels, you gotta get out of there. You aren't safe. These guys are playing for keeps. You gotta listen to me. Don't trust anybody. Not anybody!" The connection was hastily broken.

All his concerns and suspicions came rushing back. Alex ran a weary hand through his hair. Who the devil was Matt? Obviously not Nicki's boyfriend, given the "Ms. Michaels" and the youthful sound of the voice. But then, who?

Alex used her bathroom, careful not to flush the commode, though he took a chance and ran water in the sink, using a washcloth to wipe the sleep from his face. He wandered out to her kitchen and helped himself to a sandwich and a soft drink. She still liked root beer, he discovered. And vanilla ice cream. He was just finishing his snack when he heard the front door open.

"Alex?"

He met her in the dining room.

"What's the matter?"

"I wasn't sure you'd still be here."

"Like I told you, Nicki, I don't have any place else to go. What's wrong?"

"I just had a conversation with Officer Jackstone. I agreed not to press charges against Thad Osher if they'd keep him away from me. Chief Hepplewhite will be back tomorrow and your sister's fiancé is supposed to start as his second in command in three days."

"Lee Garvey," Alex acknowledged. "That should help."

"I told Officer Jackstone that you came to the front door right after he left. He wasn't happy I let you in, but I explained we were old acquaintances."

"Acquaintances?" he asked softly.

A blush stole up her neck. "Yes," she said defiantly.

"Who's Matt?"

Her face went blank. "Who? Oh. Matt! I can't believe I forgot about him! He's a local teenager. He was in the alley this morning and took off when the shooting started. I'm pretty sure he wasn't hit."

"I didn't see him."

"He told me he saw the murder, Alex. He can actually identify the murderer."

Alex set his jaw. "You'd better listen to your messages."

Hesitantly, she headed for the bedroom and hit the Play button on the answering machine. Alex studied her reaction, but all he saw was puzzled concern.

"What 'guys' is he talking about, Nic?"

"I don't know."

"He thinks you do."

"I can't help that."

Her temper was rising. So was his. "Did you actually see the murder, Nicki?"

She looked away, then sighed. "No. All I saw was you running away."

He brushed that aside. "Why did you tell the police you saw the murder?"

"I did practically see it."

"Nicki…"

"Look, did it ever occur to you that Thad Osher might be the killer?"

If she'd been looking for a distraction, she'd picked a doozy. His mind sifted over the possibility.

"I admit, I don't like him," she continued, "so I'm prejudiced. But if we could connect him to Thorton Biggs somehow—"

"What's going on Nicki? Talk to me."

Nicki sank down on the bed. "I can't. I gave my word."

"To whom?"

"I can't tell you."

"Well, you'd better tell me something. A man is dead and someone tried to kill you this morning."

Nicki jumped up. "Let's go find Matt. He saw the whole thing. He knows who the killer is and probably even the reason behind the killing."

"Nicki—"

"He lives with his aunt and uncle when he's home. He's mostly on the street. He and his uncle don't get along. Jake Collins was sort of taking him under his wing, until Matt disappeared last month."

"Disappeared?"

"Matt may have stolen a car from the restaurant parking lot. There have been a lot of car thefts…" she paused. "Why do you look like that?"

"Like what?"

"Like something is suddenly making sense."

Alex hesitated. He owed Nicki. Besides, a little more

knowledge might guarantee that she would take a few more precautions for her own safety.

"Thorton Biggs owned an auto body shop," he told her.

"So?"

"That may be the reason he was killed."

"You think he had something to do with the stolen cars?"

"Yes. If Matt was working for them as well, he probably knows everyone involved. Where does he live?"

"Off Main Street. Are we going over there?"

"I am. You're going to stay here."

Nicki shook her head. "Unless you walk, you don't have any way to get there. The police impounded your transportation. They have a warrant out for your arrest, Alex."

"Yeah."

"I told them I was sure you weren't the man I'd seen in the alley that night."

"We aren't finished with that discussion, you know."

"I am. Let's go find Matt."

Alex decided not to pursue the argument right then. Finding Matt took precedence. "You think Matt could be at his aunt's?"

"It's worth checking out. His aunt and uncle work in D.C. They tend to get home pretty late on Fridays so he may be there. It will at least give us a place to start."

"What about your shop?"

"I close at six on Fridays. Today I closed early. No one will be surprised. There weren't any customers at this hour. The danger is getting you down to my car. There are apt to be people in the parking lot right now."

"No one will give us a second glance unless we act suspicious."

"Or the police are watching."

"It's a five-man police force, Nicki. They don't have enough men to do that sort of surveillance."

"Maybe not, but Sergeant Osher hates both of us right now."

"Let me worry about Osher."

"Gladly."

Nicki's apartment and the one next door shared a narrow covered porch out back and a set of metal fire steps leading down to the lot. As far as Alex could tell, no one appeared to be paying the building any attention. Cars were parked with people coming and going, but mostly at the two ends near the bank and the general store.

No one spared them a second glance as they walked to Nicki's coupe and climbed inside.

"Your neighbor isn't the curious type?"

"Mrs. Coulton? No. She'll be moving out in a few days. She's in her eighties, has cataracts and needs a hearing aide. Her children are moving her into a nursing home."

"Too bad. She sounds like the perfect neighbor."

Nicki shook her head at his teasing. She still drove with reckless abandon, Alex discovered. Studying her profile, he was glad to see at least some things hadn't changed.

"Are you happy with your life, Alex?"

The question surprised him. He thought about the past few months and shook his head. "Not lately."

"It isn't too late to make some changes, you know."

"Yeah? Would any of them involve you and me?"

He expected a scathing retort. Instead, for a moment he saw a spark of excitement before she sent him a brooding look.

"Why are you wasting your life running around with people like Vic Unsdorf, Alex? You're so much brighter than that. Is it because your dad was accused of being a thief and a killer? Do you really think you have to live down to that sort of reputation?"

He tensed. The desire to confide in her surprised him.

"What happened to my dad has nothing to do with my life now."

"Sure it does. His death shaped your life, Alex. Yours and Kayla's. Your sister learned to hate the police. But she got over it. She's actually going to marry one now."

"I know."

"How do you feel about that?"

"I just wish he was already on duty here in Fools Point. Lee's a good cop. The cop who shot my dad was just a kid. Overeager and trigger-happy. The whole thing was a horrible accident. Dad had nothing to do with that robbery and murder in Frederick. He was just unlucky enough to be driving a car that matched the getaway car. I hate what happened to him, but I came to understand how it went down. Dad was innocent. When he reached for his wallet, the kid got scared and fired. The only ones who got it wrong were the media. They were the ones who labeled Dad a thief and a murderer."

"But that was enough to ruin your life."

"Not really. It shaped me, like you said, but I'm not a criminal, Nic."

"Then why are you hanging around with losers like Unsdorf and Barry Fairvale? You know Barry was arrested in connection with that bank robbery down in D.C. last month?"

"I know. The police questioned me too."

"See? That's exactly what I'm talking about. Why don't you go back to school? You're too smart to be hanging around with a bunch of losers."

He found himself touched by her concern. "Isn't that our turn?"

"Huh? Oh. Yeah. Matt's aunt and uncle live near the end of the street."

"The dilapidated place on the right?"

"Yes."

"Wait here in the car."

"No. I'm coming with you. He won't come to the door if you knock, Alex."

"And you think he will for you?"

"He might. He did try to warn me. Why don't you wait? I'll talk to him and convince him to help us."

Alex tensed, wanting to protest, but her words made sense. He watched her walk up onto the porch uneasily. Something about the neighborhood bugged him. It was too quiet. The house looked too deserted. And a warning prickle snaked its way up his back.

Alex stepped out of the car.

"Nicki! Wait!"

Puzzled, she turned. "What's wrong?"

Long ago, he'd learned to listen to his instincts. "Come away from the door."

"Why? What's wrong?" she asked again.

"It doesn't feel right."

"What doesn't? Alex?"

His eyes swept the deserted neighborhood. The sense of danger was stronger now. "Get back in the car," he ordered softly. "Now, Nicki."

She hesitated only a second, then she started down the steps, reaching inside her purse. "Here."

Surprised, Alex walked forward and took his gun from her hand. "Get in the car."

Nicki hurried past him. Suddenly Alex swore. His eyes fastened on the device taped to the front door.

As if that was a signal, the rear of the house exploded.

Chapter Four

Nicki screamed as the explosion rent the air. Alex ran for the back of the house. She began running as well, stumbling when the ground sloped down to allow for a walk-out basement.

Nicki skidded to a halt as she came parallel with the steps of the backyard deck. The sliding glass door under the deck had been shattered from the force of the blast. A chunk of the house had been blown away leaving a gaping, smoldering hole. Part of the deck above was gone as well.

Alex started toward the opening, but he looked up as she came into view.

"Get back!"

Before she could move, he flung himself at her, knocking her down in the grass. Wrapping his arms around her, he rolled them down the slope, away from the house.

Stunned and breathless, she peered into Alex's dark gaze. "What—?"

A second explosion rocked the air.

Alex buried her beneath his body. The concussion jarred the ground beneath them as a hail of objects rained down. Only his quick action saved them from the deadly flying shards of glass. Wood fragments pelted them as the force of the second explosion shattered the rest of the back deck.

"What happened?" she gasped when she caught her breath. Alex released her and sat up.

Splinters of wood and glass mingled with patio furniture, filling the backyard with rubble. Several spearlike boards stood upright in the hard-baked ground. One quivered in the air, frighteningly close to where they lay. Tongues of fire licked the frame house, ignited by the blast.

When she started to move, Alex pressed her back down. "Stay still. There may be more bombs."

"Bombs?"

"Someone attached them to the doors on the house. Maybe some of the windows as well, I can't tell."

"That's insane! Things like that don't happen here."

Alex gave her a rueful look. "They do now."

He surveyed the surrounding houses, then the tree line behind them. Suddenly, the gun appeared in his hand. Nicki stopped breathing.

"When I tell you, run for the house next door." His words were low and urgent. "Call the police. Tell them the house is on fire, but booby-trapped."

Fear lanced her mind. "What are you going to do?"

"There's someone watching us from the trees."

She placed her hand on his arm. "No, Alex." But he didn't seem to hear her plea. His hard gaze was focused on the field and trees at her back. He was going to go after the person, she knew it as surely as if he'd spoken his thought out loud.

"Go, Nicki. Now. Run!"

The uncompromising insistence of his tone brooked no argument. Horrified, Nicki climbed to her feet and began to run. She glanced over her shoulder. Alex was up and running too. Only he was running away from her toward the trees, gun in hand.

Nicki felt sick with fear. There wasn't a single window left in the back or side of the house.

People started to pool outside. Several teenagers came running over. They were first on the scene.

"Get back!" she yelled to them.

"Is it a gas main?"

"No. Someone set explosive devices around the house!"

"You mean bombs?" They eyed her with shock.

"What about Matt?" one of the teens demanded.

That prompted a whole new fear. "I don't know," she admitted. She turned back toward the house.

Flames shot up the back. The summer had been dry. The remains of the wooden deck acted as kindling. Soon the entire house would be involved. Were more bombs waiting to detonate? Was Matt still inside?

Alex sprinted out of the woods toward her. Her relief was staggering. He no longer held the gun in his hand. She ran to meet him.

"Are you okay?" Blood dripped down his arm from a gash.

"I'm fine, Nicki. It's just a scratch."

"I was afraid."

Alex smiled at her and touched her arm reassuringly. "Whoever was back there took off."

"It was probably just someone who heard the explosions."

"Or the person who detonated them. Either way, there wasn't much point in chasing him. He cut through the trees toward Back Lake Road. He probably had a car parked there for a fast and easy exit."

The trio of teens ran over to them.

"Hey, man, you're bleeding."

"It's just a scratch."

"Did Matt do this?" one of the boys asked, shock vying with excitement.

"Do you have any reason to think he might have?" Alex demanded.

"No, man! I mean, he and his uncle don't get along, but he's not the type to blow up their house, you know? I mean, Matt's okay. He's not depressed or crazy or anything like those kids you see on the news. He isn't even interested in stuff like that."

"Do you think he's inside?" the girl asked, shoving a wild mane of red hair back behind her ear.

Despite the chaos around them, a hushed air of expectancy fell over the group. Nicki saw Alex's hesitation. She could almost hear what he was thinking.

"You don't think he could be, do you?" Nicki asked.

Alex started running toward the burning house.

"Alex, no! Wait!"

He didn't even break stride. "I have to check."

"But there may be more bombs!"

"Keep the others back!" he yelled over his shoulder. "And pull the car onto the street so you won't block the fire engines."

"Alex!"

She watched in horror as Alex continued toward the burning house.

"I'll go with him," one of the boys offered, but a woman who'd come over to join them grabbed his arm.

"You will not, Jeremy Marshall! You'll wait right here!"

"But he might need help."

"It's too dangerous."

Nicki watched Alex approach the burning structure. She held her breath as he darted inside the gaping hole beneath the fire and disappeared. The steps leading up to the deck suddenly collapsed in a hail of sparks.

"Alex!"

"Man, that fire's really starting to catch now."

"Did anyone call the fire department?" Nicki demanded.

"I did," the woman responded.

As if to prove her words, the distant wail of the fire trucks could be heard approaching.

Nicki turned away. She stemmed her impulse to go after Alex. His last order had been to move the car and he was right. They were going to need an escape route. The explosions would bring the police as well as the fire department to the scene.

The keys dangled in the ignition. As Nicki started the engine, she looked at the front door of the house. Because she was looking for it, she saw a dark canister-like object, taped there. She could easily have blown up along with the front of the house.

And Alex was inside!

Trembling with fear for him, she drove the car more than halfway down the short block. She parked far up on someone's grass so she wouldn't block any part of the street.

People arriving home for dinner were sidetracked by the unexpected diversion. Didn't they understand the danger? There was at least one more unexploded bomb! Nicki rushed back to join the throng.

"Keep back!" she warned. The first group of teens had edged closer to the house. The adults were clustered together talking excitedly.

"There's at least one more explosive device on the front door," she told them. "There may be more. Everyone needs to move back."

"How do you know?" A man in a business suit demanded.

"You can see it! People, you need to get back!"

The youth closest to her turned to his friends. "Remember when that guy blew up in his car out near 270? Man, there wasn't enough of him left to identify. I sure hope Matt isn't inside that house."

So did Nicki. But Alex was. Why didn't he come out?

"Yeah. Hey, didn't Matt know that guy? Wow, what if the same people came back here to murder Matt too?"

Matt had known the man in the car bombing? Nicki wondered at their connection while her attention remained riveted on the house.

Why didn't Alex appear?

Rattled as she was, she knew Thad Osher could be arriving at any moment. Smoke drifted in the sluggish, evening heat. Nicki heard the distant crackle of flames as the fire continued to spread. Her fear changed to panic.

Where was Alex?

She edged closer. A front window abruptly shattered as a chair smashed its way through the glass from inside the house. Nicki ignored her dredging fear and ran onto the porch to help.

"Nicki, get back!"

Alex shouted at her as he attempted to shove someone through the window.

"Let me help!"

"Okay. I'm going to try and pass him out to you. Grab him under the armpits and pull."

Matt was limp and covered in cuts. His face was blackened by smoke. She tugged at him while Alex shoved from behind. Seconds later, she staggered under Matt's deadweight. Alex climbed out and they each slung one of Matt's limp arms around their shoulders. Together, they made their way off the porch.

Nicki blinked as someone ran forward and snapped a picture. The screaming fire engine rounded the corner and roared up the street. The din and confusion were overwhelming. Belatedly, others started forward to help, but Alex yelled at them to get back.

"There could be more explosions!" To Nicki he said, "Set him down here in the grass."

They eased Matt onto the yellowed front lawn of the

house next door. Paramedics hurried toward them. The fire department began setting up equipment. Someone began herding people back, away from the house.

Alex checked Matt for a pulse. After a moment, he gave Nicki a reassuring nod. "He's unconscious, but still breathing."

"Step aside," the paramedics ordered.

"He was inside when the bomb went off," Alex told the man.

"Bomb?" Two startled heads whipped in Alex's direction.

"Someone set explosives all over the outside of that house. Who's in charge?" Alex didn't wait for an answer. With a swift glance around, he stood and ran toward a uniformed fireman giving orders.

Nicki stepped back to allow the emergency medical technicians room to work. People milled around her. She melted back into the crowd and inched her way to where Alex stood talking with the fire chief.

The older man nodded and began issuing new orders. Alex caught her eye. He indicated she should head toward the street. He stepped behind a fireman, out of her line of sight. A moment later, Nicki realized why. Thad Osher had arrived. If he saw either one of them, he'd arrest them on the spot and ask questions later. Nicki skirted around the fire engine. Alex was waiting.

"Where's the car?" he asked.

"Down there."

"Let's go."

The coupe was hemmed in by two police cars.

"We're trapped."

"Not for long. Give me the keys."

A few deft twists of the steering wheel and Alex was free to drive across the tightly manicured lawn. In seconds, they were clear of the traffic jam and heading for Main Street. No one noticed in all the confusion.

Behind them, another explosion rocked the neighborhood. Nicki sank back against the seat. "I don't believe this."

Grimly, Alex glanced at her. "Someone doesn't want Matt to tell anyone what he knows."

"My God, Alex. He's just a boy."

Alex shook his head. "Not anymore. He's playing in the big leagues, Nic. Remember the message he left you?"

"He said they were playing for keeps. But who?"

Alex shrugged. "There's good money in stealing cars, Nicki. You said yourself that he has an unhappy home situation with little supervision. That's just the sort of scenario that would cause a kid to get caught up in something like this. This could have been meant as a warning."

"A warning! They blew up his house!"

"Yeah, and a few months ago, they blew up a man."

Something cold settled in her stomach. "One of those boys said Matt knew the man who was killed."

Alex looked startled, then thoughtful. "This is all tied together."

"I don't understand."

"Neither do I. Not completely, but let's make some assumptions. Thorton Biggs ran an auto body shop and maybe a chop shop on the side. Matt earned money by bringing him stolen cars. The victim who blew up near the interstate last January was an undercover FBI agent investigating the car ring."

"I didn't know that," she interrupted.

"Not many people do. They kept it out of the papers, so don't mention it to anyone. But do you see a pattern emerging here?" He steered into the alley next to her store and parked looking deep in thought and very troubled.

"How do you know so much about all this?"

"Have you forgotten the people that I know?"

He cast her a sardonic look and she realized he was right. If anyone would have inside information, it would be people like Vic Unsdorf and Barry Fairvale and others she could name.

"Why do you hang out with them, Alex? Vic's a troublemaker and Barry was arrested for bank robbery. You're better than that. Why don't you leave? Get a good job, go back to school. Do something positive with your life before it's too late."

"Why Nicki, I think you care."

"Don't tease me, Alex. Not now. Not about this. You aren't like those other men."

He reached out and lightly touched her face. She wanted to curl right into that hand. Alex had always had a special way of touching her. His smile was gentle, taking her back to those hot summer days so long ago.

"How could I have forgotten this?" he murmured. "No one else ever believed in me the way you did, Nic. I wish I could leave and take you with me. But I can't. At least, not yet."

"Why not?" She gripped his shoulders, wanting to shake him. Wanting to keep him safe from the sort of horror she'd just witnessed. Alex winced. She realized she'd squeezed his arm right above the cut he'd sustained when the deck exploded.

"I'm sorry. I forgot you were hurt."

"It's okay."

"No. It isn't. Please listen to me Alex. You've got to leave. Think of your sister. Kayla's going to marry a cop who'll be working here in Fools Point. You don't want to put her in a position where she's caught between the two of you."

A sad, almost wistful look entered his expression. "I won't. Lee's a decent guy."

"I don't understand you."

His smile was gentle. "It's going to be okay, Nicki, one of these days I'll explain everything."

"What's wrong with now?"

He released her and sat up straight. "Now, we're going to get *you* out of here."

"What?"

"Come on."

He got out of the car. She had no choice but to do the same. She watched as his eyes swept the parking area closely. The traffic, both pedestrian and automobile, was near the bank's drive-in window. No cars were parked anywhere near them. Still, his alert stance made her shiver despite the heat and humidity of the late afternoon.

He walked around the car and stood almost protectively beside her as he surveyed everything around them. Remembering the shooter this morning, Nicki tried not to shudder.

"You don't think the person with the gun will come back, do you?"

"We aren't going to take any chances."

They walked to the steps leading up to her back porch. Alex's tension only increased her own nervousness. Alex had to take the keys from her cold fingers and unlock the door for her.

"I feel so cold all of a sudden," she said.

"Delayed shock. You'll be all right in a minute." He turned on the kitchen light. Dusk was dropping its mantle over the sky and her apartment was filled with shadows. Ginger came running to greet them.

"What about Matt?"

"He'll be okay too. I found him on the basement stairs trying to get out. He's got a lot of cuts and bruises, but I don't think he was seriously hurt." Alex laid a hand on her arm. His fingers were warm and comforting on her bare skin.

She turned into that warmth, grateful when he wrapped his arms around her and pulled her close against the hard wall of his chest. He smelled of smoke and sweat, but she didn't care. It just felt so good to be held. Ginger twined herself about their legs.

"Nicki, I think you should go out of town for awhile. Maybe visit your aunt in Wisconsin."

She pulled her head back from his shoulder in surprise. "I can't go out of town. I've got a business to run."

"Not if you're dead."

"What?"

"You came forward as a witness to the murder, Nicki. It's only logical that you'll be next on their list."

The possibility scared her right down to her toes. He squeezed her and stepped back. Instantly, she missed the comfort of his touch, but she was drawn to the sight of blood on his arm. The cut was oozing and he had another scrape across his knuckle.

"You're hurt."

"Just scratches."

"It's a little deeper than a scratch." Ginger meowed loudly for attention, but Nicki ignored her. "You don't want an infection."

"We don't have time for this, Nicki."

She opened the cupboard where she kept the first aid supplies. "What are you talking about?"

"Matt told you they played for keeps. You just saw a demonstration of what he was talking about up close and in person. This place could be next."

Nicki couldn't breathe. She set the iodine bottle down with a thump. The very idea that someone might try to blow her up was horrifying. "You're trying to scare me."

"Darn right I am. You *should* be scared, Nicki."

She shook her head, trying to put the pieces together, pushing the fear to the back of her mind where it hovered ominously. She grabbed a clean dish towel and wet one end.

"Nicki, we need to go. There isn't time for this."

"We'll make time. Hold still. This is going to sting."

Obviously placating her, he stood stoically while she cleaned the cut and applied a topical cream to prevent infection. She hadn't noticed how well muscled Alex was until now. There was raw masculine power beneath his lean physique that promised safety—and more.

"You aren't involved in this car ring are you, Alex?"

His eyes studied her without emotion, yet she had a feeling she'd just hurt his feelings.

"Not in the way you mean."

"What other way is there?"

He didn't answer. She taped the wound, refusing to give in to an urge to stroke his skin or test the strength of those corded muscles.

"Why can't you just leave, Alex?"

"You said you didn't call me to meet you in that alley. But someone did. Someone pretending to be you. That means it was someone who knew about the two of us—who knew that I would come if you called."

His last sentence punched the air from her lungs. *Someone…who knew that I would come if you called.* The simple words stunned her. She filed them away to examine later, because he was still speaking, and what he said settled in her mind like ice.

"Think about it, Nic, there can't be too many people around who would have that particular knowledge. I was careful that summer. Our…association wasn't a widely known thing. Whoever knows about us, wanted me in the alley the night Biggs was murdered. And they used you to get me there."

"Who?"

He wouldn't look at her. He turned to wash his hands in

her sink. Then he used the other end of the stained dish-towel to wipe the smoke from his face. There was a tic in his lower jaw.

"Alex, how do you know all this?"

"No more questions. I need to use your telephone. And you need to pack a bag."

"I told you, I can't leave."

Without warning his expression grew hard, almost hostile. Alex was suddenly a potentially dangerous man. She had never seen this side of him directed at her before.

"You no longer have a choice, Nicki. Whether you want to come with me or not, they are going to come after you. Now you've wasted enough time. Pack a bag. We're leaving here in five minutes."

Nicki backed away from him. Her eyes were wide, wounded, and definitely frightened. Alex buried his remorse. If he didn't get her out of the line of fire she was going to become the next target. He couldn't let that happen.

She went silently into the bedroom. Knowing it was too late for regrets, Alex found her telephone and made two quick calls. He was finishing the second call when Nicki returned to the kitchen trailing a large suitcase.

"And you'd better cover the kid fast," he said into the phone. "I've gotta go."

"Who were you talking to?" Nicki asked.

"Don't worry about it. Have you got everything?"

She let go of the strap. A surge of anger lent color to her pale cheeks. "Don't you dare start acting all macho on me. I'm moving out of my home because of you but—"

"No you aren't. You're moving because of what you *said* you saw in that alley the other night."

Anger sheeted off her in waves, but she dropped her eyes. The telephone rang in his hand. Reluctantly, he handed it to her. "Tell whoever it is you'll call them back."

She snatched it angrily from his hand. "Hello? Oh my God, Ilona!" Instantly, anger changed to concern. "I've been so worried. Where are you? Are you okay? What? Yes. Of course I did. Yes, I told them."

Nicki looked away from him, but not before he saw her expression. Guilt. What had she done? He eavesdropped shamelessly, wishing he could hear both sides of the conversation.

"I couldn't! You know why. Ilona... No, look, it's more complicated than that."

Her eyes slid to him and away once more. This time fear mingled with the guilt. She walked to the window and turned away from him. The slim curve of her back was knotted with tension. She was gripping the receiver hard enough to leave prints in the plastic.

"Ilona, please! You don't understand. You have to... No! We need to talk. I need more information. No! I told you, I can't! You're wrong! He couldn't have!"

Her other hand reached out to grip the window curtain, bunching it in a way that was sure to leave wrinkles. Something brushed his leg. Startled, Alex jumped. Ginger looked up at him and mewed.

The cat purred happily when he lifted her and began to stroke her head.

"Ilona..."

Nicki went still. He sensed her caller had hung up.

Alex set the cat down. He walked over and laid a hand on her shoulder.

"What's wrong?"

Nicki sighed. "My friend's in trouble." She turned, lifting her head. "Her boyfriend beat her up."

Some of the coiled tension inside him relaxed. "And she doesn't want to report him?" he surmised.

"No. I don't know how to help her."

"If she won't go to the police, you can't help. Domestic

violence is the most difficult crime of all because the victims so often choose to remain victims.''

"You don't understand."

"Sure I do. Either she gets away from him or she'll continue in a no-win situation."

"He's married."

"All the more reason for you to stay out of it."

He brushed a strand of hair back from her face. Silky. Just the way he remembered. His hand lingered to stroke her hair, even though he knew he shouldn't. Her eyes widened just a fraction. It was always like this between them. He only had to touch her to create that surge of awareness between them.

"You can't solve everyone's problems, Nic. It's enough that you care."

"You don't understand."

"I understand your friend has to help herself."

He told himself he wouldn't give in to his driving need to kiss her. He told himself he'd step back. He'd give them both more space.

He should have saved his mental breath.

His thumb rubbed her cheek. "Your skin is still so soft."

"I—" her breath caught "—thought we were in a hurry."

He took his time lowering his head, giving her time to retreat. "We are."

Their lips were inches apart.

"This isn't a good idea," she breathed.

"You're absolutely right."

He kissed her. Softly. Tenderly. Achingly. And she responded with all the sweet passion he remembered. He was suddenly nineteen all over again, wanting with a youthful passion the one person who made him feel whole and complete.

Her lips clung, stirring to life all sorts of impossible feelings. And when they parted to allow him better access, he deepened the kiss, blocking the aggressive craving that demanded from her all the things his body insisted it must have.

Past and present fused as Nicki's arms circled his neck. She grew languid and pliant in his arms. Her body molded against his. A perfect fit.

His control began to slip. He kissed her mouth with greedy hunger, spurred by her answering desire. He never wanted to stop. He kissed her cheek, her jaw, drawing her hair aside to expose the sensitive region of her neck that had always heightened her response.

She arched eagerly, answering with hastily placed kisses and painless bites on his jaw and neck.

Caution flew out the window. His lips returned to her mouth, demanding more as his body began a sensual assault. Gone were the timid responses of the girl he had known, replaced by the sensual power of the woman she'd become. The taste and scent of her stoked the flame of his need higher and higher.

Their mouths fused. Their tongues dueled. Her breasts pressed against his chest. He slid his hands to her buttocks, bringing them together in closer contact. Letting her feel how much he desired her.

"You still taste like sin," he murmured against her ear, biting gently on the lobe. Eyes, half-closed in passion, she shivered, parting her lips.

He ran his tongue across the bottom lip, excited by the quiver that ran right through her. "You were always so responsive. So giving."

"Alex!"

"You aren't going to tell me to stop, are you Nicki?"

She pulled back slightly, desire a liquid film in those dark expressive eyes.

"I don't want you to ever stop."

Alex groaned. He cradled her face in his hands. The trust in her expression sucked away his good intentions to stop. He needed to possess her almost as much as his next breath.

"We can't do this, Alex."

"I promise you, we can."

His mouth enslaved her lips, demanding a response. The slight hesitation faded under his sensual onslaught, but that moment of hesitation weakened his resolve. It reminded him of all the reasons they shouldn't be doing this.

He poured his frustration, his yearning, into a blazing kiss of desire before he finally stepped back, every bit as shaken as she appeared to be. She swayed, her features softened in sweet passion.

Mind over body, the battle raged inside him. He wanted to pull her down right there on the kitchen floor and finish what they had started.

Her eyes questioned. Acquiescence was there in her face. She wanted him. But the timing was all wrong.

Alex ran troubled hands through his hair. They were shaking, he realized. His entire body vibrated with hot hunger and unfulfilled desire.

"I never forgot you."

"But you didn't come back."

The pain in that declaration nicked another notch in his heart. "I couldn't. You went away to school. I thought you'd forgotten me."

"How could you believe that?" She stepped forward and laid a hand on his cheek. He shuddered.

"Do you really think any woman forgets her first lover?"

"That shouldn't have happened."

"Don't you dare belittle what we had!"

He clasped her shoulders. The bones were delicate. Fragile. Like Nicki.

"Never. You were the only perfect thing in my world, Nic."

"Then why did you leave me?"

He stroked her face gently. "You were sixteen. Even then I was too old and jaded. Too destined for trouble."

"You were nineteen and scared," she corrected.

"Yes."

Her hands fell to her side. He sensed her emotional withdrawal. "Why didn't you come back?" There was no accusation, only remembered grief.

"I couldn't."

"Were you in jail?"

He shouldn't have felt shocked or hurt. The question was logical. "No. I wasn't in jail."

"You didn't even come home for your mother's funeral."

"It was too late when I heard she'd died. Too late for a lot of things."

"Did you marry?"

"No. I came close once." He hated to admit the truth of that, but there was so much else he couldn't tell her.

"What happened?"

"She didn't taste like tomorrow or smell like flowers after the rain."

Nicki closed her eyes. He knew she was remembering as well.

"We parted amicably. She married someone else. Why didn't you ever marry, Nicki? Whenever I thought of you I pictured you married with a couple of kids and a houseful of pets."

"I've got the pet."

"Nicki…"

"I was taking care of my family. That didn't leave a lot of time or even opportunity to meet anyone. Then, when the boys left for school, I was busy trying to establish this store. I never was the social butterfly sort, Alex.''

"No. You never were. I'm sorry, Nic.''

"We all do what we have to do.''

She didn't know how true those words were. Or how much he'd come to hate that fact.

"Let's get out of here.''

"And go where?''

Before he could answer, the telephone rang once again. Nicki answered, her sad eyes still locked with his.

"Hello? Hope? What is… Slow down! I can't understand you. What? When? But he's alive?''

Her eyes filled with raw pain. His gut clenched at the sight.

"Okay, Hope, where are they taking him? Fine. Go with Brent. I'll meet you at the hospital. Hope, he's going to be all right. You'll see.''

But the fear beneath her words plainly indicated she didn't believe it. Alex knew the inevitable had happened.

"I'm on my way.''

"Your father?'' he asked as she disconnected.

"He had a heart attack. They're taking him to the new Morgan hospital outside Frederick.''

"Let's go.''

Chapter Five

"Alex, you can't go with me. The police might find you."

"We'll worry about that later." He grabbed her suitcase and hustled her toward the back door.

"Wait! What about Ginger?"

"We can't take her to the hospital with us. We'll come back and get her afterwards."

They had to pass Matt's development to get to the interstate. The fire trucks had been joined by ATF officers, state police cars, a host of unmarked cars and the media. Alex knew they were lucky to have gotten away when they had.

Nicki didn't seem to notice. She stared straight ahead, biting on her upper lip. Alex reached for her hand. Her fingers were cold despite the warmth of the evening.

"Your dad's tough, Nicki. He's going to be fine."

"I know. I just don't understand why he wouldn't go for surgery when they wanted him to, Alex. They could have prevented this from ever happening."

"Well, at least now they'll do the surgery and fix him up whether he likes it or not."

She squeezed his fingers. The emergency room parking lot was full. Alex spotted a familiar police car near the entrance and realized it was just as well. He couldn't go in that way with Thad Osher hanging around. Alex was surprised Osher wasn't still at the scene trying to supervise things. He must have been usurped.

"Nic, I'll drop you at the door and find a place to park. I'll join you inside in a few minutes."

"Maybe you'd better wait out here."

Obviously, she recognized the car as well.

"It'll be okay. I'll go in through the main entrance. Odds are, they'll send your dad upstairs once they have him stable. I'll meet you there, okay?"

"All right. Thanks, Alex."

He watched until she was safely inside, then drove around to the main lot and found a parking spot where he could back in and survey the scene. Everything looked perfectly normal. The new building glowed in the reflected spotlights. People moved back and forth, intent on their own reasons for being there.

Carrying a gun inside ran a risk. If he bumped into Osher the gun would create problems, but it would be easier to protect Nicki if he was armed. Still, the danger here should be minimal. He slipped the gun under the front seat and got out of the car.

Inside, two kindly gray-haired ladies manned the information desk.

"I need to check on a patient who was brought through emergency a short time ago," he told the women with what he hoped was a sad smile. "He suffered a heart attack and I was wondering if there is any way you can check to see if he's still there or if he's been moved upstairs already so I don't waste a lot of time."

Their eyes softened in compassion. "Actually, I can," one told him. "My daughter works in the emergency room. What's the patient's name?"

Minutes later, Alex was in the elevator heading to the cardiac care unit. He spotted Nicki immediately. She was talking with a younger woman whose light blond hair was a stark contrast to Nicki's wild, brown-black hair. He would never have recognized Hope. The bright-eyed, gawky youngster had turned into a lovely young woman, even if her features were all distorted by tears at the moment.

"I got Big Man away from him and called for help," she was saying, "but his lips were turning blue, Nicki. If Brent hadn't been there, he'd have died. We started CPR right away, but I was so scared."

"It's okay, Hope. You did fine. Everything's going to be okay."

Nicki held her sister tightly, rubbing her back in comfort. One fact struck Alex immediately. While the sisters looked nothing at all alike, their voices were amazingly similar. Could Hope have been the woman who called pretending to be Nicki?

Why? She couldn't be more than—what?…twenty-three or four? Much too young for any of the players in the auto theft ring. Then he thought about Matt and frowned.

"Excuse me."

Alex stepped aside to allow a tall, whipcord-lean man to enter the waiting room. The man headed straight for the two women. Nicki released her sister and turned to embrace the newcomer. One of her brothers, Alex realized. Brent, from what Hope had said. Both of her two brothers had been kids the last time Alex saw them, and he wouldn't have recognized either one now.

As Nicki and Brent hugged, Alex stepped out of the waiting room, feeling like an intruder. He'd come to give his support, but Nicki had her family.

Alex decided to check on Matt and give them some privacy. He needed to talk to the teenager anyhow.

Unfortunately, the boy was still in the emergency room. There was no way Alex was going to get inside unnoticed. He spotted Thad Osher in the hall with a cluster of men. The sergeant wore his usual scowl as he listened to some thing one of the others was saying. Alex got close enough to hear that they were trying to reach Matt's aunt or uncle so they could keep the boy overnight for observation.

Alex retreated to the stairwell while he debated his options. He headed back upstairs to Nicki. As he started to open the stairwell door on three, familiar voices on the other side made him pause.

What was Vic Unsdorf doing here? And why was he talking with Nicki? Alex cracked the door instead of opening it. Vic faced him, but his attention was on the woman. A scowl lined his harsh features.

The blonde shook her head and gestured.

A surge of relief went through him. Hope, not Nicki. She really did sound like her sister. Hope spoke urgently. He couldn't hear her words as they moved closer to the bank of elevators, but she kept casting furtive looks down the hall toward the waiting area. Obviously, she didn't want anyone to see her talking with Unsdorf.

Interesting.

Alex opened the door a little further in an effort to overhear them, but the elevator doors suddenly whooshed apart. An orderly, pushing an empty gurney, stepped out and hurried down the hall. Vic Unsdorf stepped inside.

"I'll take care of it," he promised.

Hope turned away. She half ran down the hall without once looking toward Alex. But Vic's eyes narrowed in Alex's direction as the doors slid shut.

Alex pelted back down the stairs to intercept Vic. Only, the elevator had already disgorged its passenger by the time he burst through the door on the main floor. Vic was nowhere in sight.

Alex scanned the area, then darted outside. There was no sign of Vic anywhere. Alex wasted a few more minutes searching without success.

Maybe it was just as well, he decided. Vic didn't trust

him anymore. Alex had made some bad choices after he first got to town. The police, especially Thad Osher, had become interested in several of his acquaintances, making them interested in him as well. Unsdorf didn't like that much attention from the locals.

Hope was now his only lead. Vic had a string of blond female friends, but they tended to be mature blondes with a lot more cleavage than Hope could display. Maybe Vic had been drawn to Hope's natural innocence, but what would Hope see in someone who was practically old enough to be her father?

This was turning into a three-ring circus. Alex felt like he was the high wire act. It would be a real shame if it was Hope who fell off.

CONCERN GNAWED ON her insides. Nicki left the Cardiac Care Unit and walked to the waiting area with her head bent. She'd never seen her father look so frail. The monitors and tubes would have been frightening enough, but he appeared almost withered, and so pale, he nearly blended in with the stark white sheets.

If her father knew they were there, he gave no sign. The only noise came from the monitors surrounding him. Brent only stayed a minute before he left and went in search of the doctor. Nicki remained, talking to her father. She hoped the aimless conversation would reach beyond the coma and pull her father back to them.

When the nurse finally suggested she leave, Nicki found the waiting room empty. She had glimpsed Alex briefly when she greeted her brother, but he'd disappeared before she could call him over and introduce him. Now she didn't know what to do. She scanned the hall for her brother or sister. At the far end, a familiar spill of platinum blond hair caught her immediate attention.

"Ilona?" Nicki broke into a run.

Ilona stopped abruptly, her expression as stunned as Nicki felt.

"What are you doing here?"

"Never mind *me,* what are *you* doing here?" Ilona countered.

"My father had a heart attack."

"Oh." Nervously, Ilona looked around. "Come on."

Nicki followed her into the nearby rest room. Ilona's long, siren painted fingernails bit into her palms. She chewed at the matching lipstick, looking thoroughly distracted.

"Why didn't you identify that Alex Coughlin person for the police?" she demanded.

"Because I think you made a mistake."

"A mistake!" One hand shoved back a film of hair from her forehead. "How can you say that? I was right there. I saw him kill that man!"

Nicki's gaze swept the empty stalls nervously. Her friend's voice was taking on an hysterical note. They were the only ones inside right now, but that could change at any minute.

"Ilona—"

"Don't you understand?" Ilona pressed earnestly. "He tried to kill me."

"What are you talking about?"

"The murderer. He saw me that night. He came after me on his motorcycle right after I talked to you. He tried to run me down. I was lucky to get away!"

Alex drove a motorcycle, but Ilona couldn't possibly know that.

Ilona's heavily mascaraed eyes filled with moisture. There was no doubting her fear, but Nicki stubbornly shook her head. "I think it was someone else, Ilona."

Alex had darted into a burning house rigged with explosives to rescue a boy he didn't even know. How could a man who would do that walk up and shoot a person in cold blood?

"Are you crazy? Do you think I'm stupid? I know what I saw, Nicki."

Her voice was stridently positive. Anger glinted in her light gray eyes. Nicki hesitated. Was *she* the one who was wrong? There had been that one moment in her apartment tonight when Alex had looked so cold. So dangerous.

Like a stranger.

"I know he was your first lover and I'm sorry, Nicki, honest. But the man is—"

"How did you know he was my first lover?"

Ilona frowned. She stared at Nicki blankly. "You told me about him."

Had she? Nicki couldn't remember. Her relationship with Alex had always been something private, yet she and Ilona had shared several confidences during the time they'd roomed together.

"What difference does it make?" Ilona demanded. She turned and began to pace the small room. "Now I have two men to fear! He's going to kill both of us, you know. He can't let us live to testify."

"I—Ilona, I still think you're wrong. I don't know who or what you really saw, but I can't believe it was Alex."

"That's great. Just great."

"Don't you see? I didn't see the murder. How can I identify anyone? What if I did and I was wrong? You have to come forward and tell them what really happened. Chief Hepplewhite should be back in town tomorrow. He's a good man. You can trust him, Ilona, I promise."

"I can't trust anyone."

Tears leaked from the corner of her eyes. Ilona had applied her makeup so skillfully that Nicki could barely make out the remains of the bruising on her delicate face. The long sleeved black tunic covered her arms, hiding the deeper bruises and hugging her figure in feminine softness. Part of Nicki could scarcely believe this was the same battered woman who'd come to her pleading for sanctuary only a few days ago. She looked so coolly assured.

"Ilona, was the man who hurt you Thad Osher?"

Ilona's eyes widened, then closed shut. Nicki took a step in her direction, afraid Ilona was going to faint. Instead, she opened silvery blue eyes that were hard and cold. The tears had vanished.

"Nicki, you've always been a good friend. If you can't help me then you can't. I have to go."

"No. Wait." She grabbed her arm when Ilona would have brushed past her. A sickly heavy perfume clung to Ilona's clothing.

"You aren't going to identify him, are you?" Ilona demanded. "Not even after what I've just told you."

"I can't." Ilona was wrong. She had to be wrong. "I think you saw someone else in the alley that night. It was so dark, you could have a made a mistake. Alex isn't a killer, Ilona."

Her expression grew sad. Ilona touched her gently. "I hope for your sake that you're right, Nicki. Because if you aren't, he will kill you too."

She broke Nicki's grip and sailed into the hall.

"Ilona, wait!"

But Ilona hurried away, her stiletto heels clattering loudly on the tile floor. Nicki watched her go in despair. She wanted to help her friend, but she didn't know what to do. She simply couldn't believe that Alex was a murderer.

Hands clasped her forearms from behind. With a gasp of fear, she spun around. Alex steadied her, but his attention was on something beyond her. Nicki looked back. Ilona was the only person in sight.

"Who was that?"

"Ilona." She breathed the name, staring at Alex. Because once again, his features hardened, becoming alien to her. Alex could kill she realized. Anyone could kill with enough motivation. What would be enough for Alex?

Fear coalesced in her stomach. What if Ilona was right?

"Wait here."

"Alex?"

He didn't run, but he moved down the hall with surprising speed.

Fear sank its icy talons deep in her abdomen. Alex had been in the alley that night. He carried a gun with the same casualness she carried a purse.

And anyone could kill.

Why was Alex chasing after Ilona unless her friend had been right?

"Nicki? You okay?" Brent's voice penetrated the fog of her fear. His face was wreathed in concern as he came up to her. "Hey, what is it? Is it Dad?"

"No. No he's fine." She drew a shuddery breath. "At least, everything was okay when they told me to leave."

But then she had learned the man she once loved might be a murderer after all. And he'd just gone after the one person who could identify him.

"You're done in, Nicki. Why don't you come home with Hope and me and try to get some rest? I don't think you should go back to your apartment tonight."

No, she couldn't go back to her apartment. Not tonight. Maybe never. Because Alex knew where she lived. He knew how to get inside past locks and deadbolts. And if he killed Ilona, he'd know that he had to kill her as well.

Brent's arms gripped her shoulders. "Nicki?"

She stared into his face. A man's face, not that of the baby brother she'd helped raise. "When did you grow up so completely?"

His frown deepened. "You're not going off the deep end on me here, are you?"

"That's certainly one explanation." She managed a wobbly smile. She was scaring him. She couldn't involve her family in this. Especially not now. "I need to talk to—"

Brent looked past her shoulder. Nicki turned her head. Alex strode toward them, his hard expression unreadable.

"Nicki?" His gaze assessed Brent. He gave the younger man a nod of acknowledgment before turning his look back to her. His expression softened. "What is it? Did something happen?"

She was barely aware that Brent had released her. Dimly, she heard the PA announcement that visiting hours were over. She studied Alex from a new perspective, trying to be objective. He was a large man with the limber, muscular build of an athlete. He moved with lazy assurance—a predator's natural grace.

And that simile was a little too unnerving right now. Predators killed.

Alex's eyes went soft with worry. "Is it your dad?" he asked gently.

"He's holding his own." She managed to say.

Her gaze dropped to his forearm where the gauze she'd wrapped around his cut showed a small red stain below the short sleeve of his black, torso-hugging T-shirt. A cut he'd gotten saving the life of a fifteen-year-old boy who could identify the murderer.

"You're bleeding again."

"Don't worry about it."

"I'm Brent Michaels," her brother interjected. He moved protectively beside her.

"Alex Coughlin."

The two clasped hands, but once again she was reminded of the animal kingdom. Males sizing each other up as they prepared for battle. Brent seemed to stand taller, his attitude becoming vigilant.

"I remember you," Brent said. His tone said he didn't like what he remembered.

"I can imagine." Alex smiled ruefully, without humor. "We need to talk, Nicki."

"About what?" Brent demanded.

She placed her hand against Brent's shoulder, surprised, but grateful for his instant defense. "It's okay, Brent. Alex and I are...old friends," she told her brother.

She was looking at Alex when she stumbled over the words. His eyes turned bleak. For an instant she glimpsed a pain she could almost feel. It was gone in the blink of his eyes. He continued to regard her without any expression at all. She sensed him waiting with resignation for her to denounce him. Wasn't that what his peers had done in high school?

"Did you catch up with Ilona?" she asked.

"No."

Just that single word. Yet it was a challenge of sorts.

She knew Brent watched them through slitted eyes. When they were growing up, she'd assumed the role of protector over her brothers. Now those roles were reversed. Brent was fully prepared to do whatever was necessary to shield her. The thought warmed and reassured her.

Two nights ago she'd had to make this same choice. Her lover or her former roommate and friend.

"Alex isn't what he appears, Brent."

Alex flinched at her words. He stared hard at her and waited tensely.

"He went into a burning building tonight to rescue a boy. Don't let the clothes and his attitude fool you. Beneath the outward aggression is a good man." And she prayed her instincts were right.

Tension seemed to visibly drain from Alex. Humor mingled with gratitude as he regarded her. "What's wrong with my clothes?"

"Well for one thing," she said with a smile, "they smell like smoke."

His lips curved. "Yeah. I noticed that."

"And T-shirts aren't exactly a fashion statement anymore."

"Darn, I must have missed that in the style section."

"Did I mention that your boots need polishing?"

"No." His eyes smiled. "I think you left that one out."

"Why am I starting to feel invisible here?" Brent cut in.

Alex slid an arm around her shoulders. The gesture was intentionally possessive and she knew it. If Brent hadn't been watching them so closely she might have protested. By accepting his touch, she offered her brother the assurance he needed that the situation was okay.

"I don't think your sister should spend the night alone," Alex told Brent.

"That's what I just told her." Brent's voice was agreeable, but his expression remained alert. "She's going to spend the night at the house with Hope and me."

"Good. I'll drive her there so we can talk."

"All right. But be sure you come inside. I'd like to have a few words with you myself.'"

That was a little too much for Nicki who pulled free and narrowed her eyes at both of them.

"I think it may have escaped your attention gentlemen, but with the advent of cloning, it's only a matter of time before the human male is completely obsolete. I've been taking care of myself for some time now. I see no reason to change that status."

Alex shared a rueful look with Brent as Nicki strode toward the elevators.

"Ouch," Brent said.

"Yeah." Alex pulled her car keys from his pocket and jiggled them. "Don't worry, I'll take care of her."

"You'd better. But, I'm glad I'm not the one sharing a car with her on the way home."

Alex grinned. "I'll have her home by eleven, Dad, I promise."

"See that you do," Brent said. And it was hard to tell if he was joking or not.

Alex reached the elevator before the doors closed. Since there were several people already inside, neither of them spoke. He wondered if she was seriously annoyed, or only mildly irritated. What had Ilona told her to put that initial expression on her face?

He stood aside while the rest of the elevator disembarked. Nicki strode past him. He ran a hand through his hair and followed her outside. His arm was still bleeding, but he had a feeling sympathy was going to be in short supply this time.

He pressed his hand against the injury and stepped out into the night. Her conversation with Ilona had caused a dramatic change in Nicki's attitude. Too bad he hadn't been able to reach the woman in time to get a good look at her. He wanted to ask her a few pointed questions.

Nicki waited for him. "Where's the car?"

"Last row on your left." He nodded in the appropriate direction. "Want to chew on me now or wait until we don't have an audience?"

She whirled to face him. A group of people passed next to them, talking animatedly. Nicki clamped her lips together and set off for the car at a brisk pace.

"Right. No audience," he muttered.

Alex followed slowly. He rubbed the scratch on his knuckle as he scanned the well-lit lot. The parking area had already emptied pretty thoroughly, though there were still a number of cars scattered around.

Suddenly, the hairs at the back of his head began to prickle a warning. He paused and looked around warily. His hand inched toward his weapon and stopped. He'd left the gun in the car.

"Nicki!"

His sharp tone caused her to stop. She was only about ten paces in front of him and she turned in question.

"Wait," he ordered.

Her jaw set and her chin lifted defiantly. Before she could object, a small, dark car suddenly gunned its engine. The vehicle pulled from its parking spot without lights and raced toward them down the aisle.

Alex started running. Nicki wasted time turning back to look for the car. Someone nearby yelled a warning. It was already too late.

Alex shoved Nicki in front of him between two parked cars. The left front fender of the speeding car grazed his hip, sending him hard against her back. They fell to the gritty asphalt as the car sped off.

"Alex! Are you all right?"

His hip throbbed. Blood trickled down his arm. He'd torn the knee out of his jeans. Probably scraped his leg in the process. Just what he needed—more injuries. His ribs still hadn't entirely forgiven him for that beating he'd taken back in June.

"I'm fine, Nicki. What about you?"

"Shaken, but otherwise okay."

"Are you two all right?"

The cavalry had arrived in the form of two stout women.

Nicki stood. She moved okay, he decided. Nothing broken. He followed her example more slowly. At the moment, he felt every one of his thirty-four years. "I'm getting too old for this," he grumbled.

"You make this sort of thing a habit?" Nicki demanded. Fear hovered in her voice.

"Only lately."

"Are you hurt?" the first woman asked. "I saw that car hit you."

"The only thing hurt here is my pride," he told her. "I should have moved more quickly."

"The car actually hit you?" Nicki exclaimed.

"The fender bumped my hip. It's okay. Nothing permanent was damaged," but he was pleased by her concern nonetheless. "Did anyone happen to get the license plate?"

"There wasn't one," the frizzy-haired woman said. "I looked."

"Thanks."

"You wait right here while I summon security," the first woman ordered.

"No!" Nicki's voice joined his in instant protest.

"Thank you," he said, "but we have to get home. The sitter says the baby is throwing up. We don't have time to be filling out a lot of paperwork for the police. Besides, it won't do any good when we don't even know the make or license number of the car."

"A late model dark blue Buick sedan," the redhead told him authoritatively. "Here's my card. If you decide to report the incident, you can give this to the police. We'll be happy to testify to what that driver just did. Probably some young kid on drugs."

Alex didn't argue. "Thank you. Thank you very much."

"You're welcome. I hope your baby is okay."

"So do I. Come on, honey."

Nicki, who'd remained silent through this exchange, let him take her arm and hustle her away from the scene. The women watched him open the door for Nicki and limp around to get in behind the wheel. His hip was sore. He was going to have a good-sized bruise.

He glanced at the card the woman had given him and back to where they stood. Mindy Smucker, the card read.

Well, Mindy Smucker would remember the incident and them. She'd probably also remember the make, model and license number of Nicki's car as well.

"Our baby is sick?" Nicki asked.

"Buckle your seat belt. The two of them are still watching. We need to get out of here before security shows up."

"Alex, your arm is bleeding."

"Yeah. So's my knee, but don't worry about it. I've had worse. Are you sure you're okay?"

"Wonderful. Couldn't be better."

But her hand was shaking so badly he had to insert the seat belt in the clasp for her. He squeezed her arm gently in reassurance and started the car.

"I can't believe that just happened," she said. "Why would someone be so reckless in a hospital parking lot?"

Alex glanced over to see if she was kidding. She wasn't. "You thought that was an accident?"

"Oh, God. Yes," she said softly. "I did."

He spared her another glance. Her hands clenched together in front of her. Fear and anger warred on her face.

With a wave at the two women, he pulled out of the lot, but he kept a lookout for a blue four-door Buick sedan or anything else that looked or felt wrong.

"That wasn't an accident, Nicki."

"You can't know that," but her voice lacked any real assurance.

Steering the car toward the highway he sighed. He didn't have the energy to argue at the moment. "Why was your friend Ilona at the hospital tonight?"

Nicki went still.

"I know she said something to upset you and I'm guessing that something had to do with me."

"What makes you say that?"

"A hunch. What sort of car does she drive, Nicki?"

She gasped as the implication sank in. Alex pressed

home his advantage. "I'd really like to know why a woman I've never even met hates my guts."

"She thinks you shot Thorton Biggs."

"Why?"

Nicki shifted. For a minute he thought she wasn't going to answer.

"She witnessed the shooting."

"For crying out loud! That alley must have been busier than Grand Central Station at rush hour. How many other people were back there that night?"

"I don't know."

"Well why didn't she come forward and tell the police what she saw?" When Nicki didn't answer, he glanced over and saw the hurt and confusion on her face. "Talk to me, Nicki."

"I told you, her boyfriend beat her up. She was staying in my apartment."

"And she didn't want to get involved," he said in resignation.

"It's more than that. Her boyfriend is a cop. I think he might be Thad Osher."

Alex whistled tunelessly. Pieces began sliding into place. "So that's why you suggested Osher might have done the shooting."

"In a way. The first thing Ilona said to me that night was that he'd found her. I assumed she meant her boyfriend. Then she told me she saw the shooting."

"And you put the two together. It's a logical deduction, but where's the connection between Osher and Biggs?"

"I've no idea."

"You didn't see the actual shooting, did you Nicki?"

"No." He sensed her relief with the admission. "Ilona did. She dialed 911 and then realized she couldn't come forward with what she'd seen."

As Nicki unfurled the events, it all made sense. Nicki

was the loyal type. Her nature was such that she couldn't do anything else but try to protect her friend. He had no complaints coming since that same loyalty had kept him protected as well.

"If she saw the murder, she knows I didn't kill him, Nicki."

"I know, but I think she must have seen you loitering across the street earlier. She was really nervous the whole time she stayed with me, always looking out the windows, jumping whenever the phone rang. If she saw you there that night and the real murderer looked something like you, it would be easy to see how she might have come to confuse the two images."

"I don't think so." He turned onto the exit for Fools Point.

"I don't either," she admitted finally.

Alex waited. After a moment, Nicki sighed.

"I think Ilona saw her boyfriend kill Thorton Biggs. I think she's so afraid of him that she identified you instead because she saw you there."

Alex nodded. "Makes sense. I need to talk to her, Nicki."

"I don't know where she's staying. When she left my apartment that night, she wouldn't tell me where she was going. I don't think she really knew herself. And tonight, I never thought to ask her."

"I'll find her. I'll drop you off at your dad's place—"

"Wait. We have to get Ginger, remember?"

"Why don't I come back for her tomorrow?"

"We have to pass right by my place. I can't leave her there all night. I don't know how much food she has in her bowl."

"Nic, she won't starve… Okay, never mind, we'll stop. In and out fast, all right? You grab her and her bowl and we're out of there." Not a person or another vehicle moved on Main Street. Fools Point still rolled up its sidewalks after nine. The alleys were worse. Barren and isolated and pitch-dark, the back of the buildings were just as they had been the night of the shooting.

"You need to get that light fixed back here," he told Nicki.

"Maybe you'd like to take a crack at convincing public works for me?"

"I'll see what I can do."

He stopped the car directly behind her store.

"Aren't you going to park?"

"We aren't going to be here that long." He held her in place when she released her seat belt.

"What?"

"Wait a minute."

He scrutinized the area. No one. Nothing. Yet he had that same crawly feeling that he'd gotten in the parking lot at the hospital. He reached down and felt for his gun.

"What are you doing? What's wrong?"

"I don't know that anything's wrong," he told her. "I just don't like this, Nic."

"Because of that car tonight?"

"That too."

She fell silent as he continued to study the alley.

"All right, now listen. If anything happens, you get back in this car and take off. Understand?" He separated her house key from the keys still hanging in the ignition.

"You're scaring me, Alex."

"Good. I want you scared and alert. Like Matt warned you, someone is playing for keeps."

"Wait. If you think there's that much danger, Ginger will probably be okay for the night."

"We're here now." He flashed her a cold smile and stepped out of the car. He held the gun in his hand. "Let's get her and get out of here."

The alley was too quiet. The feeling of wrongness nearly made him shove her back in the car and take off. He continued to sweep their surroundings as they climbed the stairs, their footfalls ringing on the metal steps. Nicki lagged behind him. She nervously watched the parking lot as well. Suddenly, she paused halfway up.

"Alex, look! It's Ginger! She got loose." Nicki ran lightly back down the steps.

His nerves were screaming a silent warning. Alex turned and started after her. His calf brushed something strung across the step.

They had just run out of time and luck.

Chapter Six

The bomb exploded. The concussion threw Alex down the remaining steps. He thudded against the roof and side of Nicki's car. His ears rang. His body felt deflated.

"Alex! Alex!"

"Get in the car." He managed to stand. There was no way he could drive. "Get us out of here. Now!"

His head pounded. He couldn't quite make his eyes focus. He felt Nicki's hands on him. She guided him into the passenger's seat and called to the cat. He wanted to tell her that there wasn't time, but he couldn't summon the energy required to speak. There wouldn't be one bomb. Not after what they'd done to Matt's house.

Nicki opened the driver's door and slid inside. She thrust a bundle of trembling fur into his arms and threw the vehicle into drive. The cat squirmed in a frenzied effort to escape his hold as they barrelled down the alley.

"I'll have you at the hospital in minutes."

"No hospital."

"You're injured!"

"No hospital!"

A second explosion rocked the neighborhood. The tires squealed in protest as Nicki careened onto Main Street—away from the highway. Clawing his arm, the cat leaped into the back seat. Nicki raced to the traffic light. She ignored the red signal and turned left. He'd expected her to go right, toward her dad's place.

A police siren wailed somewhere nearby. Alex closed his eyes. He ignored the well of blood on his arms. In fact, he barely noticed the small wounds. He still felt curiously detached. Was he going to embarrass himself by being sick, or simply pass out? Squeezing his eyes shut, he tried to hang on. He couldn't afford to do either one. That would leave Nicki defenseless. Not that he'd done her much good so far, he thought without humor.

"Need to get to a phone," he muttered. Somehow, he couldn't make his sluggish brain explain. He needed to tell Nicki…something. He needed…

"Alex! Alex!"

Nicki pulled into the doctor's parking lot and turned off the engine. She and Dr. Leslie Martin didn't move in the same circles, but Leslie's father had been her childhood doctor. She only knew Leslie to say hello to, but the doctor was the closest source of help. In Nicki's mind, that was all that counted.

Alex had slumped sideways. His head rested against the passenger window. He wasn't moving. Terrified, Nicki reached for his neck. As soon as she found a pulse, she was out of the car. She ignored the office entrance and raced to the front of the house, praying the doctor was home. She left her finger on the doorbell, banging against the door with her free hand.

Each second passed like minutes. The door finally opened. Leslie stood there in a cream satin robe, loosely belted at the waist.

"Please, you have to come!" Nicki said breathlessly. "He's unconscious. I don't know how badly he's hurt."

"Where?" The doctor didn't waste time with other questions. Obviously ready for bed, she brushed aside a loose fall of brown hair and stepped outside.

"In my car. On the side in your parking lot."

"I'll go down through the office," she said. "That way we can get him right inside. Meet me at the office door."

"Hurry!"

As Nicki raced back to her car, a third explosion shattered the night. Despite the distance and the row of buildings between them, the sound was distinct. Her mind shut down. She couldn't deal with that right now. Couldn't think about bombs or her apartment. She had to concentrate on helping Alex.

She opened the passenger door. Alex practically fell out in her arms. "Alex!" She caught his head and felt something warm and sticky on her arm.

His eyes fluttered.

"Alex, wake up. You have to help me. I can't carry you. Stand up."

He blinked, tried to focus on her and failed. But, like an automaton, he obeyed her command. He got to his feet and swayed. She slung his arm around her shoulders, praying she could support him if he started to collapse.

Ginger started to climb out, but another explosion sent her darting back inside. Nicki closed the door with her foot. Alex suddenly buckled. She nearly went down under his considerable weight. Leslie appeared and grabbed Alex's other arm.

Between them, they half carried, half dragged the stumbling Alex inside her home office.

Leslie guided them down the hall to the first examining room. "You're going to have to help me get him up on the table. Does this have anything to do with those explosions I'm hearing?"

"The first one. It caught him in the back. He flew right down the last few steps and landed against the car."

"All right. You dial 911 while I—"

"He doesn't want to go to a hospital."

"No hospital!" Alex affirmed.

Leslie looked at Alex sharply. Recognition flickered in her eyes. She sighed audibly. "All right. Let's see how badly he's hurt."

GROWING UP AROUND horses, Nicki and her siblings had learned a thing or two about medical skills and working with large, injured animals. That knowledge and experience made it easier for her to assist the doctor as she tended to Alex.

Getting his clothes off required both of them. Despite his efforts to help, his coordination was impaired. "Just hold still," the doctor ordered firmly.

She cut away the black shirt and stripped off his pants with a professional detachment Nicki envied. Looking at Alex's bare chest only served to remind Nicki of the way her hands had once explored every inch of his hard flesh.

His body was trim and well muscled. As Nicki helped remove his jeans, she couldn't help but notice that the boy she remembered had developed into a terrific male specimen.

The doctor fired questions at him the entire time she worked. "Alex, tell me what hurts."

"My head's the worst."

His hand attempted to reach for the back of his skull.

"Never mind, I'll check it out. How's your vision?"

"Blurry at first, but it seems to be clearing."

"Were you unconscious at all?"

"No."

The doctor looked at Nicki who said, "I thought he passed out for a minute or two, but he might have just closed his eyes."

"I did," Alex assured her.

"Okay. Can you roll over?" the doctor asked.

Since his coordination was still off they had to help, but

they eventually got him onto his stomach. He had multiple cuts across his back and shoulders. None were severe. The worst injury was to the back of his head where a large gash bled profusely.

"Head wounds bleed a lot," Leslie assured Nicki, probing the site through his thick hair. "Fortunately, this one isn't deep. It's not even going to require stitches. We'll get some ice on it."

"He was hit by a car earlier tonight," Nicki told the doctor. "He hurt his knee and his hip, I think."

Leslie Martin pursed her lips as she regarded him. "Staying out of trouble as usual, huh?"

Alex grunted in response.

"Okay, I don't think there's any permanent damage to your head—at least, none due to these injuries," she said dryly. "But I want a couple of x-rays to be sure."

She ran experienced hands over his back and sides, pausing when she reached his left hip. Even before she tugged at the elastic on his briefs, Nicki saw the start of a nasty bruise only partly hidden by the white cloth.

"Is this where the car hit you?" the doctor asked.

"Yeah."

"Okay." She probed the area and he grunted a soft protest. "We'll run an x-ray here as well as his head and that knee." Alex attempted to glare at her over his shoulder, but she ignored him. "And I want to check your ribs. It will be a miracle if you haven't injured them again. He was supposed to be taking things easy," she added for Nicki's benefit.

"Oh?"

Leslie scrutinized her. "Alex is one of my patients. I assumed that was why you brought him here."

Nicki shook her head. "You were the closest source of help."

"Good enough. Let's get you up," she said to him. "I'll

get a wheelchair and we'll move into the back room so I can take some x-rays.''

"I can walk," Alex protested.

"I'm glad you think so, but you aren't walking anywhere," she told him firmly. "If you can sit up without falling over, I'll get the wheelchair and make things easy on all of us."

"I don't need one. I can manage."

He did manage to sit up, but he teetered enough that Nicki stood by ready to catch him if he fell off the examining table. He stopped protesting about the wheelchair. Getting up on the x-ray table seemed to tax his strength. He was in obvious pain.

"What else hurts, Alex?" the doctor asked.

"What doesn't? The concussion practically flattened me."

"He was limping before the bomb exploded," Nicki put in.

"That's just a bruise," Alex argued, but a grimace spoiled his glare.

"So it appears, but since I'm the one with the medical degree we'll take a look."

Nicki waited outside the room while the doctor took a series of x-rays. After she finished, she motioned Nicki back inside the room.

"Stay with him while I develop these pictures. I don't want him falling off the table."

Alex frowned wryly. "No problem. I don't think I have the energy to roll that far."

"See that you don't."

Nicki reached for his hand.

"Why is it all the women in my life are so bossy?"

"Gee, I don't know. Could it have anything to do with the fact that we have to be in order to get your attention?"

He slanted her a look. "You always got my attention, Nic."

"Uh-huh." But his expression made her heart skip a beat.

"Are you positive you weren't hurt?"

"I was below the blast. Fortunately, so was most of you."

"We both owe that cat of yours a can of tuna. But I'm sorry, Nicki."

"For what?"

His eyes clouded with regret. "For getting you involved in this."

"I think you've got that wrong way round. I'm the one who got *you* involved, remember?" She squeezed his hand. "You saved my life."

"Actually, I nearly got you killed. He rigged some sort of trip wire on the step."

"He?"

"Bombers are usually males. I should have listened to my instincts and gotten you away from there."

"I insisted, remember?"

Alex grimaced. "I knew things didn't feel right as soon as we got there."

"More of your hunches? What did the doctor mean when she said you were supposed to be taking it easy?"

Alex closed his eyes. Nicki had given up getting an answer when he finally spoke.

"I had some trouble back in June." He opened his eyes and regarded her bleakly. "I was trying to help my sister and Lee when a couple of guys jumped me and used me for a punching bag. They cracked a couple of ribs."

Nicki sucked in air. All sorts of thoughts and admonishments went through her mind. It took real effort to keep them inside. Alex already knew what she thought of the people he hung around with. Lectures wouldn't do any good.

"You do lead an exciting life, don't you?"

"Also a charmed one," Leslie scolded from the doorway. "You're in better shape than you have any right to be, Alex. Do you have a place to spend what's left of the night?"

"What time is it?" he asked.

"Almost one-fifteen."

"It can't be," Nicki protested.

Leslie raised her eyebrows.

"Your brother is going to kill me," Alex said fatalistically.

"I won't let him. But he isn't going to be real happy with either one of us."

Leslie checked the back of his head again, handed him an ice pack, and set about cleaning up the assortment of cuts and abrasions that covered him. As Nicki helped, she grew increasingly aware that he was nearly naked. She dabbed at cuts with the antiseptic lotion, trying to stay focused so her ministrations didn't give way to a subtle caress. She told herself it was because she was so relieved that he was alive, but she knew that was only a partial truth.

"I was going to take Nicki out to her dad's place," Alex told the doctor. If he was uncomfortable being undressed in front of the two of them, he didn't show it, though his eyes did have a tendency to linger on her and Nicki knew it. He winced as she dabbed at his scraped knee.

"And then?" the doctor asked.

Alex shrugged and grimaced. His hand went to his face as if to rub away the signs of his pain.

"Okay. I have extra rooms upstairs," Leslie said. "You can both spend the night here."

"I'm not sure that's a good idea," Alex argued.

"Why not? How could he find us here?" Nicki questioned.

"Anything's possible."

Leslie looked from one to the other before her gaze fastened on Alex. "I won't ask who you're talking about, but Chief Hepplewhite is back," she said quietly.

They shared a look of understanding that locked Nicki out. She wondered about it, just as she wondered about the doctor's relationship with the chief of police.

It was widely, but quietly speculated that Leslie and Chief Hepplewhite were more than friends. Nicki had heard the rumors, but like most of the town, she'd ignored the gossip. She liked Chief Hepplewhite. His wife was confined to a wheelchair and as far as anyone knew, the woman was unable to speak or move. People claimed she was practically a vegetable, but no one knew why or how. There were all sorts of speculations, but whatever the truth, Chief Hepplewhite took excellent care of her. Other than pity for a pair of star-crossed lovers, no one thought a thing of his relationship with the doctor.

"We'll talk to him in the morning," Alex told her. "The chief's going to have his hands full tonight, but Nicki's car is in plain sight in your parking lot."

"Is that a problem?"

"Yes."

"She could move it around up top. I can pull my car out of the garage if you want to put it inside."

"Good idea."

"Oh, my gosh. Ginger! I just remembered my poor cat's out in the car," Nicki explained.

"Ah, I wondered about those scratches on his arm."

"She didn't like the bombs going off," Alex said.

"Smart kitty. Okay, you wait here while we move the cars and bring the cat inside. Keep that ice pack on the back of your head. It will cut down on the swelling."

"I appreciate your help, Doc, but that car's been out there unattended for a couple of hours now. I don't want either of you going near it."

Nicki gasped. "You don't think—"

"We aren't taking chances. Someone wants us dead, Nicki. I'll move the car."

She planted her hands on her hips and glared at him. "What makes you invincible?"

"Practice." He managed a sideways grin. "Plus I know what to look for. Where's my gun?"

The doctor didn't seem at all fazed by the question.

"I don't know," Nicki answered. "You must have dropped it when the bomb went off."

Alex cursed. Still holding the ice pack to the back of his head, he started to stand, swaying slightly.

"Hold on," Leslie protested. "You can't go out there in your briefs."

"Who's going to see me at this hour?"

"We will. I'll see if I have some pants you can wear."

"I doubt we wear the same size, Doc."

She didn't smile in return. "I'll be right back."

Alex sighed. "Nicki, while we're waiting, you'd better call your brother and let him know what happened."

"At this hour?"

"Trust me. He'll be up. And Nic? Don't tell him where we are."

"Why not?"

"If he doesn't know where we are, he can answer truthfully when the police show up. And they will show up. Maybe I'd better call him myself."

"No. I'll do it. He'll worry otherwise." She used Leslie's office phone and called the house. Brent answered on the first ring.

"Nicki! Where the hell are you? Are you okay?"

Alex had been right. From what she'd observed, he generally was. "Brent, listen. I'm fine, but someone blew up my apartment tonight."

"What?!"

"I'm okay. I'm with Alex."

"I'll kill that bastard."

"He saved my life, Brent. We're safe, but we have to talk with Chief Hepplewhite. I'm not coming out to the house until tomorrow. I didn't want you to worry, okay?"

"No, it is not okay!"

Leslie returned with a pair of men's dress pants and a white shirt.

"What do you mean someone blew up your apartment? What's—"

"I've got to go, Brent. I'll call you tomorrow."

"Nicki! Don't you dare—"

She hung up and faced two sets of curious eyes. "My brother's going to kill you," she told Alex.

"He'll have to get in line. What have you got, Doc? I see I'm going formal."

"Sorry, I couldn't find any scruffy jeans, but these should fit," she told him.

"They'll do fine. Thank you. Besides, Nicki told me I needed to change my style."

"I'll let you get dressed while I move my car out of the garage for you. I'll leave the back door to the house unlocked so you can get inside afterward."

Alex shook his head. "I'd better move your car as well. I think it would be better if you two stay inside."

Leslie hesitated a moment, then nodded. "I'll get my keys."

"Thank you."

"Yes, thank you," Nicki seconded.

"Don't worry, he'll get my bill," she promised with a small smile.

Alex shrugged into the shirt, finding it only a little loose on his frame. The sleeves were too long so he rolled them up, moving stiffly. He reached for the pants, but Nicki was already there.

"Let me get them started while you're sitting down. That way you won't have to bend over."

"I'm okay, Nicki."

"Really? Well I'm not strong enough to pick you up if you fall."

"I'm not going to fall."

"Not if we do it my way."

Noting the stubborn set of her jaw Alex decided it was easier not to argue. Besides, he felt rockier than he wanted to admit. He knew he was going to be sore and stiff for several days to come. Nicki pulled the dress pants up his legs as if she did this sort of thing every day. He would have felt foolish if she hadn't paused self-consciously when she reached his thighs.

The slight pink color in her cheeks was soothing to his battered ego. At least she wasn't totally blasé about the situation. He felt darn uncomfortable sitting in his briefs before two fully dressed women, even if one was a doctor and the other had already seen—and touched—nearly every inch of him.

"Okay to stand now?" he asked Nicki. She wouldn't meet his eyes. He stood, waited for the moment of dizziness to pass, and pulled the pants up the rest of the way. Leslie had been right, the fit was close enough that he didn't even need a belt to keep them on. He wondered who they belonged to.

"Do you really think someone may be out there?" Nicki asked.

"I don't intend to guess or take chances. I'll need a flashlight."

"Right here," the doctor said as she entered the room with her keys and a high-powered flashlight.

He nodded his approval. "Thanks again."

"I'll go up and unlock the back door."

Nicki laid a hand on his arm as Leslie disappeared again. "I don't think you should go out there alone, Alex. You aren't even armed anymore."

"The gun hasn't done me much good so far. You can wait inside by the door while I check the car, Nicki. I'll hand you Ginger as soon as I'm sure the car is safe."

An automatic protest swelled on her lips. Impulsively, he kissed her on the nose. "Trust me."

He stood on the porch several long seconds, scanning the night, aware of Nicki at his back. There was the usual mix of night sounds, but the commotion from the fire department was also audible. Periodic wafts of wind carried a now familiar scent of fire. He only hoped none of Nicki's neighbors had been hurt by the explosions.

Satisfied that there was nothing wrong in the immediate vicinity, he checked the car doors, the trunk, the undercarriage and finally the hood of Nicki's car. There was no sign that the vehicle had been tampered with in any way.

Ginger followed his progress mewing piteously, frantically pawing the windows to be let out. When he was certain it was safe, he opened the door and caught her by the scruff of her neck. The scratches she'd already inflicted stung despite the ointment the doctor had applied and he didn't want a matching set.

Nicki came onto the porch and took the squirming animal into her arms.

"Get her inside, Nic. I'll meet you in the house after I shift the cars around."

"Are you sure you should you be driving?"

"No." He slid behind the wheel and started the engine. As he backed up and started out of the parking lot, something slid across the carpeted floor. So, thankfully, he hadn't lost his gun after all. He drove to the garage side of the house and retrieved his weapon, moved the cars around, took Nicki's suitcase from the backseat, and closed the garage before limping back to the house.

Nicki and Leslie were getting the cat settled in a bathroom. In lieu of litter, they'd shredded newspaper in a plastic dishpan. The doctor was in the process of opening a can of tuna when he entered the kitchen.

"She's got fresh water, bath towels for a bed, and this tuna should make up for any deficiencies in her accommodations."

"She'll be fine. I don't know how to thank you," Nicki said.

"It isn't necessary." Leslie cast an experienced eye in his direction. "You need to be in bed."

"Yes, ma'am." The truth was, he felt shaky with exhaustion and he ached everywhere. He thought of all the things he should be doing right now and dismissed them.

"Headache?" Leslie asked.

"Yeah, but no double vision or anything."

"Come with me," Leslie ordered.

Forty minutes later, Alex finally lay in a large double bed, waiting for the pain pills to kick in. He stared at the ceiling while his mind replayed the day in Technicolor. There was a soft rap on his door. It opened before he could call out.

Nicki stood framed there dressed in a short nylon nightgown. Her hair hung loose around her shoulders.

"Alex?" she whispered hesitantly.

"I'm not asleep, Nic. What's wrong?"

She slipped inside and closed the door. "I know you're probably going to think...well, I'm not sure what you'll think."

Her teeth were chattering, he realized.

"I was just wondering if you'd...if I could..."

Alex pulled aside the blanket and sheet in invitation and shifted to one side. She hastened onto the bed.

"You need to understand that I didn't come here for sex, Alex." She was shaking all over.

"Well, darn." But he said it gently to let her know he was teasing. He pulled her against his side, glad he'd kept his briefs on after all.

"I'm just so cold. I can't seem to get warm."

"Delayed shock," he told her. "I'm feeling it too." He hugged her closer, rubbing her back briskly. Her hair was damp and smelled of shampoo. Lucky her. She must have taken a shower. The doctor had ruled it out for him until morning. A sponge bath just didn't feel the same.

"I know this is crazy, Alex. I'm a basket case now that it's all over and we're safe… We are safe, aren't we? At least for tonight?"

"We're safe, Nicki. But we've been running on nerves and adrenaline most of the day. Our bodies are letting us know how much they don't appreciate the abuse."

"But what—?"

"Shh. Try to let your mind relax. Take it someplace far from today. Someplace soothing. A favorite memory often works."

"You sound like you've done this before."

"Once or twice," he admitted. He stroked her cheek, running his hand down the column of her throat. As tired and battered as he felt, her practically nude body pressing against his after all these years was a powerful temptation. His fingers encountered a chain around her neck.

He felt his way to a small, heart-shaped charm at the end. Was it the cheap little gold heart with the ruby chip? His heart gave a leap at the thought.

"What's this? A gift from some admirer?"

"Yes."

Funny, he hadn't expected that to be her answer. Nor did

he expect the small shaft of jealousy that bit him. He had no right to feel anything where she was concerned. He'd given up those rights a long time ago.

"You gave it to me," she said.

"You kept it all this time?"

"That afternoon by the lake is one of my favorite memories."

"Mine too." He kissed her forehead unable to find words for the sudden bout of emotions that swept him.

"Our lives were pretty complicated back then," she said.

"Yeah, but at least no one was trying to blow us up."

"True."

The silence that fell between them didn't need words. Alex was pretty sure she was reliving that special day as clearly as he was. He continued to stroke her gently. At some point he realized she'd stopped shivering.

"I don't think you ever knew how much our time together meant to me, Nicki," he told her quietly. "I was out of control back then and mad at the world. You were my anchor. I kept thinking I couldn't do anything that might come back and hurt you. So indirectly, you kept me out of serious trouble."

"I'm glad."

She nestled more firmly against his chest. Her head fit comfortably in the crook of his arm. Alex stroked the damp hair back from her face. Her eyes closed. Her breathing relaxed. So had his, he realized. He closed his eyes, savoring the familiar feel of Nicki wrapped in his arms. She yawned. He watched, but she didn't open her eyes. When he thought she must be asleep, she spoke quietly against his chest.

"Why didn't you come back for me?" The question held no trace of accusation.

"Right now, I'm wondering the same thing, Nicki." He stroked her arm and yawned widely.

"Good."

He smiled at her sleepy-voiced statement. They needed to do some serious talking, but not right now. Right now was a time out. Morning would come soon enough.

He yawned again and his eyes fluttered shut. When he opened them the next time, dust motes drifted in the sun-filled room. The clock on the dresser said it was after eight. He needed to get up and get moving despite the immediate protest from every muscle in his battered body.

Nicki's hair had tumbled forward to obscure her features, but one of her arms was wrapped protectively around his chest. She'd thrown a leg across one of his, twining them together in a position that instantly stimulated several parts of him.

There were a million and one things to take care of, but he lay still, reluctant to disturb her even though she was definitely disturbing him. What would life have been like if he'd made different choices?

"Good morning." Nicki woke clear eyed. She pushed hair from her face and gazed at him.

"Good morning."

Her gaze altered as she became aware of their position. The air suddenly charged with new energy. Instead of pulling back, Nicki reached out to clasp the side of his face.

Alex took that as an invitation to do what he'd been wanting to do since last night. He kissed her. He only meant to test her reaction, but he should have known better. All coherent thoughts sailed away the moment his lips settled over hers.

Nicki kissed him back, her body pressed to his in silent invitation. Her breasts flattened against his bare chest. He felt them clearly through the silky threads of nylon.

As she opened her mouth to deepen the kiss, his hand covered her breast. She made a low sound of pleasure deep in her throat. His groin tightened. He ignored his aches and pains as her pointed nipples pressed home her own desire while her bare leg rubbed up and down the length of his, teasing, tempting. The satiny friction of her gown added to the sensations, especially when he felt the short gown riding higher up her thighs.

Desire burned straight through him. His entire being concentrated on pleasuring Nicki. She was so responsive to his slightest touch. The small sounds of her excitement spurred him on. She quivered when his lips sought the sensitive skin of her neck. And she moaned as his hand slid up the smooth length of her inner thigh, to cup the moist warm place that her gown no longer protected.

"Oh." Her breathing became fast and erratic. Or maybe that was his.

"Let's get this gown off, Nicki. I want to see you."

"Your injuries," she protested.

"I think we discovered a miracle cure."

"Really?"

"Mmm. Maybe we can patent it." His fingers groped for the material and she pushed them aside. With a siren's smile, she sat up, lifting the hem of the gown and drawing it over her head without hesitation.

Alex caught his breath. "You're beautiful, Nicki."

She held still, letting him look his fill, loving him with her eyes. He touched the tip of one nipple, watching it pucker tightly. She shivered when he traced a path lightly over her abdomen, never once taking his eyes from hers.

"Lie still. I'm going to kiss you," she breathed.

Alex found he couldn't lie still. The moment her mouth covered his, he kissed her with a desperate hunger that had lain in ambush until that moment. Nicki responded fervently. Her hands clung to his shoulders, stroking and kneading as their mouths fused. He swallowed the small sounds of her enthusiasm that added volumes to the blood-pounding need now driving him. This was Nicki. Nothing else had ever felt so right.

He moved his hand to the center of her pleasure, kissing his way down her sensitive neck.

"Yes!"

His fingers probed her entrance, pleased to find her as eager and ready as he. His mouth claimed one raised nipple. She arched against him in instant reaction.

"Alex!"

She scored his sore shoulders with her nails when he found the small nub with his thumb. The tension in her throbbing body matched his own. He wanted to slow things down, to prolong this heady sensation, but his body had other ideas.

"I need you, Nicki."

"Yes!"

Alex kissed her hard and fast as he rolled over her. Their gaze locked in a communication that needed no words. He claimed her mouth even as he claimed her body. She twined herself tightly around him as he surged inside.

Thoughts couldn't put words to the emotions he was feeling. This felt so incredibly right. He wanted the sensations to last forever. But almost immediately, she began to shudder. Her body began to contract around him. He knew there wouldn't be time for slow. They were both caught up in the maelstrom of need. He drove to his own release as she pulsed beneath him.

Gradually, his heart rate slowed and the world came back into focus. All the aches and pains he'd pushed to one side resurfaced with a vengeance. He rolled over, drawing her against his side so her head lay against his damp chest. He felt utterly enervated, yet on another level, more rested than he had in years. Alex kissed her temple lightly, stroking her arm, vividly reminded of the past.

"I would have thought it was impossible, but I think we got better at this," she said sedately.

He grinned. "I forgot how good you were at reading my thoughts."

"We always did seem to be in tune," she agreed.

"I don't ever want to move from this spot."

"Me either. But we have to. Don't we?"

"Unfortunately," he agreed reluctantly. "I need to take a shower."

"Want me to soap your back?"

He kissed the tip of her nose. "More than anything. Think we'd ever leave the bathroom?"

"No, we'd probably drown. But what a way to go."

He laughed. And he realized it was the first time he'd laughed in a long, long time.

"Later, you greedy woman." He touched the delicate skin of her neck. "I left marks. I'm sorry."

She touched his shoulder lightly. "That's okay, so did I."

Before he could protest, she pulled away and threw her legs over the side of the bed, reaching for the discarded nightgown. The graceful curve of her back captivated him.

"You really are beautiful, Nicki."

"I'm glad you think so," she said flashing him a smile. She pulled the gown down over her head. "I'd better go use the other shower before temptation gets the better of us."

"Too late."

She offered a saucy grin and opened the hall door. "Oops. Leslie left you a present." She bent over to retrieve a pile of clothing. "Look, even a disposable razor."

Alex propped himself up on an elbow, unable to take his eyes off her. "Remind me to send her a garden of roses."

"Sounds about right."

"Want to come back to bed?" he invited.

"Yes. So I'll see you in a couple of minutes." She dropped the clothing onto the dresser and disappeared out the door with a wink.

It wasn't until he was standing under the stinging spray of the shower rinsing the shampoo from his sore head that he realized he hadn't used any protection with Nicki. The thought stopped him cold, hands motionless in his shampoo-lathered hair.

Never, not even his very first time, had he ever forgotten to use protection. He didn't have to ask if she was on anything. He knew from the tightness of her that it had been a long time since Nicki had taken a lover.

He stood there letting the water pulse against his back, searching for a sense of panic. Remarkably, all he could think was how exciting it would be to watch Nicki grow large with his child. He had a feeling she might not view the situation in exactly the same way. At least, not right now.

He cut off the water and toweled himself dry, moving stiffly as various muscles protested. He ignored them and focused his thought on Nicki instead. He had a lot of explaining to do. The conversation was no doubt going to get a bit touchy.

Leslie had left him a fresh pair of slacks and a dress belt this time. There was even clean underwear and socks. The new white shirt had short sleeves. Unfortunately, they exposed the ugly line of scratches where Ginger had marked her fear. He used the antiseptic cream Leslie also had left, then regarded himself in the mirror, startled by the transformation.

How long had it been since he'd worn anything besides jeans and T-shirts and the occasional leather jacket? With a decent haircut, he could pass for a normal businessman.

He took the gun from the floor beneath the bed where he'd put it last night, discovering it made a heavy bulge in his pocket. He shoved it down inside his boot instead. After making up the bed, he gathered his laundry and went in search of a telephone. He found Leslie in the kitchen reading the morning newspaper over a cup of coffee.

"Good morning. I thought you'd be with patients this morning."

"I had a couple of cancellations so I came up to see if I could fix you anything to eat. How do you feel?" She assessed him with critical eyes.

"Sore all over and my head is pounding, but better than I have any right to feel, thanks to you."

"No double vision? Ringing in your ears? That sort of thing?"

"Just the headache and a pile of aches too numerous to mention. Okay to help myself to some coffee?"

"Of course. There's some analgesics in the cupboard next to the sink. Can I fix you—?"

"No. Thanks, Doc, but I don't need to be waited on. We'll grab something when we leave."

"You made the front page."

"What?" He took the proffered paper and stared at the picture prominently displayed. The photographer had caught him and Nicki supporting an unconscious Matt as they staggered away from the burning house. From the journalist's point, it was a terrific picture. Alex swore.

"Going to talk to John?" Her shrewd eyes continued to assess him. "He and I don't have a lot of secrets."

He'd wondered about the rumors concerning the police chief and her.

"Well, in this case I'm glad or you probably wouldn't have been as quick to help last night." He took a gulp of the hot coffee he'd poured, waiting for the caffeine to jump start his system.

"Oh, I would have helped, but I would have called him at the first opportunity."

Alex nodded. "You haven't spoken with him yet?"

"No."

"When you do, tell him I'll be in touch. I want to check out a couple of things first."

"Does Nicki know?"

He frowned. "Not yet."

"You'd better tell her. Soon," she added pointedly.

"I planned on it. The last thing I ever wanted was for her to get involved in any of this."

"Well, you may be interested in what Mildred Kitteridge had to say this morning."

Despite severe arthritis, Mildred still ran the town's general store.

"Thad Osher came across a truck broken down near the Huntington Horse Farm this morning."

She glanced past him and he knew without looking that Nicki had joined them.

"The rig was filled with stolen cars. The driver was Vic Unsdorf."

Alex cursed. This was the real reason Leslie had come up here. She stood, rinsed her cup, and laid a set of keys on the counter.

"Why don't you leave Nicki's car in the garage? You can take mine. I won't need it today. There's also a house key. I have to get back downstairs." She turned to address Nicki. "I fed Ginger this morning and I'll let her out when I come back up this afternoon. Help yourselves to whatever you need. And Alex?" She gave him a meaningful look. "Nicki was right. It *is* time for a change of wardrobe."

Chapter Seven

As soon as the doctor disappeared Nicki turned to Alex. "What was that cryptic remark all about?"

"She's not fond of my clothing choices either. Do you want something to eat?"

She shook her head. "I need to see about my dad."

"Then let's go." He picked up Leslie's car keys.

As she followed him outside, Nicki tried to ignore the missing sense of intimacy that should have encased them. Alex seemed preoccupied. Was he regretting what had happened between them? Or was he merely upset over Vic's arrest? The arrest must have come as a shock if the two of them were friends.

Surreptitiously, she studied Alex's profile as he turned out onto Main Street. This was the first time she'd seen him with his face freshly shaved, his hair neatly combed, and dressed in something besides a T-shirt and jeans. His bad boy image had been dangerously sexy, but this new look turned him into a strikingly handsome man in a different, more commanding sort of way.

Why was he wasting his life hanging out with losers like Vic Unsdorf?

As she started to ask him that question once again, the building she had called home captured her full attention. She'd thought she was prepared for the sight. She'd been wrong. The destruction was much worse than she'd expected.

The entire front of her shop and the entrance leading to the apartments upstairs were nothing but rubble and gaping holes. None of the three shops in her building were open. The police had roped off the sidewalk between the two alleys, cutting off access to the area. The camera store had suffered extensive damage, while cracked and shattered windows marred the hair salon.

"Alex? Do you think they got Mrs. Coulton out okay?" Her elderly neighbor's apartment centered over the camera store. The apartment over the hair salon had its own entrance, but those tenants must also have been terrified, if not injured, by the explosions.

"I'm sure they did. Leslie would have heard something if anyone had been hurt last night."

"I suppose."

His hand suddenly snagged hers. The remoteness faded, replaced by a tender expression of concern. "There was nothing you could have done about this, Nicki."

"Except by not lying to the police in the first place?"

Alex tossed his head impatiently. "It's too late for looking back. We need to figure out who is bent on getting rid of the witnesses."

Did he know he'd said "we"? They drove past Matt's street and she shuddered. Alex released her hand. As they neared the interstate, Nicki eyed the burned out shell of the Bide-Awhile Motel and decided Fools Point was starting to resemble a military zone.

"Technically, I'm not really a witness," she muttered.

"The murderer has no way of knowing that."

Nicki rubbed her face wearily. "I was stupid to lie to the police."

"Don't worry about it."

"But I hampered a murder investigation."

"Right now, Nicki, that's a minor issue."

Alex resumed his silence, but she no longer sensed that impenetrable distance between them. Alex drove with single-minded purpose. He wasn't at all bothered by the heavy traffic around them. He slid smoothly in and around slower vehicles and didn't seem concerned that his increasing speed was just asking for a ticket.

"How did Hope come to know Vic Unsdorf, Nicki?"

They were approaching the hospital when the question came out of nowhere.

"She doesn't."

Without saying a word, he conveyed his dissatisfaction in her answer.

"She doesn't!"

"They were talking together last night, Nic. She acted like she didn't want anyone to see them together. I can't say I blame her, but that wasn't a coincidental meeting."

"You must be mistaken."

"Vic's got a thing for blondes. He usually likes them older, chestier, and with more experience, but maybe he made an exception in Hope's case."

"No way. My sister isn't involved with someone like Vic Unsdorf!"

Alex frowned. She longed to reach for his hand again. She desperately needed a physical connection to him. His words and their implication were scaring her.

"They were talking urgently," Alex told her. "I heard him say he'd take care of something. Hope didn't look happy."

Fear trickled straight down her spine. Alex wouldn't lie about this, but Hope and Vic Unsdorf?

"How would Hope even know someone like him?" she demanded frantically. "Hope spends all her time working with horses. Trust me, if it doesn't eat hay or know how to muck a stall, she's barely aware of its existence. She hasn't had a social life since she graduated from high school. I've been nagging her about that for some time now. She'd never have an opportunity to meet someone like him.''

Alex scowled.

"You know who he is," he pointed out.

"Of course I do. He's lived around here for years."

Alex arched his eyebrows.

"That's different," she protested. "I know *who* he is. I don't know him *personally*! Whatever you saw, it couldn't have been Hope and Vic Unsdorf. The man's almost old enough to be her father."

Alex didn't argue. His silence did that for him. Technically, Vic Unsdorf was only a few years older than Alex. But that still made him a lot older than Hope.

As Nicki stared at Alex she realized her words had erected a barrier between them. She'd hurt him by not taking his words at face value. But didn't he understand? Hope was her sister. His words had dragged her baby sister into this craziness that surrounded them. After what they'd shared this morning she'd expected…

What? What exactly had she expected from him? A declaration of undying love?

She should have kept in mind that Alex hadn't come to her last night—Nicki had gone to him. She was the one who climbed into *his* bed. And she was the one who'd wrapped herself around him in the night and all but begged him to make love with her this morning. Maybe he was regretting their action.

Shame mingled with guilt. While they'd made love, her father battled for his life and investigators picked over the rubble of her life. Rubble that her lies had caused. Rubble that now affected every person connected with her.

Alex sliced through her melancholy thoughts with a question.

"Have you ever noticed how much your voice and Hope's sound alike?"

Her fear went from a trickle to a full-blown waterfall, cascading right through her. While she'd made this connection right away, she'd hoped he wouldn't.

"Nothing will make me believe my sister is involved in murder."

"I don't think she is. At least not directly."

"Then what are you implying?"

"Unsdorf may be using Hope."

"How?"

"Let's say they do know one another somehow. Let's say Unsdorf asked Hope to make the phone call that lured me to the alley that night."

"No!" Nicki struggled to contain the torrent of fear.

"It's the only scenario that makes sense, Nicki."

And that was exactly the problem. Her sister was one of the few people who knew about Nicki's connection to Alex. Hope had asked her to go out back and search for the missing bracelet right after Nicki locked up for the night. That would have put Nicki out back shortly after nine. Alex's caller had wanted him out back right after nine.

It had to be coincidence!

"I won't have my family dragged into this, Alex. Especially not now. My father could die!"

"I know. And I'm sorry. The timing is cruel, but if Hope is involved with Unsdorf you can't ignore the situation. We'll need to protect her."

"Protect her?" Fear solidified, turning to dread. "You think Hope's in danger?"

"She is if she made that call."

"Oh, my God."

"I'll talk to her," he promised.

"No! *I'll* talk to her."

Alex sighed. When his hand would have reached for

hers, Nicki drew back. She hugged herself tightly and wondered when this nightmare would end.

"What does he do for a living?"

Suddenly, it seemed important to know because she couldn't see a connection between Vic and Hope no matter how she tried.

"Whatever's profitable." Alex shrugged. "Recently, he was driving trucks for Yosten Lumber."

"Gunnar Yosten's dead."

"I know." Alex's voice emptied of emotion. His features became so cold and empty the transition was shocking.

"He was shot to death by the police," she continued, desperate to take that horrible lack of expression off his face. Why was it there in the first place?

"Was he?"

Her confusion intensified. Then she remembered that Alex had worked for Gunnar as well. Would Alex also do whatever was profitable?

"Unsdorf worked for Gunnar part-time. He needed to show a legitimate job up front." Alex's voice resumed without emotion. The starkness of his expression, combined with the lack of inflection in his tone sent chills over her arms. "Vic transported stolen cars to Baltimore the rest of the time."

She couldn't prevent a soft gasp. "You knew this?"

"I suspected it," he said. "The situation isn't what it seems."

"You think Vic Unsdorf killed Thorton Biggs?"

Alex hesitated. She was almost relieved to see him frown as he considered her question.

"It's possible. I've wondered if that murder wasn't simply a falling out among thieves."

Relief swept her.

"If Unsdorf didn't do the killing himself, I'll give you

odds he knows who did,'' Alex said thoughtfully. ''Are there garages or body shops out past your dad's place?''

''Not that I know of. Why?''

''Because I can't figure out what Unsdorf was doing in the middle of nowhere with those cars. The key to transporting stolen vehicles is to be unobtrusive. You get on the highway and you blend in. A car carrier on that road would stick out for miles.''

You get on the highway and you blend in. Alex spoke like he had firsthand knowledge.

She eyed the hard thrust of his jaw. She longed to touch those smooth planes. Anything to remove the remote hardness that was settling over him again. Whatever thoughts were going through his head weren't good ones.

Why was it so difficult to remember that Alex wasn't one of the good guys? Wanting wouldn't make it so. When he was touching her, making love with her, it was easy to forget the inflexible core of steel inside him. But she'd seen the tough side of him. Her passionate lover was the same man who'd knocked down Osher inside her shop the other day.

If this was a movie or a novel, she'd suspect he was a cop working undercover. But cops and good guys don't beat up other cops. Even slimy cops like Osher. Still, she resisted the idea that Alex was one of the bad guys. Bad guys don't rush inside burning buildings to save people.

Alex backed the car into a space at the hospital and turned to face Nicki.

''I need to explain a few things to you.''

''Yes. You do.'' Only she didn't think she could stand hearing any more truths right now. Her thoughts were already in chaos. ''Can it wait until I check on my father?''

He hesitated and she reached for the door handle. She needed a little time and distance from Alex to think. She could not and would not believe Alex was a murderer, but that left the door wide open for other charges.

"All right," he said reluctantly. "But afterwards we have to talk."

"You won't say anything to my sister?"

He ran a hand through his hair, obviously frustrated. "Not until after you visit with your dad," he agreed.

"Thank you."

They started toward the hospital in silence. Nicki automatically slowed her pace when she noticed him limping.

"Are you sure you're okay?" she asked.

"A little stiff, that's all. Nicki, should I be apologizing for this morning?"

The question zipped through her with the power of an electric charge. His expression was hooded, but she recognized the uncertainty in his inflection.

"I'd rather you didn't."

"Good."

Relief and satisfaction rippled in his voice. His expression softened. Somewhere inside her, the coldness that had been spreading began to thaw. He wasn't sorry they had made love.

God help her, neither was she.

In the Cardiac Care Unit's waiting room they found Hope standing between both her brothers. Hope looked as if she hadn't slept in days.

Alex stopped barely inside the doorway as Nicki went forward to greet her family. Alex realized Hope was watching him covertly from troubled eyes. Her gaze plunged to the carpet when she realized he'd noticed her. No doubt about it, she was guilty of something. He chafed under the promise he'd made to Nicki.

"They're going to do the surgery this morning," their brother Gavin was explaining to Nicki. "The doctor says the situation is critical. The nurse says we can all see him before they prep him.''

"He's conscious?"

"He has been since shortly after we left last night," Brent confirmed.

Alex stepped aside to allow a slender young nurse entrance. But the woman stopped, surveyed the room, then spoke directly to him. "Excuse me, but would you be Alex Coughlin?"

Alarm zipped through him. There was nothing ominous in her expression, so Alex nodded reluctantly. Everyone else stared openly.

"Mr. Michaels is demanding to see his family. He specifically asked for you and his daughter Nicki." Her gaze picked Nicki from the group. "He's becoming quite agitated over this so the doctor is going to allow all of you back there at once. We can do this since he's the only one in the unit right now, but please, we ask that you don't upset him any further. We can only give you a few minutes."

Alex found his shock mirrored in Nicki's expression.

"Why does he want to see Alex?" Hope demanded.

"I couldn't say, Ms. Michaels, but your father was most insistent. If you'll all come with me, please."

"Let's go," Gavin said. His probing stare focused on Alex.

Nicki came forward and took his hand. "Please, Alex."

With a sinking feeling, Alex took her hand. "We should have had that talk outside," he tried to warn her. She just shook her head and started after the nurse, tugging him beside her.

Alex would have given a lot to refuse to go with her right now. He had a feeling he knew what was coming, and the words should have come from him, not her father. But the soft plea in Nicki's eyes was more than he could withstand. With a knot in his stomach, he stepped into the CCU ward.

Bernie Michaels lay withered and shrunken against the stark white linens. The gray pallor beneath his weathered skin gave him a corpselike look that was unsettling. Alex didn't doubt for a moment that Bernie Michaels was dying. There was little left of the large, forbidding man who had cornered him fifteen years ago. Only his dark blue eyes still shone with keen intelligence as they fastened on Alex.

"Breeding always tells," he said. The voice still carried the remembered strength of the man he'd been.

Alex heard Nicki or Hope inhale sharply, but he didn't look at either of them. He strode to their father's side. "Thank you."

The shrewd eyes glinted with humor and a touch of respect. "Knew you were a good investment."

"You and nobody else," he agreed.

"Oh, there was someone else."

Alex knew he meant Nicki.

"My mistake was sending you away back then."

"No, sir. It wasn't a mistake. You were right. We were too young."

Bernie Michaels closed his eyes in acknowledgement. "We could've worked it different."

"Perhaps."

"I never expected you to pay me back."

"I know. But without that money, I wouldn't have—"

"What money?" Nicki questioned. Her father waved the question aside.

"You'd have made it," Bernie said. "One way or another, you'd have made it. You were like my kids. Stubborn. Determined. Are you still with the FBI?"

This time the gasp came from more than one throat. Alex didn't turn around, but his body tensed. That had torn it.

"Yes, sir."

"Knew you were bright."

"Not so bright, Mr. Michaels," he said sadly, wanting to look at Nicki, but afraid of what he'd see on her face. "Not lately, anyhow."

"Ha. Even John Hepplewhite likes you. But that's not why I wanted to see you. Damn doctors want to do some fancy cut-and-paste job. Don't like it, but don't guess I can convince anyone to leave me be."

"No, sir."

"Well, I've been a fool where my kids were concerned." For the first time, his gaze encompassed the others standing silently around the bed. "Happens when you love 'em and don't know how to show it."

"Mr. Michaels," a nurse interrupted firmly, "we need to clear this room and—"

"Get out of here until I'm finished talking to my family!"

In that moment, Alex saw the Bernie Michaels he remembered. He didn't turn around, but he heard both of Bernie's sons hustling the nurse from the room.

"Dad, please. Try to save your strength."

Nicki moved to take his hand on the opposite side of the bed. A lone tear trickled down her face.

"None left to save, girl. You look just like your mother. Soft and delicate. I don't think I ever told you that."

"No." More tears hovered in her eyes. Beside her, Hope began weeping openly.

"Should have. Always meant to. Fortunately, you got my grit. You're a stayer. I raised two beautiful daughters, didn't I, boy?"

"Yes, sir. I always thought so."

Bernie Michaels smiled. The expression of pride took away the faded look of him.

"Also raised a fine pair of sons. But I made mistakes. Can't fix most of 'em." His gaze returned to Alex. "But

I'd like to fix this one. Promise me you'll take care of Nicki for me.''

"Dad! Nothing's going to happen to you."

Bernie ignored his daughter. His gaze locked on Alex. "Promise me."

The fierce blue eyes seemed to penetrate his soul. Shaken, Alex looked at Nicki's stricken face then back down again. "I'll do my best." He had a sinking feeling it was a promise he might not be able to keep.

"Good. You take care of this man, Nicki. I'd be proud to call him son. Hope, stop that sniveling and come closer."

Alex stepped away from the bed. Her brothers had returned and he knew everyone stared at him. Everyone but Nicki. As Bernie continued talking to each of his children, Alex barely registered his words.

His cover had been ripped away, but that didn't matter anymore. If he was right, his investigation had been seriously compromised a long time ago. That was the real reason he'd been set up that night. They'd wanted him out of the way. What could work better than pinning a murder charge on him?

Alex swore to himself. He knew what really bothered him was that he hadn't been the one to tell Nicki the truth. Her confusion was as plain as if she'd expressed it in words.

When she led a sobbing Hope from the room past the nurse who'd returned with reinforcements in the form of the surgeon, Alex followed slowly.

"You can talk to your family again after the surgery," the doctor was telling Bernie. But Bernie Michaels had closed his eyes. He'd accomplished what he set out to do.

"You're FBI?" Gavin demanded at his side as they reached the waiting room.

No one else was nearby, so Alex nodded. "I'd appreciate it, if none of you would mention this. To *anyone*."

He stared at Hope, whose tear-streaked face blanched so white he thought she might faint. Nicki hugged her and glared.

"I've been working undercover. If the wrong people learn my identity, it will totally compromise the investigation." He didn't add that it would also get him killed. They could figure that out.

Hope sagged into a chair and buried her face in her hands.

"Does this have something to do with what happened to Nicki's shop?" Gavin demanded.

Alex studied the younger man. He was taller than Alex. Leanly muscled like his brother. Her brothers made a formidable pair. "You're a lawyer, aren't you?" Alex asked.

Gavin nodded.

"You'd better tell your family exactly what happened, Nic."

Anger pulled her mouth into a tight line, but Nicki didn't address him. With a conciseness that would have pleased his superiors, she summed up the recent events.

"I can't believe you lied to the police, Nicki." Gavin frowned at his sister.

"People lie to the police all the time," Alex defended softly.

"I remember Ilona," Brent put in. "Blond, stacked, the sort who knows all the angles."

Surprise flickered in Nicki's expression. "You remember her?"

"Hey, I was what? Thirteen or fourteen? Teenage boys do not forget women built like Ilona."

"I remember her too," Gavin said consideringly. "So what does all this mean?"

"It means this is a murder investigation," Alex told him. "The Fools Point police will be here to question Nicki. With the exception of Chief Hepplewhite, none of them know who or what I am. I'd like you to keep it that way for now.''

"All right. I understand. I'll take care of it," Gavin promised.

"There's more. You need to keep Nicki and Hope near you at all times. I have to report in. Normally, I wouldn't let them out of my sight after what happened last night, but they arrested Unsdorf this morning, so that should reduce the danger.''

Hope gaped at him.

"But Unsdorf may not be the murderer. For certain, he's not in this thing alone.'' Alex turned to her brothers. "Nicki and Hope should be safe enough until I can arrange police protection, but stay alert. Don't let either of them out of your sight. Not even to go to the bathroom.''

"Hope too?'' Gavin asked.

"Yes.''

"Mr. Michaels?'' The nurse had returned. "There are some papers that need to be filled out.''

"I'll take them," Gavin said absently.

"And I'll be back shortly," Alex told the room at large. Nicki didn't even look up. Neither did Hope, who had gone back to crying. But Brent walked him to the elevator.

"Let me give you my cell phone number. Is there a way we can reach you…if something happens?''

Alex gave him the local number. "But in an emergency, call the police. I probably won't be in my office and may not get the message.''

"Understood. You're really FBI?''

"Yes.''

"Nicki should be pleased.''

"Maybe eventually she will be.'' The elevator doors opened and he stepped inside. "Take care of her.''

"We will.''

Alex found a telephone and set their protection in motion. Then he headed for the field office in Frederick. Nothing about this investigation had gone as it should from the beginning. He had never gained the inner circle even though he knew most of the key players. He suspected someone had known who he was and why he was there from the start. Yet he'd been selected for this job precisely because of his past reputation. He should have blended in without any problem, but there'd always been a sense of mistrust that he'd never quite understood.

Maybe he'd unwittingly betrayed himself when he'd helped his sister Kayla and her fiancé. The police suspicion of him had made his old ''friends'' wary. He'd assumed the beating he'd taken back then had been related to Kayla's situation, but now he wondered. What if the beating had been intended as a get-out-of-town sort of warning?

His search through old yearbooks had given him the names of a few troubled schoolmates who had an affinity for chemistry, but in today's world, practically anyone could have figured out how to build the sort of bomb that had killed Agent Kenholt. Including a certain police officer who'd been exceptionally antagonistic from day one.

If Osher was involved in the car theft ring, a lot would be explained. Except why he had arrested Vic Unsdorf this morning.

Alex cursed. Nothing added up, but he could see where he'd given himself away a dozen times over. The night he shot Gunnar Yosten might have been the deciding incident.

In the confusion that night, Alex hadn't thought anyone had seen him. He'd reported the truth to Hepplewhite and his own supervisor. They knew he'd fired the fatal shot instead of one of the policemen at the scene that night, but they also knew he'd had no choice. Gunnar would have killed Sydney Edwards if Alex hadn't been following him, mistakenly believing he was part of the car theft ring.

Still, the incident weighed heavily on his conscience and

no doubt always would. He'd hoped never to take a person's life in the line of duty.

Troubled by the memory, Alex found a parking space and headed upstairs. Instead of reporting in, he headed for the computer section and a fellow he'd played softball with. Darrin Lange worked in information retrieval. The youthful-looking man welcomed him with a surprised smile.

"Hey, when did you get back? Thought you were still undercover on that car ring."

"I am. I need a favor."

"I should have guessed."

"Don't worry, I just need you to work your magic. The request will come through channels shortly, but I can't wait. I need as much information as you can find on a woman calling herself Ilona Toskov."

Darrin's mouth dropped open. Alex ran tired fingers through his hair. "Look, I know it's not policy, but I need this information before I meet with Lemmer. You can get authorization—"

"No, no. I'll run it. It's just an unusual name. Why do you…what does she have to do with your assignment?"

"That's what I'm trying to find out. Right now she's simply a witness."

"Oh."

Darrin was obviously uncomfortable with his request to stretch the rules. Alex had never thought of him as a by-the-book sort of person, but he didn't know Darrin very well. Obviously uncomfortable,Darrin turned to his computer.

"Have a seat, this could take a minute."

"A minute's about all I've got," Alex replied, but he sat down gratefully and rolled his tight shoulders trying to ease the strain. "Lemmer's waiting for me right now."

A fan swept back and forth on the corner of Darrin's

bookcase. The small breeze rustled papers without really disturbing them.

"I see they never got the air-conditioning fixed back here."

Darrin didn't look up. "They're working on it."

Alex nodded. Papers lifted and fell on the bulletin board beside Darrin's desk. Alex perused the cubicle restlessly until his gaze landed on a file in a pile on the corner of the desk. The dead agent's name practically jumped out at him.

Kenholt, Joseph Jonah.

"They've got you working on something to do with Kenholt's death?"

Darrin looked up blankly. Alex nodded toward the stack of files.

"Huh? Oh. No. Lemmer carried it in here one day. I've been meaning to get it back in the files." But he shifted uncomfortably in his seat.

"Darrin, if you're worried my request is going to cause you grief—"

"No, no. Don't worry. Here we go." Surprise scored his features. "We've got a file on her."

Alex was mildly surprised himself. He hadn't expected an FBI file on Ilona.

"Ilona Toskov. The family were Russian immigrants back in the sixties. Both parents deceased. She has one brother, Pavel. There's a flag next to him. Want me to run it?"

"Yeah. Print out what you have on Ilona while you pull up the brother's file."

"Printer's in the corner outside Kirtle's office."

"Okay."

Alex stepped out of the cubicle as Darrin hit the Print key.

He collected the sheets as they spewed from the printer and began reading as he walked back to Darrin's office.

"DEA has the flag," Darrin announced.

"What does the Drug Enforcement Agency want with Pavel Toskov?"

"The guy's a chemist. I know there's a joint project right now that's looking in to all those designer drugs that have been turning up around here."

"Ilona has a chemistry degree as well."

"I saw that."

The words were right. The tone was all wrong. Alarms began tripping in his head. Darrin's demeanor from the moment he'd mentioned Ilona's name had been all wrong. And the story about Lemmer leaving the file on a dead agent in his office didn't ring true at all.

"Brother Pavel has suspected ties to the Russian mafia through an uncle and some cousins," Darrin added.

"Nothing on car thefts?"

"No. But he does have a connection to the Baltimore harbor."

"Bingo. Run me a hard copy of his information too."

"Sure. You sit and read Ilona's file. I'll get it for you. I need to stretch my legs for a minute anyhow."

"Thanks."

The minute he left the cubicle, Alex stood and reached for the files on his desk. Kenholt's file wasn't there any more. Alex flipped through the stack. No time to go through his desk, but as the fan lifted the edge of a sheet of paper on his bulletin board, Alex froze. A fuzzy snapshot had been tacked beneath the top papers. A photograph of Darrin and a tall blond woman under a cherry blossom tree arm in arm.

Darrin's wife was a short brunette.

Alex started to lean closer for a better view when he heard someone greet Darrin. He barely made it back into his seat in time.

"How's married life treating you?" Alex asked. He'd

heard how surprised the department was when their perennial playboy had married a nice young woman he'd met on a skiing vacation the year before.

"Fine. Great. You ought to try it sometime."

"Maybe I will."

"Yeah? Anyone I know?"

"Nope. I notice there's no picture."

"Sure. My wife's picture is right over there."

Sure enough, a brunette who barely came to his shoulders. Of course, the blonde could be a sister or cousin or just about anyone.

"I meant of Ilona and Pavel."

"Oh, yeah. The computer got hung up. Want to wait for it to clear?"

"No, that's okay. I'll take these printouts over to Lemmer's office before he sends out a team to hunt me down. Thanks, Darrin. I owe you one."

"I'll remember that."

Don Lemmer really was waiting, Alex discovered. He ushered Alex into his office, but Alex didn't take the offered seat. "We have a problem," Alex began without preamble.

"Yeah, your cover was blown to smithereens."

Alex nodded. "And I suspect the origin of the leak may have come from down the hall."

Lemmer's eyes narrowed. "What are you talking about?"

"Darrin Lange had a hard copy file on Kenholt sitting on his desk a few minutes ago. He said you left it there."

"No."

"That's what I thought." Tersely, Alex related what had just occurred. Lemmer turned to the phone and issued a series of orders.

"You'd better be sure about this."

"I'm only sure that his actions were highly irregular."

"So were yours."

"Yes, sir. I couldn't see the picture over his desk clearly and the woman was in profile. She could be anyone."

"But you think it was Hope Michaels?"

"More likely, Ilona Toskov."

There was a subtle rap on the door.

"Come in."

"Sir, Darrin Lange left for the day."

With Lemmer on his heels, Alex headed for the cubicle. The computer was still warm. A search of his desk proved the file was definitely gone. So was the photograph.

Lemmer turned to the man who'd reported Darrin's disappearance. "Pick him up."

"Yes, sir." The man disappeared, at a trot.

"What's your theory?" Lemmer asked.

"I don't have enough information to form one. At least not yet." Alex thrust the printouts into Lemmer's arms. "But my gut's telling me I need to get back to Nicki right now."

"Since your cover is gone, take your identification with you this time."

"Yes, sir."

Alex went to his own cubicle. He grabbed what he needed and paused long enough to call Chief Hepplewhite. Carolyn patched him through immediately.

"This is Alex. My cover's history. I'm on my way. Tighten the net on Nicki and Hope. All hell could break loose any minute. I'll explain when I get there. And, John, keep Osher away from them."

Chapter Eight

Nicki paced restlessly. Hope wouldn't talk to anyone, but at least she'd stopped crying. Her sister was too upset to press for answers. They were all aware that the surgery was taking too long, and despite the start of a pressing need, her brothers were adamant that Nicki not leave their sight.

To top it all, she couldn't stem her petty feelings of betrayal. *Why hadn't Alex told her what he really did for a living?* Why hadn't he trusted her?

Nicki was almost relieved when she spotted Ilona peering into the large surgical waiting room. Nicki strode over to greet her friend before her brothers could intercept her.

"Ilona?" While groomed impeccably as always, Ilona seemed nervous. "What are you doing here?"

"I tried to call you to check on your father. I know how much he means to you, but when I got no answer I drove by your apartment. Oh, Nicki, it's so awful. I was terrified that you'd been killed. I took a chance and came back here to the hospital to see if maybe..." Ilona hesitated, looking past her.

Nicki realized both her brothers had taken protective positions on either side of her. "Gavin, Brent, this is Ilona."

Gavin assessed her with his impenetrable lawyer's eyes. Brent, however, gave her a cold stare. "I remember. You're the one who put my sister at risk."

Ilona gasped. "What have you told them?"

"The truth," Brent assured her.

Ilona would have turned and fled, but Nicki grasped her arm. "Ilona, they're on your side." Sort of, she amended silently. She saw Gavin raise his eyebrows and gave both her brothers a stern look. "You're my friend," she added for emphasis. "Besides, Gavin's a lawyer. He can help us."

"Oh, God! You told a lawyer? I've got to get out of here."

"Don't worry, it's not contagious," Gavin teased gently. When she continued to look stricken he added, "Hey, even as a lawyer I don't usually terrify people." Turning to Brent he added, "Must be you, little brother. Why don't you keep Hope company? See if you can get her to talk a little."

The two exchanged a look of understanding. The look would have exasperated Nicki except that she was so relieved when Brent strolled over to Hope who sat with her back to them, wrapped in misery.

"I have to go," Ilona insisted. "I only wanted to come by and see how your dad was doing."

Nicki held onto her arm. "Stay, please."

For a second, it was touch and go, but Ilona finally relaxed. Nicki led her to a chair in the far corner away from the other people who sat in the immense waiting room waiting for reports on their loved ones.

She held Ilona's brilliantly manicured hand. Fear and consternation still dominated her lovely features. "Gavin and I only want to help."

"It's too late for that."

"Battery is still a criminal offense," Gavin said mildly. "You can press charges against the man who hit you."

"No!" Ilona stared hard at Nicki. "Exactly what have you told him?"

"Beyond the fact that you're in trouble, very little," Gavin assured her before Nicki could respond.

"I don't know any details of your private affairs," Nicki added. "But I did tell him that you were the real witness to the murder and why you were afraid to come forward."

"Oh, God. You shouldn't have said anything! There's no way you can help me now."

Nicki flushed. Guilt rode her conscience, even though she knew it shouldn't.

"I'm sorry, Nicki. I know I shouldn't have asked you to lie like that. And I'll understand if you tell the police the truth about that night."

"Even the police aren't above the law," Gavin told her. "We *can* go after the man who hurt you."

"Oh, I'm so confused. I don't know what to do."

"Why don't you let us help you," Gavin offered.

"My brother's a pretty good lawyer if I do say so," Nicki told her.

"Thanks. You've been a true friend all along." Abruptly, Ilona's eyes widened as she stared past them. "Oh, no. He's here! He'll kill me!"

"Who's here?"

But Ilona jumped to her feet. Nicki looked over her shoulder and spotted Thad Osher near the entrance to the room. He was talking with someone out of their line of sight and he did not look happy.

"Osher was your lover?" Gavin asked.

"Yes." She hissed the word and pivoted. Her ridiculously high stiletto heels made no sound against the carpeted floor as she hurried toward the far end of the room and the doors marked No Admittance.

"Ilona, wait!"

Hope jerked her head around at Nicki's cry. Ilona plunged through the double doors. Brent restrained Hope when she rose to follow Ilona. He said something to his sister, who flashed Nicki a frightened glance.

Before she could wonder what that look was all about, Gavin loomed over her looking fierce. "I'm going to have a talk with Sergeant Osher."

"No." Nicki gripped his arm.

"Are you afraid of him too?"

"Of course not. But he makes my skin crawl, Gavin. He's one of those sleazy types who looks at a woman as if he were undressing her with his eyes."

"I think he needs to learn some manners."

"You will not go near him! I don't want you having a run-in with him too."

"What do you mean, too?"

"Alex decked him the last time Sergeant Osher tried to talk to me. They hate each other. Stay away from him, Gavin. He's nothing but trouble."

"Decked him, huh? I'm liking Coughlin more by the minute." Gavin flexed his fingers.

"Don't you dare go over there! I mean it! You said battery was still a criminal offense and you're an officer of the court. I will not have you assaulting a police officer no matter how disgusting I find him. Besides, Alex said you were supposed to stay with me."

Nicki could easily picture her respectable brother being hauled away for assault, given the mood he was in.

"Hey. Take it easy, sis. I'm not sure if I should be insulted that you don't think I can handle someone like Osher, or flattered that you care enough to want to protect my delicate knuckles."

"You dope. I just don't want you to cause a scene in front of all these people. If they're in this waiting room, they have enough problems."

"Good point. He's leaving anyhow."

Thad Osher scowled furiously at the person he was talking with. His glance swept the room. Nicki's gaze collided with his. Chilled by the anger she saw there, she was relieved when he turned and strode out of sight. His companion stepped into view.

"Chief Hepplewhite!" She exhaled on a sigh of relief. She had always thought it interesting the way the chief's striking white hair camouflaged his actual age. A person had to look closely to see it was weather and not age that had lined his face. He wore a confident air of authority as he strode toward them. Nicki realized Alex carried himself the same way.

"Nicki. Gavin. How's your father doing?"

"We haven't heard anything yet," Nicki replied. "But he's been in there longer than they said he would."

Gavin laid a reassuring hand on her shoulder. Nicki acknowledged her brother with a grateful look. What scared her a little was the realization that the touch she longed to feel belonged to Alex. If only he was here.

"Can we help you with something, Chief?" Gavin asked.

"Unfortunately, I have to ask Nicki a few questions about what happened last night."

"Have you started traveling in pairs?" Gavin nodded in the direction Osher had taken.

Hepplewhite's face lost his friendly expression. "The initial investigation belonged to Sergeant Osher. He intended to ask the questions."

"But now you're going to ask them?"

Hepplewhite rubbed his jaw. "I understand Nicki and Sergeant Osher have some issues. I suggested it might be better if I talk with her instead."

"Issues?" Nicki queried. "Well, I guess that's one way to put things."

"I was told you might want to file charges against Sergeant Osher. Is that still your intent?"

Nicki felt Gavin come to attention. "I haven't discussed this with my brother yet so I'm not sure I have grounds for more than a nuisance suit."

"I'd like to hear the details," he said.

"So would I," her brother rejoined.

"You acting as her counsel, Gavin?"

"For now."

Hepplewhite nodded. "Let's sit down."

"You're going to do this here?" Gavin asked.

"I didn't think you'd want to leave right now. There's no one sitting near us at the moment. Is this all right?"

"Of course," Nicki assured him.

"Then I'd like you to start with the night of Thorton Biggs's murder, if you wouldn't mind, Nicki."

She recited everything, only omitting references to Alex. There was no need for her brother or the chief to know about Alex's late night visit to her apartment, or the crazy resurrection of their old attraction.

Chief Hepplewhite had a number of questions. Especially about what Ilona had said and how Thad Osher had behaved. Nicki answered without pulling any punches.

"She actually stated that she and Thad were having an affair?"

Gavin interrupted. "She said yes when we asked if Osher was her lover," he corrected.

Nicki glared. "It's the same thing."

Hepplewhite extended his hand in a bid to keep the peace. "How did you and Alex Coughlin come to have your picture on the front page of this morning's paper?"

The doors at the far end of the room opened before she could answer. Her father's surgeon appeared. With a brief apology to the police chief, she and her brothers and sister surged forward, surrounding the doctor anxiously.

"Your father is in critical condition," he told them. "Our surgery went well, but I discovered a mass in your father's chest, tucked behind his heart. They're running a biopsy right now, but I'm fairly certain it's malignant. The cell growth is abnormal. We'll need the biopsy to positively identify the mass.''

"You didn't remove it?" Brent demanded.

"I'm sorry. The location makes the tumor inoperable. We'll have to wait and see exactly what we're dealing with when the results come in.''

ALEX LOCATED JOHN Hepplewhite near the recovery room. The large man stood looking out a window, completely alone.

"What's happened?"

"Bernie Michaels has inoperable cancer.''

Alex swore.

"The surgeon just got word from the lab downstairs. He's going over options with the family, but the situation isn't good. You want to brief me while we wait?''

Alex ran a hand through his hair feeling helpless. What he wanted to do was go to Nicki and offer whatever comfort he could. On the other hand, she was with her family and he had a job to do. A job that meant keeping Nicki and her sister alive. Alex gave Hepplewhite a terse rundown on what he'd discovered.

"So you think this Darrin Lange fingered Kenholt and you?''

"Looks that way. Either intentionally, or unintentionally. Hard to say until we pick him up, but the fact that he ran is pretty damning.''

"How does Thad Osher fit into this?''

"That's what we need to determine. What do you think of him?''

Hepplewhite scowled. "On a personal level, I can't stand the man. I inherited him with the job. I've had complaints, but nothing actionable—until you hit town.''

Alex raised an eyebrow.

"Yeah, I know. Makes you wonder if he knew who you were from the start."

"And that would mean he's totally involved in the car theft ring as well as the murder of Agent Kenholt."

"Then why would he bust Vic Unsdorf this morning?"

"Good point. I wondered the same thing myself." Alex rubbed his jaw thoughtfully, trying to make sense of Osher's actions. "Nicki suggested Osher might have killed Biggs. She thinks her friend Ilona is covering for him out of fear."

"I hope she's wrong. I want to believe he's just gung ho to do his job. I know he's a womanizer. Most of the complaints I've had have come from women, but he's been careful not to step over the line. Damn it, if he's dirty, I need something I can use."

"I'll do my best."

Hepplewhite nearly smiled. "That, I don't doubt. By the way, ballistics confirmed the gun in your car was the murder weapon."

"Who owned it?"

"Well now, that's going to be a little embarrassing. It belongs to Lee Garvey."

Alex gaped at him.

"Remember back in June when Lee's car was stolen? Well, his backup piece was under the seat."

"Lee's not going to be happy."

"Nobody's happy. The good news is, this ties nicely back to the car theft ring and there's a partial print that doesn't belong to either one of you."

"Always nice to know I'm not the primary suspect anymore."

"Yeah. Your being near that alley at just that time can't have been a coincidence."

"They knew who I was from the start—where I lived,

what I drove, even my past connection to Nicki. No wonder I couldn't get an inside track.''

Hepplewhite nodded. ''You might be glad to know that your soon-to-be brother-in-law starts work tomorrow.''

''Lee's a good man.''

''I agree.''

''So where's Osher right now?'' Alex asked.

''I sent him back to Fools Point. He came over here to talk to the Williams boy.''

''I'd like to talk to Matt myself.''

''Well, you'll have to find him first. He tricked his guard and took off again.''

Alex muttered an oath.

''I agree. The kid's slippery as greased lightning, but we need to know what he knows.''

''He's probably afraid you'll bust him for boosting cars.''

''You know, there are days I wonder why I ever wanted this job.''

''I know exactly what you mean. What are you getting out of Unsdorf?''

''The name of his lawyer,'' Hepplewhite said wryly. ''He's got a record so he knows how to play the game.''

''I'm pretty sure he's the one who arranged to set me up. I'll have a few words with him this afternoon. Maybe we can strike a deal.''

''Good luck. I'll let Carolyn know you're coming in. Oh, and I had your car taken over to Dr. Martin's. Your bike's back at your place.''

''Thanks.''

''Looks like they're done,'' Hepplewhite said. ''Give me a call later.''

''I'll do that,'' Alex replied, but his attention had moved to Nicki, who stood beside her brothers.

He headed toward the group, unsure of his welcome. Brent saw him first. Nicki turned around. Tears had dried on her face. His heart lurched. He took an uncertain step forward and Nicki launched herself straight into his arms.

"Oh, Alex."

He caught her, holding her tightly, feeling her body quiver with grief. "I'm sorry, Nic. So sorry." He stroked the slender curve of her back as she wept silent tears.

Gavin caught his attention. "We're going back to the house. You're welcome to join us."

"Thanks. I'll bring Nicki with me."

She looked up, wiping the moisture from her face with the back of her hand. "I'm okay. We need to get my car."

"And mine."

"I thought the police had yours."

As her family moved away, he nodded. "Chief Hepple-white's having it delivered for me."

"What about the gun they found?"

"It's the murder weapon," he confirmed, "but my prints weren't on it. I'll give you the details later. Do you want to talk about your dad?"

"It's cancer and it's in an advanced state. They can do chemo, but not radiation because of the location. The heart surgery went fine, but I'm not sure we did him any favors. I think he knew about the cancer, Alex. I think that's why he didn't want to have this surgery done."

Alex stroked her hair in sympathy.

"They let us see him for a few minutes, but he was still unconscious. They're moving him back to the Cardiac Care Unit as soon as he's stable. We have to come back later."

"Okay. Let's go pick up my car. I'll run you out to the horse farm."

On the way back to Fools Point, Nicki talked about her father and their family. Alex knew she needed the catharsis of speech, so he prodded her to continue. By the time they reached the doctor's house, Nicki was spent. Her eyelids drooped with fatigue.

"I didn't mean to go on like that."

"Hey, I learned more about you and your family in the last fifteen minutes than I would have otherwise."

"You should have told me to shut up."

Alex smiled. "Not a chance. I like listening to you."

"Why didn't you tell me, Alex?"

He sighed, knowing what she meant. "I had a job to do."

"Was last night and this morning part of your job too?"

"You know it wasn't." He turned onto Perry Road, glad they were almost at the doctor's. He wanted to be having this conversation where he could give it his full concentration. "I deliberately stayed away from you when I came back to town so I wouldn't have to lie to you."

"I see."

He parked the doctor's car in the grass and twisted to face her.

"I doubt it. You once asked me why I never came back to Fools Point. Kayla had some pretty strong views about authority figures after our dad was killed by that police officer."

"I know. It's sort of ironic now that she's engaged to a policeman. What does she think about your career choice?"

"She doesn't know."

"Your own sister doesn't know you work for the FBI?"

"No."

"What does she think you do for a living?"

"Pretty much what you thought, I guess." He shrugged. "I've been evasive about my job because I didn't want to upset her. It wasn't hard. Mostly we've exchanged telephone calls, cards, and simple notes. I've never been assigned to this area in my job capacity before."

"You're telling me she still doesn't know?"

"No one knew, except Chief Hepplewhite."

"And my father."

"Yeah, well," he shifted uncomfortably.

"Why did Dad know? And what is this money he was talking about that you repaid?"

Running his hand through his hair, Alex sighed. "Your dad found out I was seeing you that summer I graduated high school. If you recall, I was feeling pretty wild back then."

"I remember."

They shared a wistful smile. "Well, your dad came to me and offered me a deal. He'd pay for my college education if I left town."

"You mean if you left me."

"I'm sorry, Nic, but yes. He pointed out how young you were. How young we both were. And he offered me an opportunity to make something of myself."

"All your big dreams."

Alex lifted her hand. "He offered them to me on a silver platter."

"Why didn't you tell me?"

"That was part of the deal. I had to leave and not look back."

"And you always keep your word."

He hated causing her more hurt. "Actually, I did come back once. Before my first assignment. You were away at school and I talked to your dad. He was real proud of you, Nicki."

"And that's when he learned you were FBI?"

"Yes. When I got this assignment, I figured by now you'd be raising a family, teaching in some school somewhere…" He shrugged.

"You paid Dad back."

"Yes." The beeper on his belt went off. "It's my office. I need to go inside and use Leslie's telephone."

"I'll take my car and head back to the house."

"No! Let me see what this is first and I'll follow you, okay?"

"Why? You don't trust me to drive to my father's place?"

"No, because we still need to talk. Matt Williams is still missing."

"So?"

"So someone tried to kill both of you. Until we figure out who's behind all this, I don't want you going anywhere by yourself."

"The bathroom is going to get awfully cramped."

He squeezed her fingers before letting her get out of the car.

Nicki followed him into the house where they were greeted by an eager Ginger. Nicki lifted the animal and began stroking its head while Alex reached for the telephone.

Lemmer picked up on the other end, snarling his name in Alex's ear. "It's Coughlin," Alex identified.

"Darrin Lange went straight home," Lemmer told him without preamble. "He pulled his car into the garage. When he got out, the car exploded. He was killed instantly. The seat was wired with a pressure sensor that activated when he sat down. As soon as he got out of the car, it went off. No one else was injured. Do you want to talk to his wife?"

"I do, but I need to stick here. Matt Williams disappeared this morning. I need to find him ASAP."

"They're eliminating all the witnesses."

He swallowed down a lump of fear. Nicki was one of those witnesses. "Yeah. That's how it looks to me too. I'm going to talk with Unsdorf. Maybe offer him a deal. See if you can set that up for me. Lange's death might actually get him to open up since our boy Vic is probably on the elimination list as well.''

''Good thought.''

''Can you pick up Ilona Toskov and her brother? And we need 'round the clock on Nicki and Hope Michaels. I'll check back after I talk with Unsdorf.''

''I'll see what I can do.''

As he hung up, Nicki braced him. ''Alex? What happened? Why are you having someone pick up Ilona? I didn't even know she had a brother.''

Gently, Alex told her how Darrin Lange had died. ''We aren't taking any more chances, Nicki. I want to round up everyone who has even a possible connection to this case so we can get some answers. We need to talk with your sister as well as Unsdorf.''

''I'm going with you.''

''Not to see Unsdorf.''

''Where will I be safer than City Hall?''

She had a point. ''Okay. We'll put your car back in the doctor's garage and take mine. I don't want to draw attention to Leslie by leaving my car here.''

Alex made her wait while he checked his car for unwanted devices. Nicki agreed to stay with Carolyn, the police dispatcher and office assistant, while Alex went inside to talk with Vic Unsdorf.

Unsdorf took in his new look with quickly hidden surprise. ''Don't tell me you're a cop?''

''FBI,'' he confirmed.

Unsdorf swore and slapped the table. ''No wonder I was told not to trust you.''

''Who told you that?''

''Go to hell.''

''Vic, I need information.''

''Tough.''

"What does Hope Michaels have to do with Thorton Biggs's murder?"

Vic clamped his mouth in a tight line.

"You do know Toskov is using bombs to remove all the players, Vic."

Something flickered in his eyes. The expression came and went too fast to identify.

"Life's a bitch," he sneered.

"This jail isn't exactly bomb proof, Vic. You're a sitting target."

"Go to hell." But Vic fidgeted in his seat. For the first time, Alex saw genuine nervousness.

"We already have most of the knowledge we need to bring this whole thing crashing down around the principal players. Why don't you see what sort of deal you can make?"

"Go to—"

"You're repeating yourself, Vic." Alex stood. Laying his hands flat on the table, he towered over the other man. "I thought you were smarter than this. You want to play hardball. Fine. We'll play hardball. If you change your mind, have them give me a call."

"Go—"

"Yeah, yeah." He straightened up without taking his eyes from the other man. "At the rate witnesses are blowing away, I'm betting you'll get there a lot sooner than me."

Alex knew he'd struck a chord. How long it would take for the fear to work on Unsdorf to where he might cooperate was anybody's guess. He left the man with Officer Jackstone and found Nicki still sitting in the outer office talking with Carolyn.

"Tell the chief I'll be in touch," he told her. The pretty brunette smiled and nodded as Nicki said a hasty goodbye.

"Did he tell you anything?" she demanded.

"No. I'll give him some time to brood. Vic's a tough guy, but he's no more anxious to die than the next person. All they've got him on is possession of stolen merchandise. If he cooperates, he's looking at a seriously reduced sentence and he knows it."

"So now what?"

"Now we go talk with your sister."

BRENT WAS ON his way out as they arrived. "I'm picking up some carryout. You two want anything?"

Nicki realized she was mildly hungry so she and Alex added to Brent's order.

"I'll call it in from the car. Hope's inside lying down," he told them. "Gavin and I were going through Dad's papers. The situation's pretty grim, but I'll let him tell you about it."

"Did the hospital call?"

"No. We're going back over after we eat."

"All right."

Inside, they found Gavin in their father's den. "Do you need some help?" Nicki asked.

"Brent and I were trying to make sure everything was in order."

"He said it isn't."

Gavin's gaze flew to Alex before returning to meet hers. "No."

"What's wrong?"

"Dad doesn't have health insurance anymore."

Shocked, she stared at her brother. "Of course he does."

Gavin shook his head. "The hospital called. His insurance isn't valid anymore, Nicki. They dropped Dad after the start of the year for nonpayment."

She folded herself into a nearby chair. "Are you sure?"

"Brent's the accountant, but even I can look at a checkbook and read the bottom line. I had no idea the situation here was this desperate.''

"Hope said they were doing fine.''

"She lied. This place is so far in the red I'm not sure how they've kept things together this long. If it wasn't for the horses he's been boarding and all this money Hope's been depositing every month, they wouldn't have a roof over their heads any more.''

"That can't be right.''

Gavin gestured toward the computer. He stood to allow her in front of the machine. Nicki recognized the spreadsheet, having set up the software herself when she was still running the house. It took her several minutes to scroll through the information on the screens. She heard the men talking in low voices at her back, but she ignored them to concentrate on the numbers in front of her.

The current picture was every bit as bleak as Gavin had said. And it appeared last year had been just as bad. But what scared her more than everything else, was the sum of money Hope had been depositing in the household account for almost a year.

"I don't understand. Where is Hope getting this kind of money?''

"Good question.''

Nicki looked at Alex while her heart began to pound. She saw sympathy, but also intense interest. "You think she's doing something illegal.''

"Not necessarily.'' Alex regarded her brother. "Hope has some sort of connection to Vic Unsdorf. We know he's involved in the auto theft ring operating out of this area and we believe Thorton Biggs was also connected to the ring.''

"That's why you were here undercover?''

"That and to investigate the car bombing of the first agent who tried to infiltrate the group.''

"I think we'd better go and wake little sister," Gavin said thoughtfully.

"I'm awake."

Everyone turned to find Hope standing in the doorway. She looked wan and pale as death, but she strode into the small room with her head held high.

"I don't know anything about a car theft ring. My only connection to Vic Unsdorf is the money he's been paying me every month."

Gavin quickly stepped forward. "Hope, perhaps you'd better not say anything more."

She shook her head, her long blond hair swinging against her shoulders. "It's okay, Gavin. I haven't done anything criminal."

"Hope—"

"I leased some of Dad's land. That parcel on the other side of Rumble Creek."

"The old Maybry place?"

"Yes. I was going to ask Dad if we couldn't sell it off since we've scaled everything down, but then I was approached about leasing the land instead."

"Dad agreed to lease it?" Gavin asked.

"Well, no. Not exactly."

"What, exactly?"

"I used that legal program Nicki installed on the computer to draft a lease."

Gavin muttered something under his breath.

"I didn't tell Dad because he might have said no and we needed that money. Vic didn't want to buy the land, but his rental offer was more than generous, so I agreed."

"Oh, Hope," Nicki protested, "why didn't you tell me?"

"Or any of us?" Gavin demanded.

"Because this was my problem. Nobody else cares about

the horses or this land. I'm the only one who wanted to see it succeed. So I had to find a way to make it pay."

"You're wrong," Brent said from behind her. "You aren't the only one who cares. I've been saving like crazy so I could buy into Dad's operation."

"What?"

The scent of the takeout food filled the room. Brent regarded them steadily, his hands filled with bags. "I've discovered I'm not cut out to sit behind a desk all day. I miss working with the horses."

There was a moment of silence before Gavin took command. "All right," he said, "let's move this discussion into the dining room. It looks like we need to have a family council."

"Would you like me to leave?" Alex asked softly.

Gavin studied him. Her brother and Alex were almost the same height, Nicki realized. They were both good-looking, confident men and both had an air of authority about them.

"No," Gavin said finally. "I think you should stay. Dad made you an honorary son, remember? Besides, I have a few questions for you myself."

"Nicki?"

Alex's expression clearly asked her opinion as to whether he should stay or go. She stood quickly and walked to his side. Sliding her arm around his waist, she gazed up at him. "You'd better come with us. We may need a referee before this is all over. Besides, we haven't eaten all day."

He smiled first with his eyes. By the time the smile reached his mouth, the tautness in his body had dissipated and he was reaching to smooth back a strand of hair that had fallen forward on her face.

"You're right," he said quietly. "Suddenly, I'm starving."

Gavin's voice broke the subtle spell Alex's eyes were

weaving inside her. "Come on, gang, I'm starting to feel like a voyeur. Let's eat."

"Alex?"

He chuckled and stroked her cheek sending ripples of instant longing through her.

"One of these days," he said softly, "there's going to be time for just the two of us."

"You think?"

"I know."

Chapter Nine

"You could have ridden to the hospital with your brothers," Alex pointed out as Brent's tires crunched gravel on his way down the long driveway.

"No, I couldn't." Nicki offered him a smile as she started for the passenger's side of his car.

"Hold it. Let me check the car first."

"Why, for heaven's sake? You just checked Brent's and it was fine. They've both been sitting right here in our driveway while we were inside."

"That's exactly why."

Nicki blinked at his grave tone. "Alex, you can't really think someone walked up to the house and planted a bomb in your car while we were sitting at the dining room table having lunch."

Alex didn't bother to respond. She watched as he began the same painstaking search of his own car as he'd just made of her brother's.

"Doesn't it make you wonder why the bomber was confident enough to walk up to your place and rig a bomb in clear view of the main street of town?" he asked.

"Of course it does. The whole thing terrifies me, but what does it mean?"

He closed the hood and moved to the driver's door. His inspection was careful and thorough.

"There are two apartments at your place, Nicki. How did he know only you would be apt to go in or out? He either knows a great deal about you, or he doesn't care who he kills."

While horror magnified his words, Alex reached for the door handle on the driver's side. Nicki held her breath, letting it out on a long gust when nothing happened. Still, fear lay like a lump in her chest while he examined the interior of the car with his eyes. Then he squatted down and peered under the driver's seat.

"Damn."

The whispered oath stilled the very breath in her body. Nicki took three steps forward. His head jerked in her direction.

"Get in the house."

Fear slammed her with the force of his order.

"You don't mean—"

"Go! Now!"

Nicki obeyed, running for the front porch. Alex rose slowly beside the car. He held the gun in his hand once more as he scanned the front yard, the fields and the barn down the hill from the house.

"Alex?" The world seemed to suddenly still.

"There's a bomb under the front seat," he said quietly. "The bastard knew my car. Get inside."

Her hand shook so badly she could barely get the front door unlocked. Nicki sensed him come up on the porch behind her though his feet made no sound against the wood.

"That's impossible," she whispered. "How can there be a bomb? We were right inside the whole time."

Alex didn't answer. As soon as she opened the door he headed for the telephone. She gripped the back of the old covered rocker, sick with fear. The bomber had stood right outside her father's house, calmly rigging a device to kill them when at any second they could have looked outside and seen him.

"What about Brent's car? If your car had a bomb...?"

"I checked his car, remember? His car was clean." Alex punched in a series of numbers, striding toward her, the portable phone in his hand.

"But what if you missed it?" Horror gnawed at her insides. "They could be killed."

"Nicki."

She met his eyes, dark with an emotion she couldn't identify. Her fingers dug into the worn fabric.

"Your family is safe," he stated.

The words carried the weight of a promise. And Alex never broke his promises. His gaze roved beyond the window, sweeping the fields as he spoke his name into the receiver. "Send the bomb squad out to the Michaels farm," he ordered tersely. "Yeah. Under the seat of my car. You'd also better alert the team en route to the hospital. Her family's all in one car. No, it's clean. I checked before they left. Yeah. Take her into protective custody. The brother's a lawyer, but I don't think he'll argue. Uh-huh. I'll be here." He looked directly at Nicki. "It's possible the person responsible is still on the premises. Call Hepplewhite. Tell him to use sirens."

Nicki stared speechlessly at Alex while panic washed her mind empty of everything else. "Hope and Gavin and Brent—"

"Are fine," he told her. "Get behind the chair in the far corner of the living room."

Her father's chair. The one that commanded a view of the entire room. Nicki obeyed blindly, fear searing a hole right through her. In her mind's eye she saw Matt's house exploding, and the devastation of her own home and business.

Alex's arms came around her. He turned her so he had

a view of the room over her shoulder. "It's okay, Nicki. I promise. Everything will be okay."

"How can it be okay?!"

He held her for an eternity while she struggled to cope with the horror. Finally, they heard sirens in the distance. Nicki drew in a deep, shuddery breath. "I'm all right, Alex."

He kissed the top of her head. "I know you are."

Not until there were footsteps on the porch did Alex move away from her with the terse instruction to stay put. She recognized Chief Hepplewhite's gravelly voice, but there was another man with him. A voice she didn't recognize.

The men entered the house, tensely alert. The tall, good-looking stranger obviously knew Alex. He cocked his head to one side and grinned.

"Seems to me like you're trouble no matter which side of the law you're on," he said. "Still, I think I like you better on our side. You do realize your sister is going to be spitting mad."

"Yeah," Alex agreed. "So I think I'll let you explain things to her."

"Thanks a lot, pal," Lee replied. "I'd rather stay here and face bombs."

This must be Lee Garvey, she realized. The man who was going to marry Alex's sister, the newly hired second-in-command of the police force in Fools Point.

"The call said you think the suspect is still here?" Hepplewhite asked.

"Not really," Alex replied. "He's had plenty of time to get away, but we should check to be sure."

"Stay with Ms. Michaels while Lee and I have a look around."

"Fine. Where's Osher?"

The men shared a pained look. "We don't know. He

never reported in after lunch. Carolyn's been trying to reach him on the radio, but we aren't getting a response. His wife hasn't seen him.''

All three men looked grim.

''We've got a pickup order out,'' Hepplewhite added.

''Think he's our bomber?'' Lee Garvey asked.

Nicki edged closer to Alex. He reached out and drew her against his side. The proprietary gesture wasn't lost on the other two men.

''Anything's possible,'' Alex told them. ''You'd better put your jail on high alert. This guy is doing his best to get rid of everyone involved.''

Hepplewhite nodded. He began issuing orders on his radio as he stepped outside, Lee Garvey on his heels.

''You okay?'' Alex asked Nicki.

She drew in a deep breath, thankful for the reassurance of his arm around her shoulders. ''Just wonderful.'' she managed.

His lips brushed her hair. ''Yeah. You are. Hang in there.''

''Sure thing. I'm not too crazy about my other options.''

He squeezed her shoulders. She could feel the tension in him as well. She knew he wanted to be outside with the other officers, but he didn't let go of her. She was selfishly glad. At the same time, she knew she shouldn't prevent him from doing his job.

''Go join them. I'll wait here.''

Alex chucked her under the chin. ''Why don't you help me make a sweep of the house, instead?''

Fresh panic tried to suffocate her. ''You think he got inside?''

''No,'' he reassured quickly, ''but like I told John, it pays to be thorough. Come on. You can show me your old bedroom so I can see where you used to lie and dream about me.''

Nicki found herself responding to his teasing with a weak smile. "You just wish."

"You mean you didn't? I'm crushed."

"It would take a building."

Alex gave her a reassuring smile. "Stay behind me."

"Don't worry. People with bombs scare the willies out of me."

"Me too. However, I plan to savor this moment. It's probably one of the few times I'll be able to have an order obeyed in this relationship."

As strange as it seemed, joy negated her fear. While it wasn't a declaration of love, at least Alex implied they'd begun a relationship rather than reliving an old affair.

Alex peered into every room from the basement to the attic. Neither her sister nor her father's beds were made, but the rest of the house was relatively tidy. Her brothers had staked out their old room, the largest bedroom in the house. Trophies coated with dust, still marked their territories, reminding her of the past.

"Alex?" Hepplewhite's voice called up the stairs.

"All clear here." He squeezed her hand gently. "You find anything?"

"Nothing that didn't have at least four legs. The bomb squad's pulling up."

"We'll be right there." Alex kissed her lightly and led her downstairs and outside. The bomb squad took control of the scene and Nicki watched as they talked with Alex, Hepplewhite and Lee Garvey before setting up their equipment. As the bomb squad set up a perimeter, they were moved well down the driveway.

They watched for some time before Alex finally said, "This is going to take awhile. Let's try and get you to the hospital so we can check on your dad."

"Need a lift?" Lee Garvey offered.

"Thanks, but I'm going to need a car. Would you drop us at Doc Martin's? We left Nicki's car in her garage."

Lee raised his eyebrows. "Do you think that's safe?"

"We'll soon find out."

Alex refused to let Nicki climb in back. He sat behind her, adjusting himself so his hand touched the back of her hair. Lee cast them a speculative look, but didn't say anything.

"What do I tell your sister?" Lee asked.

"The truth. I'll come by as soon as I can so she can yell at me in person."

"I'd appreciate that. I don't want to take all the heat here. She's still getting used to what I do for a living."

Alex squeezed Nicki gently. "I know the feeling."

"Hey, I would never have objected to your line of work," Nicki felt compelled to correct. "If you'd ever bothered to tell me what it was. It's certainly better than what I thought you did for a living."

"Yeah?" Lee said. "What was that?"

"Whatever was profitable."

Alex grinned ruefully, obviously understanding her reference.

"I'm sure Kayla will be relieved by your occupation as well," she told him haughtily.

The two men shared wry smiles. "That remains to be seen."

The easy atmosphere of the car faded, however, once they arrived at the doctor's office. While she waited in Lee's car, the men examined the garage, the car inside the garage, and the doctor's car as well.

Finally Alex motioned Nicki to join him.

"Thanks, Lee. I'll talk with you later. We need to get to the hospital."

"I hope your father will be okay, Ms. Michaels," Lee offered.

"Thank you. And it's Nicki."

"Nicki," he agreed with a devastating grin. The man was almost as good-looking as Alex. He tapped two fingers against his forehead in a mock salute to Alex and got back in his car and left.

They drove to the hospital, caught up in private thoughts. Her family looked bleak when they saw her entering the Cardiac Care Unit. A man and woman in business suits stood alertly beside them.

"Are you okay?" Gavin demanded as soon as he spotted them.

"Chief Hepplewhite told us what happened," Brent added.

"We're fine, thanks to Alex." Nicki assured them. "How's Dad?"

"He's conscious and alert. They just threw us out of there. They'll only let people visit at timed intervals."

"The surgery went well," Brent added.

"But?"

Gavin looked from Alex to Nicki. "His cancer is advanced, sis. There are some new protocols they can try, but the prognosis is bad."

Brent nodded and put his arm around Hope, who stood silent and mournful. "It's only a matter of time."

Alex's arm tightened around her. "How much time?"

"A few months at most."

While his words wrenched her heart, Hope looked at her, dry-eyed. "Can we take him home, Nicki? I know he doesn't want to stay here."

"As soon as the doctor says he can be moved, we'll take him home."

Understanding and agreement passed from one face to another. In this they were united. They would make their father's last days as comfortable as possible.

"Can you call off my watchdogs?" Hope asked Alex.

"Sorry. You need to let them protect all of you."

"But Dad—"

"They won't release him for a couple of days yet, Hope," Gavin said.

"By then I hope we can wrap up this case," Alex added.

"All right, but I have to go home now and check on the horses."

"No." Alex's voice joined Nicki's in an immediate protest.

"The bomb squad is still out at your dad's place. They won't let you near. I'll see to your animals."

Brent's eyebrows rose. "You will?"

"We will," Nicki corrected firmly.

"Uh, Nicki, I want you to go with your family," Alex said.

"What about you? That was your car, not mine."

"Look, Nicki—"

"You have no idea what needs to be done. I do. We'll feed the stock and lock down the place for the night then we can join the others."

"Hey, sis, I don't think that's such a good idea."

"Don't worry, Brent, I'll be safe enough. I have Alex to protect me."

"Nicki..." Alex hesitated, looking from one face to another.

Nicki squared her shoulders for a fight. She could almost hear Alex mentally debate the danger versus the argument he'd need to mount to get her cooperation.

His fierce expression finally softened and Nicki relaxed. She'd won. He wasn't going to send her away after all.

"All right. The rest of you go with these agents. They'll see that nothing happens to any of you."

A relationship indeed. Working together was a start. "Let's see if they'll let us in to see Dad," she said happily.

"They'll let us in," he promised.

They did after Alex held a brief, whispered conversation with the doctor in charge. Bernie Michaels was awake, but unable to talk because of the tube down his throat. Nicki felt her heart constrict at the sight of him. She struggled to keep her anguish from showing. The nurse agreed they could have three minutes. She had to make them enough for now.

"We're going to spring you in a day or so," she promised her father. "Think you can hold out until then without causing the nursing staff to quit?"

Her father gave a small nod and she saw the amusement in his pale eyes. Then his gaze shifted to Alex.

"I figured you gave me permission to date her this time, but let me make it official. Is it okay if I see your daughter?"

Bernie smiled with his eyes and nodded again.

"Don't I get a say?" Nicki demanded teasingly.

"Not a chance," Alex told her. "You might say no."

She gave him an impish grin. "I might at that."

He shook his head in mock disgust and turned to her father. "You do realize you've saddled me with a headstrong little thing. Now, I don't mind most of the time. She does have her good— Oof."

Alex made a show of being injured as she elbowed him in the side. Belatedly, she remembered that he really had been injured only the night before. Somehow, that seemed a long time ago.

"See what I mean?" Alex was saying. "Headstrong and a bully. And speaking of bullies, here comes the nurse. They're about to toss us out of here, so you get some rest and I'll take care of the mischief maker."

Another nod yes.

"We'll see you tomorrow, Dad." Nicki kissed his cheek, controlling the tears until they were outside. "Oh, Alex."

He pulled her against his body, holding her and stroking

her back without speaking until she got herself under control.

"I'm sorry."

"Don't apologize, Nicki."

"I can't bear to think of losing him."

"Then don't. Doctors are just people too. They don't know everything. And as your brother said, they have a lot of new treatments now. We'll take it one day at a time, okay?"

"Thank you."

"Come on. We've got horses to check."

"What about my—"

"The agents already took your family to a safe house."

"And us?"

"I'm going to keep you safe, remember?"

"How could I forget?"

Alex hesitated. "Would you rather be with your family tonight?"

"No," she answered honestly. "But I probably should."

"Then I'll arrange it. Let's go."

ONLY HOURS EARLIER, the driveway in front of the house had been filled with cars and fire engines and a disposal team. A small contingent of people still remained. Alex left Nicki waiting patiently while he spoke with the others on the scene. He walked Officer Derek Jackstone to his cruiser. The Fools Point policeman was the last to leave, promising to make frequent checks on the property over the course of the evening. His car raised a trail of dust as he turned out onto the main road.

Alex rejoined Nicki, lightly touching her shoulder. The small contact gave him pleasure. He liked touching Nicki. He always had. And he realized he liked more than touching her. That was why he'd allowed her to come with him. He didn't want Nicki going anywhere without him.

The house suddenly stood silent and empty as if nothing out of the usual had taken place there that afternoon. For just a moment they stood savoring the quiet.

"Come on," Nicki finally said. "You can't muck stalls in those clothes." She headed for the house.

"We're going to muck the stalls?" Alex demanded as they entered the house.

Nicki gave him a weak smile over her shoulder as she started for the staircase. "City boy," she teased.

"And proud of it," he agreed, glad to see how well she was handling the situation. Allowing himself to relax for the first time all day, he admired the view as he followed her upstairs, marveling at her resiliency.

She caught him eyeing the nicely rounded curve of her bottom and came to a stop in the hall. Her smile faltered and slowly changed, replaced by an expression of awareness that stirred his groin.

"Somehow, I don't think your mind is on mucking stalls," she teased

"You're quite perceptive."

There in the dimly lit hall, a familiar sensual energy easily replaced the relaxed sense of camaraderie that had grown between them. Lightly, Alex stroked the hair back from her face, lingering over the silky feel.

"Uh, you and Gavin are...about the same size." She moistened her lips as he traced the curve of her ear with his fingertips. His body tightened in a surge of heat. Her eyelids feathered down in acknowledgement, hiding her vulnerable expression briefly.

"Why don't you...uh, borrow a pair of jeans? Gavin's jeans."

He framed her face, noting the rapid increase of her pulse. It blended with his own accelerated heartbeat. Tenderly, he ran his palms across her shoulders, down her arms. Nicki quivered.

"Are you sure that Gavin won't mind?"

Her eyes widened when he let her glimpse the hunger growing inside him.

"We…won't tell him."

Her voice lowered to a whisper. He liked the way her breathing also changed, coming in short, inviting pants. He watched her lips part. Her tongue flicked over them, moistening the inviting surface.

"I'll wait here…in the hall…while you change."

He tipped his head to one side and closed the distance between them. Passion simmered in the glow of her eyes. Nicki took a hasty step back. Alex took another step forward. Her expressive eyes now glistened with excitement as she suddenly found her back against the wall.

"I don't mind if you watch," he said softly.

"Oh."

He flattened a hand on the wall beside her head.

She raised her chin. "You like being watched, do you?"

"Oh yeah, if the watcher is you with those sultry eyes."

"Sultry eyes?" She sounded breathless.

"Uh-huh. Hasn't anyone ever told you how sexy your eyes are?"

"No. I…no. The subject's never come up before."

The tip of her tongue brushed her lips once more. His groin tightened as he thought about how his tongue would taste those lips.

"But the horses will never get stabled if I go in that bedroom with you now."

Alex extended his other hand, effectively pinning her between him and the wall. "True. But we could always give the horses a night out eating grass."

"What about us?"

"Oh, I'm definitely hungry, but not for grass. I think I'll start with an appetizer." His mouth came down on hers, fiercely possessive. He feasted on the scent and taste of Nicki.

She responded instantly, lifting her face to his and returning his kiss with equal fervor. Her lips parted, inviting him inside the warmth of her mouth. Alex drew her tongue into his mouth, sucking hotly, even as her arms snaked around his neck to pull him closer. Nicki arched against him in blind heat.

Slowly Alex inserted his leg between hers, while their tongues dueled in a mating ritual as instinctive as it was sensual.

Nicki moaned. She parted her legs to allow him better access. Boldly, he rubbed his leg against her most vulnerable spot.

She drew back, eyes glazed in a greed that matched his own. "Alex!"

"What?" His hands slid down her body, cupping her hips to draw her against his sliding leg.

A slow smile lifted the corners of her lips. "Just...Alex." She shuddered, giving a soft moan of pleasure.

"Ah, you like that."

"Yes." The word was a tiny whisper of accord. Her hands clung to his shoulders. She strained against him. His mouth possessed her until he wasn't sure who was possessed and who was the possessor.

And his beeper went off, jerking them apart as if it had been a thunderclap.

Alex swore. "I don't believe this."

"Me either," Nicki said shakily. "You could flush it down the toilet."

He fumbled for the device and scowled, muttering something vicious under his breath. "It's Lemmer, my boss. I need to call in."

The desire that had clouded her eyes only moments ago

began to fade as the real world intruded. "I'll save your place."

Hungrily, he pulled her against him and kissed her once more, letting her feel the weight of his desire. "You do that. I plan to reclaim that place."

Nicki smiled. "There's a telephone in Hope's room," she said, pointing the direction with a hand that wasn't quite steady.

Alex found the phone and punched in the familiar number, still trying to stem the flood of desire raging through his system.

"Lemmer."

"Coughlin."

There was a slight pause. Alex didn't generally bark his name like a crazed person. He tried to control himself while Lemmer coughed. "DEA is unhappy with us."

"Why?"

"Pavel Toskov. His expensive, shiny new sports car made a nasty mess of a Baltimore parking garage this afternoon."

Alex drew in a sharp breath. Nicki entered the room holding a pair of men's jeans and a work shirt. Her face was still flushed and her lips had a puffy, well-kissed look that made him want to finish what they'd begun. He forced his gaze from the provocative sight.

"What happened to Toskov?"

Nicki tensed visibly.

"Toskov wasn't part of the mess. A delivery man lost control of a loaded dolly that careened into the side of Toskov's car. Experts are checking on why that triggered the explosion, but fortunately, no one was seriously hurt."

"So why is DEA ticked off at us?"

"They had a tracer on the car that was going to lead them to the site of his drug operation—or so they hoped. They think our investigation spooked him."

"And Pavel arranged to blow up his own car?"

"That's how it looks. They're questioning the delivery man now."

"Why aren't they asking Toskov?"

"They can't find him. He bypassed surveillance and disappeared sometime yesterday."

"Sounds to me like they should be ticked at their own people. How is it our fault they screwed up and he got away?"

"If we had notified them right away of our interest—"

"I get the picture."

"Pavel Toskov has the knowledge necessary to be our bomber. Working on the docks in import-export gives him access to all sorts of things."

"Like the ingredients to make bombs."

"Precisely. There's also the fact that the stolen cars were being shipped out of Baltimore harbor. Ilona's brother is very ambitious. Drugs, cars, maybe more. And, Alex, according to DEA, he's got a temper. He's put more than one man and woman in the hospital."

"And of course, no one pressed charges."

"Against a nice guy like that?" Lemmer asked sarcastically.

Nicki watched Alex closely. He nodded slightly to let her know everything was okay. "I need a picture of Pavel as well as his sister."

"On its way."

Alex replaced the receiver and turned to Nicki. She took the news better than he'd expected. Her hands curled into fists and she turned toward the window.

"Do you think the man Ilona saw in the alley that night was her brother?" Nicki asked.

"I'd say it's a real possibility. It would explain her fear. From what Lemmer said, Pavel doesn't mind using his fists when he's displeased."

Nicki nodded. "Poor Ilona." She turned back to the window and frowned. Suddenly, she straightened up, pressing her face to the glass. "Alex, look! That's Matt!"

Alex hurried to her side in time to see a figure slip inside the main barn.

Nicki started for the door.

"Wait!"

"But it's Matt! He must have come here looking for me. Alex, he's got to be scared to death."

"You wait here and—"

"Not a chance." She shuddered. "I'll do exactly what you tell me to, promise! Just don't leave me anywhere alone."

Alex hesitated. She had a point. The two key players were both unaccounted for right now. And given the telephone message to Nicki that he'd heard, the boy was obviously running scared. Nicki might just be able to keep him from spooking and taking off again.

"Okay, but stay close."

"Like a lover," she promised.

Alex couldn't return her smile. If he guessed wrong, she could be hurt. He didn't like it, and the closer they got to the barn, the more he didn't like it. The fields were quiet in the growing dusk.

"What would Matt Williams be doing out here?" he muttered.

"We'll have to ask him. Should I call out to him?"

"No. Wait."

Alex motioned her to stay against the barn and eased into the opening cautiously. One of the barn cats leaped down from a stall railing, startling him. It stalked away, its tail raised indignantly. Nothing else moved. The insides were darkening with the day. There were no horses in any of the stalls.

"Lights?" he whispered.

Nicki joined him and reached for a switch on the wall. "Call him."

"Matt? Matt, it's Nicki. It's okay, honey, come on out." Nothing moved.

"Matt?"

"Where does that door lead?" he asked softly.

"The tack room. Dad added it onto the barn a few years ago."

"Any other way in or out?" The opposite end of the barn was open to a corral.

"Yes, there's an outside entrance. We keep it locked though. There's the key hanging right there beside the door. The inside door is never locked."

Alex eyed the closed door. "And do you usually keep the door closed?"

"Never."

"Get outside. Now, Nicki!"

Nicki stiffened. "Do you smell smoke?"

Before he could stop her, Nicki ran for a nearby fire extinguisher. "It's coming from inside the tack room!"

"No! Wait, Nicki!"

"If we wait this whole place will catch fire! We're in a barn, Alex! And Dad is no longer insured!"

He grabbed her before she could open the door. "Better he lose the barn than you!"

A thumping sound came from inside the tack room. They exchanged startled looks. The scent was growing stronger and someone or something was inside with the smoke. Alex grabbed the extinguisher from her hands. "Go back to the house! Call the fire department."

Without waiting to see that she obeyed, Alex started for the door. He set the extinguisher down and felt the door for heat. Cool wood. The thumping noise increased. Something fell over inside. Alex took a chance and reached for the handle.

"Locked."

"Here." Nicki handed him the key.

"I told you to go back to the house!"

"You can't handle the extinguisher and the gun at the same time. And if you get killed, they'll come after me long before the police arrive."

Damn! "All right, hold the extinguisher. If anything happens, open it up and spray."

Nicki nodded. Alex inserted the key in the lock, opened the door and went in low. Smoke billowed out choking and momentarily blinding him. This was the danger point when an armed assailant could take him down. But nothing happened. The source of the fire was easy to spot once the rush of smoke thinned. A trash can piled high with old rags and other objects smoldered noxiously. On the ground some distance away lay a body, now thrashing weakly.

A horse blanket acted as a makeshift hood over his head and upper torso. Alex wasn't at all surprised to find Matt Williams underneath. The youth coughed strenuously as Nicki finished extinguishing the flames.

Alex squatted beside the boy. His hands were bound so tightly circulation had stopped. Blood ran profusely from a recent wound on the side of his head. His eyes were vague and unfocused. As Alex called his name, they rolled back in his head and the boy passed out. Alex fumbled with the ropes, unable to loosen the tight knots. Nicki passed him a knife. He didn't ask where she'd gotten it. The tack room contained all manner of objects hanging from the walls and sitting on shelves. There was even a makeshift workstation near the center of the small room.

"Is he all right?" Nicki asked.

"His pulse is weak and thready. He needs a hos... why did you close the door?"

Her gaze followed his.

Her lips trembled. "I didn't."

Alex swore. He aimed his gun and started to rise. A shot tore through the center of the door.

Alex yanked Nicki off her feet. A second shot ripped through the door and he heard it strike the makeshift table. Alex rolled Nicki against the far wall, jarring the saddles hanging there. A third shot thudded into a saddle nearby.

Alex took aim at the door and hesitated. Shooting through wood was risky business, especially with Nicki and Matt in the way. Nicki looked her questions at him without saying a word. Alex shook his head. Motioning her to stay put and stay silent, he crawled across the dusty floor back toward the boy. Matt didn't move.

Hurried sounds came from the other side of the door. There was a thump as something was pushed against the door. Alex braced himself and waited. No one turned the handle, but there were further sounds. It took him a minute to realize what was going on. When he did, his blood ran cold. Alex stood and fired.

"Alex?"

He heard the person running away. He turned without answering Nicki and went to the other door. He examined what he could see of the edges. Unfortunately, the door had weatherstripping.

"Alex, what is it?"

"I could be wrong. I hope I'm wrong. But I think our bomber deliberately drew us in here using Matt as bait. I think he rigged a bomb on the other side of the doors."

Chapter Ten

Nicki stared at him in horror. "Both doors?"

"I don't know, Nic. He could be making me think that way just so he could get away. I could be wrong."

"But if you're not..." She shuddered as she pictured what the bombs would do.

"We need to find another way out of here."

"There isn't any other way out of here."

"There has to be." Alex paced.

There were no windows. No openings beyond the two doors they didn't dare trust.

"The vents."

"What?"

Nicki pointed up. Near the ceiling of the room were two metal vents across from one another. One would lead outside, the other into the barn beyond the wall.

"That's not a lot of help, Nicki. It's too high. And too narrow."

She eyed his broad shoulders and nodded. "But it's all we've got unless you can defuse the bomb from in here."

"I'm not even sure there is a bomb."

"But you think so."

"Yeah. I do. It fits the pattern."

"Then, give me a boost. We don't have time to waste. I can get through that vent."

"It's bolted in place."

Nicki scrambled amid a shelf and turned with a tool in her hand. "Don't you love cordless tools?"

His smile came slowly. "I think there's a naughty pun in there somewhere."

"Don't you dare."

"Okay, but I love the women who wield them. If there's an ax in here I can probably punch my way through the wall," he said seriously.

"No ax."

"A saw? A hammer? Something I can use?"

"I'm sure there's a hammer, but that would take a long time, Alex." She held up the cordless screwdriver. "Lift me up."

Alex lifted her onto the worktable. He surprised them both by kissing her hard. "I don't like this, but get on my shoulders," he told her. "We'll see what you remember from PE classes."

"I was never a gymnast," she told him as she straddled his head and he staggered across the room to the inside wall.

"Then why are we doing this? Even if you get the vent off, it'll be a long fall, Nicki. You could break your neck."

She positioned the tool over the first screw. "If memory serves, there are bags of feed on the other side of this wall. Think happy thoughts, and let's just be glad Dad only put nine-foot ceilings in here."

Alex leaned into the shelving that lined the wall to get her as close as possible. The shelves would never support her weight, but they gave them both a sense of security and stability.

In seconds, the first screw was out, dropping to the floor with a loud ping.

"It's working! Alex, it's working!"

"Great."

His voice was lined with the strain of supporting her weight on his shoulders. Belatedly, Nicki again remembered his previous injuries.

"Oh, God, Alex. Are you okay? I forgot about—"

"Just hurry."

Nicki hurried. She was working on the last one when she felt him sway.

"One more, Alex, hang on."

"Hurry."

The moment it came free she tossed the grate and the screwdriver to one side. Using the bottom of the opening, she pulled herself up, balancing precariously so she could look through the opening.

"Nicki, I can't do this much longer!"

"The angels are on our side. I was right about what's below me. With luck, I won't break my neck."

"Nicki, this is a bad idea."

"It's the only one we've got."

She pulled herself up, trying not to think scared. She'd often dropped from the top of the hayloft as a kid. This was almost the same thing, right?

She wriggled through the opening, twisting as she fell to land on her back the way she'd seen stunt people do it on television. The impact jarred the breath from her body for a second.

"Nicki, talk to me! Nicki!"

"I'm…okay," she panted. She climbed to her feet. Her legs tried to wobble, but she forced herself forward, nearly falling over the bags of grain that had split open. When she came to the door she stopped. The whole world stopped.

"Oh, God, Alex, you were right. There is a bomb."

"All right. Take the key and go around—"

"I can't! The key's still in the door. There's a wire attached to it."

She heard him swear. Fear dredged her mind.

"Call Hepplewhite. Tell him to get the bomb squad back over here."

"Alex?" Her heart pounded so hard she thought it would burst through her chest. "There's a watch attached to this thing. Does that mean it's set to go off at a specific time?"

"Get out of there Nicki! Go! Now! Get help!"

Nicki sprinted for the phone on the wall inside the main door. She punched in 911 and tried to take a steadying breath as the operator answered. Her voice still came out high and shrill.

"This is Nicki Michaels. I'm at 1255 Cicada Road. We need the fire department, the bomb squad and an ambulance. Special Agent Alex Coughlin of the FBI and a young boy are trapped inside the tack room of the main barn. There's a bomb rigged to detonate at any moment. We need help right away."

The soothing voice began to ask questions in her ear. Nicki dropped the phone without listening or disconnecting. Maybe it would spur them into hurrying. Sprinting around the barn, she came to the outside door. A bomb had been affixed to that door as well. There was no timer attached to this one. Still, she had to get Alex out of there now.

Nicki looked around wildly for another alternative and spotted the answer. She might not know how to defuse a bomb, but she knew how to drive a tractor.

"Alex!"

"Nicki! Get away from here!"

"Move Matt to the northeast corner of the room. Try to cover yourselves with saddles or something. I'm coming through the wall."

"What? No! Nicki, listen to me—"

"There's no time. You have to trust me. Hurry!"

Nicki ran for the tractor, praying her father had left the key in the ignition as usual. She blessed her guardian angel tenfold when the grumpy machine started right up.

This was a Hollywood sort of play and she knew it. Probably, this kind of thing only worked in the movies where the walls were made of balsa wood and everything was choreographed with care. But she'd seen news footage of cars plunging into houses and buildings and they generally left a good-sized hole. The question was, could she get up enough speed to attain the momentum she'd need so she didn't just come to a stop the moment the tractor hit the wall.

Nicki positioned the tractor, backing it up as far as she dared. She aimed for the side away from where she'd told Alex to go. She offered a mental plea that the force of the crash wouldn't prematurely detonate the bombs and revved the poor engine.

The tractor gained more speed than she would have thought it could. It hit with a stunning impact that flung her off and into the dirt. Numb with shock, unable to catch her breath this time, Nicki could only lay there panting. Stars lit the night sky above her. A beautiful display.

She knew she had to stand. Alex was counting on her, but it seemed like such a lot of effort.

"Nicki! Nicki! Can you hear me?"

Alex loomed over her.

"It worked?"

"Yeah, love, it worked. Come on. We've got to move away from the building. Can you stand?"

"Sure."

Alex pulled her to her feet and the ground began to sway wickedly. Alex muttered something about shock. That seemed reasonable. After what they'd been through, it was hardly surprising. Somehow, Alex had gotten past the obstruction of the tractor and was free. That was all that really mattered.

"Come on, Coughlin! Move!"

Nicki's head swiveled toward the new voice. She recognized the Fools Point police uniform. "Where did he come from?"

"Come on, Nicki, stay with me here. We've got to get away from the barn."

The officer had Matt Williams in a fireman's carry. He started running into the field away from the barn.

"That's not the way to the house," she protested.

"The house is uphill. There's no time."

She stumbled and would have fallen, but Alex suddenly lifted her into his arms and began to run.

"Put me down. I'm too heavy."

Alex didn't answer. A fire truck screamed up the driveway. There were already other cars in front of the house she realized as she bobbed along in his arms.

And the tack room exploded into the night.

NICKI OPENED HER eyes and lay still, trying to figure out where she was. As the events of the night before came back to her, Ginger stirred at her feet. The cat stretched and rose, walking up the bed to butt Nicki's arm in a bid for attention.

"All right, cat."

She scratched the happy feline behind the ears and under the chin while the fuzz cleared from her brain.

"Ginger, did I break every bone in my body?" Because if there was a bone or muscle in her body that didn't hurt it was in hiding.

"Meow?"

The cat patted her arm insistently. "Sorry, cat, you'd better find the doctor if you want to be fed. I'm not up to opening a can of tuna at the moment." But she did need to use the bathroom, so she had no choice but to stand or disgrace herself.

The distance to the hall bathroom seemed interminable,

but at least she'd discovered that all her parts still functioned.

Desperately craving a long hot shower, she contemplated the bathtub. She'd have to expend a lot of energy to climb over the side of that tub. At the moment, it looked as insurmountable as Mount Everest. The knock on the door startled her.

"Nicki? Are you okay in there? Do you need any help?"

Like an incredibly old person, she managed to stand and open the door. "Just tell me one thing, Doctor, is there a cure for the way I feel?"

Leslie Martin's eyes crinkled at the corners as her lips curved in a smile. "Yes. It's called bed rest and time."

"How many years will it take?"

"Not as many as you might think right now."

"It couldn't. I was debating the dubious merits of climbing into the tub for a shower."

"I thought you might be. I came to suggest you use the shower stall I had installed in my bedroom. It only has a three inch lip."

"You are a wonderful human being."

Leslie chuckled out loud.

"Where's Alex?" Nicki asked.

"Still asleep in the other room."

Nicki lowered her voice. "Is he okay?"

"Bumps, bruises and assorted contusions. Sort of like you. The two of you have incredible luck. No permanent damage was done."

Nicki followed her into the master bedroom. "You know, things are a little fuzzy around the edges this morning. How come we ended up on your doorstep again?"

"Something lacking in my hospitality?"

"Oh, I didn't mean—"

"Relax. I was teasing you. Alex and John decided to use

me as a safe house. Do you remember being transported to the hospital by ambulance last night?''

''Oh yeah, but then they smuggled me back into someone's car. Lee's I think. By then I was having trouble staying awake.''

''I know. I was concerned when they first brought you inside.''

''I sort of remember that. What happened to Matt?''

''Matt? You mean Matt Williams? John didn't mention him. We'll ask John when he comes by again. And I can see your next question already forming. Your father is doing well. They're moving him into step-down this afternoon. Look, you shower and I'll bring you something to wear. We'll talk while you eat, okay?''

''I'm not sure how I'm ever going to repay you for all your kindness Dr. Martin.''

''I think we've gone past the formal stage. The name is Leslie. Now get your shower, but don't linger under the hot spray too long. In and out, okay?''

''Yes ma'am.''

Nicki wasn't sure which felt better. Having clean hair and clothing or a full belly. Scrambled eggs and toast had never tasted so wonderful. Even the hot tea soothed her battered body. Or maybe that was the medication Leslie had given her. Either way, as Leslie removed her plate, Nicki decided she might just survive after all.

''Did Chief Hepplewhite let my brothers and sister know what happened?''

''I'm sure he did.''

''The barn must be a complete wreck. And the animals! I forgot all about—''

''The Huntingtons took the livestock, Nicki. They even caught your barn cats, although I understand Jeff Huntington now has marks to match Alex.''

''Sheba,'' Nicki said wryly. ''She isn't fond of people.''

"Well, since the fire department was en route before the detonation occurred, the damage was confined and minimal. John said the tack room was destroyed and most of the feed, but the barn itself suffered little damage."

"We were lucky."

"You were indeed. Oh, there's John pulling up outside now." She waved to someone outside through the window. "I have patients to see this afternoon. Are you up to answering questions right now? I can tell John to come back later."

"That's okay. Thanks, Leslie. As long as I don't have to move more than my mouth, I'll be fine. Are you sure Alex is all right? Maybe we should check on him again."

One quick peek at his sleeping form had tugged at her heartstrings. He'd looked so peaceful curled on his side. If Leslie hadn't been waiting for her, Nicki might have given in to the temptation to stand there and gaze at him for awhile. She was so relieved they were both okay.

"Alex was up into the wee hours of this morning giving them statements," Leslie said. "Sleep is what he needs right now. I'll see you later." Leslie went to let the police chief inside.

Chief Hepplewhite carried a tape recorder and he wasn't alone. A man, introduced as Agent Lemmer, set a duffel bag on the floor and eyed her curiously as he proffered a firm handshake.

"You're Alex's boss, aren't you?"

Lemmer ducked his balding head in acknowledgement. "He's been temporarily assigned to my office, yes."

"Temporarily?"

"His normal jurisdiction is elsewhere. He was brought in to cover this particular case."

"Well I hope you realize just how good he is. I'd be dead right now if it wasn't for him."

Lemmer blinked, cleared his throat and finally smiled. "I understood it was you who saved him last night."

"Oh, no, last night was a joint effort. And I was referring to earlier."

"I see."

It wasn't clear what he saw, but Nicki didn't care if she was wearing her heart on her sleeve. Somehow she'd fallen in love with Alex all over again. And this time, she didn't care who knew it.

"Er, Ms. Michaels, we need a statement for the record." He nodded toward the device the chief had set on the table. "Would you mind if I tape-record this conversation?"

"No, but I don't remember much after the tractor hit the barn. Leslie said it was probably shock coupled with stress and exhaustion. This has been a rough few days."

"So I understand," Lemmer said.

"Planning to take up stunt work in your spare time, Nicki?" the chief asked with a glint in his eyes.

They were looking at her with respect, Nicki realized. She relaxed and took another sip of her cooling tea. "Not me. I can barely walk this morning. Would you gentlemen like something to drink?"

"Nothing, thank you," the chief replied.

"You're lucky you weren't killed."

"Yeah, well, I wouldn't recommend the procedure, but there weren't too many alternatives at the time."

"I understand Agent Coughlin is sleeping," Lemmer said as he put a tape in the machine.

"Yes, do you want me to wake him?"

"No. That's not necessary. Let's get started, shall we?"

Nicki answered questions as openly as possible. There was no reason to hold back information other than the private events between her and Alex. She'd given them as much as she could when Alex entered the room. Agent Lemmer clicked off the machine.

Battered, bruised, and disheveled, Alex looked every bit the image of the tough guy that he'd been projecting for so long. Stubble lined his face, giving him a dangerous, sexy look. His unruly hair needed scissors and a comb and the cuts and bruises running the length of his arms were starting to multiply alarmingly. But he was alive and her heart rejoiced at the sight of him.

His gaze was clear and it went straight for Nicki.

"Are you okay?" he demanded.

"Better than you, judging by appearances."

The two men faded into insignificance as Alex strode toward her with that arrogant, I-am-somebody way he had of moving. Even the slight limp didn't detract from his impact. An enormous surge of relief swept through her. She really loved this man.

Unaware of her thoughts, he ruefully rubbed his jaw. "I look that bad, huh?"

She wanted to tell him he looked wonderful. Instead she cocked her head and surveyed him teasingly. "Let's just say that a homeless person would probably offer *you* some help. I did tell you those slacks weren't suitable for mucking out stalls."

He still wore the shirt and slacks from yesterday, but they were torn and stained beyond repair. Brutal reminders of the way they'd spent the evening.

"Clothes don't make the man, you know."

"Good thing or the chief would have to arrest you."

Lemmer cleared his throat while Hepplewhite grinned. The heated look Alex gave her stirred new flutters to life inside her. Alex turned to his boss.

"So what's the current situation?"

"We instituted search warrants on Pavel Toskov's apartment and his business. We're raiding one of his freighters even as we speak, and the DEA is lending a hand since they've got a vested interest here. They're primarily looking for drugs, of course.''

''Think they'll find any?''

''Could be. Toskov is ambitions. Drugs, cars, guns, whatever turns a profit.''

''So where is he?''

''We got some late information that Toskov was last seen in the company of a blond woman, probably his sister. The Baltimore office hopes for more information once they finish the raid and pick up all the little people involved.''

''And Matt Williams?''

Lemmer turned to the police officer. ''Matt refuses to talk with anyone,'' Chief Hepplewhite answered.

''Actually, we're hoping he'll talk to you, since you saved his life,'' Lemmer put in.

''Not me,'' Alex protested. ''Nicki.''

Every gaze landed on her. Nicki tucked a strand of hair behind her ear. She could feel a blush staining her cheeks. ''It was a joint effort, remember?''

''Would you be willing to talk with him, Nicki?''

''Sure, if it will help. But what's going to happen to him?''

Hepplewhite shrugged. ''Depends on how he's involved. Right now, he's a victim. If we find proof he was involved in the car ring…''

''The FBI isn't interested in a fifteen-year-old boosting cars,'' Lemmer said. ''There are a number of minors involved in this that we know about, but we want the people paying him and shipping the cars overseas.''

''In other words, Toskov,'' Alex said.

''Right. If the boy is involved in theft and we can prove it, he'll be charged. But if he helps us, we can cut him a deal.''

''He'd be looking at a first offense anyhow,'' Hepplewhite put in. ''He's got a clean record until now.''

"What about Osher?" Alex asked. "Is he still missing?"

Hepplewhite nodded. "The state police found his car at the scenic rest area off 270 an hour ago. It wasn't there last night during a routine check of the site. That narrows down the time when the car must have been left."

"Could he have left it there himself?"

"We don't think it's likely. The state boys found blood stains in the car," Hepplewhite responded. "We don't know whose blood yet, but it was fresh."

"So what do you want me to do?" Alex asked his boss.

"We don't have a search warrant for Ilona Toskov's apartment. Think you can use some of that charm of yours to get the manager to let you inside for a quick look around?"

"Hear that, Nic? Some people think I have charm."

"He just doesn't know you as well as I do."

Alex grinned. "I'll see what I can do. Let me grab a shower first."

"I'd recommend a change of clothing," Nicki put in. "Charm or no charm, the way you look, the manager will have you picked up for loitering before you get inside the place."

"See the abuse I've been taking?"

Lemmer and Hepplewhite rose to their feet. "We stopped by your place and brought you some clothing," Lemmer said, indicating the duffel bag on the floor.

"Thanks. I'll check in after we talk to Matt and go through Ilona's apartment."

"Do that."

ILONA HAD AN expensive apartment not far from the Morgan hospital. They were new low-rise buildings that had sprung up right along with the hospital on the outskirts of Frederick.

The manager in the too-tight blouse took one look at

Alex and straightened her posture, practically thrusting her enhanced bustline in his face.

He didn't dare look at Nicki to gauge her reaction, but it was an effort to keep his face expressionless. He fought a strong desire to ask if there was something wrong with the woman's eyelashes the way she kept batting them at him.

Her flirting quickly changed when he identified himself as an agent. She was typically shocked, nervous and curious at having two FBI agents asking about one of her tenants. Alex had to apply very little of his so-called charm to get her to open the door for them to go inside for a quick look around.

"She seems to think I'm an agent too," Nicki whispered.

"Uh-huh. Stick with me kid and you'll see it all. This may be an expensive place, but the security stinks. She didn't even call to confirm our identity."

"True. I suspect she couldn't decide if she wanted to get to know you because of your pecs, or if she was afraid to get to know someone who looked as battered as you do."

"Thanks a lot."

"I am surprised she left us alone in here. We could steal everything in the place if we wanted to."

He scrutinized the expensive decor. "I never knew you had such a larcenous nature, Nic. Looks like there's plenty in here to steal. Who did you say Ilona worked for?"

"She never said."

"The records indicate she's a chemist. Must pay a lot better than an FBI job."

Nicki peered around curiously while Alex began a careful search through Ilona's papers.

"What are you looking for?" Nicki asked.

"Anything that might give us a clue as to her brother's whereabouts. Or hers, for that matter."

"You don't think *she's* involved with the car theft ring."

"Anything's possible." He moved into the bedroom and opened her closet. "The lady certainly has a passion for clothing."

"She always dressed nicely."

"I'll say. She could go a year without repeating an outfit."

Tucked in the back of a dresser drawer he hit pay dirt in the form of an envelope stuffed with photographs.

"Lemmer forgot to give me the picture of Ilona and Pavel. Any idea who these people are?"

"Let me see." Nicki flipped through a couple and stopped. "This is Ilona. Judging from his coloring and the set of his mouth and eyes, I'd say this could be Pavel."

Alex studied the picture. He'd expected Pavel to be a large bruiser of a man, but Ilona's brother had a slender build and stood no more than five-ten. There was a lean toughness about the man, however. A good fit for someone who liked to use his fists.

"Alex, isn't this Matt?"

A cluster of teens were grouped around a black sports car.

"Hard to be sure, but it could be."

"I don't see anyone else that I recognize," Nicki said, handing the stack to Alex.

He began flipping and almost immediately came to a stop.

"Unfortunately, I do," he said with a sigh.

Nicki looked at the picture he held. A man and woman stood beneath a cherry blossom tree. The picture was out of focus and the couple's features were indistinct, plus the woman was turned three-quarters away from the camera.

"I think that is Ilona, but I don't recognize the man."

"Darrin Lange."

"The FBI agent you told me about?"

Alex nodded. "Lange had a copy of this in his office right before he was killed. The picture went missing along with him. I don't know if they recovered it after the explosion or not."

"What does this mean? Ilona *is* involved?"

"That picture says she knew Lange."

"But it could have been an innocent knowledge. We don't know when this picture was taken or what their relationship was."

Alex hesitated. "True. Unfortunately, Lange isn't alive to give us any answers."

"But Ilona is."

"If we can find her." He held up a hand to forestall her next argument. "It's possible she had an affair with Lange and when her brother found out, he used her to gain inside information."

"Or Lange might be an old friend who told her things she innocently passed on to her brother. Don't forget, we think Pavel beats her. Maybe he beat the information out of her."

"Either way, this picture connects Ilona to a murder victim."

They finished up relatively quickly after that. There wasn't much else to find. "No checkbook, financial statements, bills, nothing personal at all. No food in her refrigerator and the cupboards are bare. Do you get the idea this place may have been for show?"

"Maybe she cleaned everything out."

"Or maybe her brother did," he agreed thoughtfully. They stopped by the manager's unit and thanked her, dodging questions while asking one of their own.

"You wouldn't happen to know Ilona's brother, would you?"

The woman fluttered her heavily mascaraed eyes. "Of

course. Hard to miss him. He's a little short, but he looks a lot like Brad Pitt. You know, the movie actor? He was here just yesterday.''

''Brad Pitt?'' Nicki asked deadpan.

''No, of course not. Ilona's brother. I saw him going inside.''

''You didn't mention that before.''

''You didn't ask,'' she said coyly.

''Was he alone?'' Alex asked.

''I think so. Ilona wasn't with him if that's what you're asking.''

''Has anyone else been here looking for her?''

''Not here, specifically, but Ilona always had a lot of company, if you know what I mean. She was an attractive woman in her own way.''

''Do you know any of the men?''

''No. I do have my own busy social life, you know. I'd just see men come to call on her now and again. There were never any wild parties or that sort of thing. She was actually a quiet tenant. Always paid her rent on time.''

''All right, thank you.''

''My pleasure.''

Her lashes fluttered madly and Alex beat a hasty retreat. He could feel Nicki silently laughing at him. ''Ever feel like you just had a close call?'' he muttered as they climbed into her car.

''Not at all. Why?'' Teasingly, she fluttered her lashes at him over eyes that gleamed with amusement.

''Very funny.''

''Hey, it's a good thing I'm not the jealous type. She was looking at you the way I look at a hot fudge sundae after a month of dieting.''

''Yeah? How's that?''

''Like I'm very hungry.''

"Well, if you lick those lips like that again, you're going to make *me* very hungry. And not for hot fudge."

"Why Agent Coughlin, are you coming on to me?"

He pulled his seat belt across his lap and grinned. "Yes, now that you mention it."

"Good." Nicki reached for her own seat belt, surprising a laugh out of him.

"Why good?"

"I just wanted to be sure the feelings I've been having weren't all one-sided."

Amusement faded instantly. "What sort of feelings have you been having, Nicki?"

Her features grew serious. "Tell me something."

"If I can."

"No. No more secrets."

Alex shook his head. "I didn't mean that. I'll tell you anything I can and if I can't, I'll tell you why I can't."

"All right. Today your boss said you were temporarily assigned to his office. What did that mean?"

Not sure where this was leading, Alex watched her expression closely. "Just what he said. They pulled me off regular duty because I grew up here. And because of the reputation I had growing up here. When I recognized some of the names under suspicion, they asked me to come in undercover and see if I could infiltrate the car ring."

"So where do you normally work?"

"I'm assigned to the Denver office."

"Denver? You mean Colorado?"

Alex nodded.

"So you'll be going back once this job is over?"

More slowly, he nodded again.

"They won't reassign you here permanently?"

"You never know. Anything is possible." He reached

out to touch her arm. Her eyes were sad when she looked from his arm to his face.

"Even miracles?"

And he knew she was thinking of her father as much as him.

"Even them."

Chapter Eleven

"The truth is, I don't know that I can be reassigned to this area, Nicki." Alex hesitated. "You'd like Colorado. It's a beautiful state."

"I'm sure it is, but it's a long way from here."

"And your family."

"Yes."

He swerved to avoid a turning car that hadn't bothered to signal.

"So you'll be leaving." While she didn't say again, the word lay there, unspoken. An insurmountable barrier.

"When this job is completed, I won't have any choice. You could come with me."

Nicki shifted. "You know I can't."

"Not now perhaps, but…"

"My family is here, Alex. My shop, my friends."

"There was a time you would have gone anywhere with me," he said gently.

"Yes, and instead you left without a backwards glance."

A retort hovered on the tip of his tongue. Instead he gripped the steering wheel and focused on the road in front of him. "Yes."

"I'm sorry, Alex. That was a cheap shot."

Alex drew in a deep breath and exhaled slowly. "Have

you stopped to wonder why we keep hurting each other over the past?''

''I said I was sorry.''

''I think it's because the hurt is still there, Nicki. I could apologize a hundred times over for the choice I made, but it won't change anything.''

''I don't want an apology.'' She crossed her arms over her chest defensively.

''Don't you? I think you do. I think you want me to say I'm sorry. That I made a terrible mistake all those years ago. But your dad offered me a chance that day to be more than a punk like Vic Unsdorf and I grabbed it with both hands. I'm not sorry, Nicki.''

''We were young—''

He shook his head in negation. ''If the situation were the same and I had to make the decision right now, this minute...'' He gripped the wheel more tightly. He felt her eyes boring into him with all the hurt she'd buried for fifteen years and his anger drained away.

''When I touch you, Nicki, it's like all the years between us vanish,'' he said quietly. ''No one else has ever made me feel the way you do. But the truth is, those years not only exist, they changed us. They formed us into the people we are today. I'm not that brash young punk. You aren't that defiantly impulsive young woman. We can't go back. Not even if we wanted to.''

''I don't!''

''Don't you?'' Her silence whipped his conscience, but he forged ahead. ''Don't you wonder if part of our attraction isn't due to our memories of the past?''

He felt her pain like the cut of a knife.

''Is that what our relationship is to you? A trip down memory lane?''

''No! Oh, hell, I don't know,'' he answered honestly. He darted a glance at her. Her eyes were tightly shut, her arms wrapped around her like a shell. "I only look at you and I get hard. I just have to think of you and I want you. And when I touch you...everything else disappears."

"Except your job in Denver," she said wistfully.

He pulled into the parking lot, waited for a van to vacate a front row spot, and parked, turning off the ignition. "Do you think that's love, Nicki? Or proximity based on feelings that are fifteen years old?"

She opened her eyes, staring straight ahead.

He sighed in frustration. He never had been any good at intimacy. He should have known better. "We shouldn't be having this conversation right now."

"Why not? This seems to me this is a perfect time to be having this conversation."

"If I asked you to marry me, right here, right now, knowing we might have to fly to Denver tomorrow or the next day, what would you say, Nicki?"

"I can't. You know I couldn't. My father—"

"I know." He gripped the wheel more tightly. "And I would never ask that of you. That's why we shouldn't be having this conversation. We've been in a life or death situation ever since the night your sister's call sent me into that alley."

"You don't know that my sister called you."

His silence was louder than words.

"If she did, she was only...well, matchmaking."

"That may have been her intention, but it was no accident that she picked that night and that time. Unsdorf must have prompted her. Care to take bets?"

Nicki looked away. "No."

"Yesterday, you risked your life to save mine," he said softly.

"Then we're even. You saved my life, too. More than once, actually." She wouldn't look at him and he couldn't decide what she was thinking.

Alex's frustration mounted. He strove for a calm, reasonable tone. "When this is over...when we have a chance to draw a breath and we don't have to fight for our very lives, we're going to talk about the future. Until then—"

"Until then," she said, turning around, "you can let go of my arm, Alex."

He hadn't realized he'd touched her, yet he held her as if he were afraid she'd run. They stared at each other, right back where they'd started the night he'd broken into her apartment to confront her.

He relaxed his fingers. Nicki promptly got out of the car. She held her head high. Her spine was unnaturally straight, but he couldn't read the expression on her face or in her eyes. He climbed from the car slowly, and not just because his body was stiff and hurt all over. He felt as if he'd just bungled the most important thing in his life.

Again.

"Let's go see Matt and get this over with," she said. "And this time you might want to keep an eye out for hit-and-run drivers. Your luck is only going to last so long."

Alex knew his luck had already run dry.

He followed her into the hospital, wishing more than anything that he could take back these last few minutes. He loved Nicki. He just didn't know if he loved her enough to give up the job he also loved.

She wouldn't understand, but his job defined him. Through hard work he'd gained the respectability he'd sought since the day his father's bad luck had branded him the son of a thief and murderer. Alex wiped his face in frustration.

Nicki waited inside the elevator for him to punch the appropriate button. She wouldn't meet his eyes and he couldn't think of anything to say. He'd deliberately timed their visit for her safety, so they would arrive well before the normal visiting hours began. It was time to focus on business. He could finish screwing up the rest of his life later.

Staff had started passing out dinner trays to the patients.

They had stashed Matt Williams in the psych ward behind controlled access and a police guard. On their way there, he wondered if he could ever find anything to say that would undo the harm his words had just done.

MATT WILLIAMS looked young and very much alone in the big white bed. His eyes lit the moment he saw Nicki, then dimmed as he saw the man standing behind her. She knew the feeling. Alex had dimmed her soul with his words and she had no one to blame but herself.

Alex had been right. That conversation should have waited for later. Much later.

"Hi Matt."

If only Alex could love her the way she loved him.

"This is Alex Coughlin. He's…a friend."

Could she ever look at him and see a friend instead of the man she loved?

"I work for the FBI," Alex said.

In Denver. Miles away from everyone she knew and cared about.

Alex stepped up to the bed. "We need your help, Matt. Nicki says you saw the person who killed Thorton Biggs."

The betrayal in the boy's eyes made her want to throttle Alex. What ever happened to subtlety and tact?

"We need to put that person away so he can't come after anyone else."

Matt closed his eyes, but not before Nicki saw the hopelessness in their depths. She walked to the side of his bed and nudged Alex aside with a glare. The boy quivered when she touched his arm, but he didn't open his eyes to look at her.

"I appreciate that you came out to my dad's place to try and warn me again last night—" she began.

"I didn't." Matt pursed his lips shut as tightly as his eyes as if regretting his hasty words. And he still wouldn't look at her.

"Then why did you come?"

The boy lay there silently.

"Everything's going to be okay, Matt. The FBI knows what's been happening. They're going to keep you safe."

Matt's eyes flew open with such naked contempt, she was stunned. Matt dismissed both of them with a scowl. There was an air of finality as he shut his eyes this time. Nicki understood that he wouldn't answer any questions, but Alex persisted as she walked away from the bed.

After awhile Alex looked at Nicki, inviting her to try again. She shook her head. They finally left, Alex promising to come back whenever Matt wanted to talk.

"You'll wait a long time," Nicki warned him.

"I wonder why he clammed up like that?"

"He's just a boy, Alex. He's alone and scared. I would be too in his place. Still, I wonder why he came out to the farm if it wasn't to see me."

"Good point." Alex hesitated. "Nicki, those things I said earlier—"

"Do you think he was following someone?"

Alex rubbed his jaw, obviously disappointed by the way she'd shut him out. "Who?"

"The bomber."

"Why would Matt do that?"

"I don't know. You're the professional. I'm just making stabs in the dark. Where are we going?"

"I thought you'd want to see your father."

"Oh. Yes, I'd like that, but this isn't regular visiting hours."

"Don't worry. My badge is better than a hall pass."

She didn't return his smile, but she was grateful. And even more so when he opted to wait outside so she could visit with her father in private.

Bernie Michaels turned his head when she entered. They'd removed many of the tubes he'd been hooked to and he actually almost smiled. "Nicki!"

"Hi. You're looking a lot better tonight." His voice was scratchy from the tube they'd had down his throat, but color lent strength to his face. Maybe the doctors were wrong.

"Well you aren't." A familiar scowl replaced the warmth. "I recognize that expression. What's the boy gone and done?"

For a moment she thought he meant Matt, but as his eyes bored into her, she knew exactly who he meant. "What makes you think Alex did anything?"

"Because you had that same shattered look fifteen years ago. Do I need to have a talk with him?"

"No." But her lips curved at the offer.

"What's wrong, Nicki?"

She blinked back unexpected tears. "There's nothing wrong. I just let my hopes get too high."

"He refusin' to marry you?"

"Of course not. We haven't even discussed marriage." Not as a viable option, anyway. "But Alex lives in Denver."

"Don't tell me you have some misguided idea that you have to stick around here and watch me die."

"Dad!"

"I'm not having it, girl. I'm dying. Been going at it for awhile now."

"No!"

He stared her down. "Dying isn't as hard as living. It's part of life, Nicki. Not something to fear. That boy loves you. He loved you then and he loves you now."

"You're wrong, Dad."

He stared at her with that familiar, unwinking stare that reduced her to immediate childhood.

"He tell you that?"

"No, of course not."

"I've lived with the guilt, watching you be sad, long enough. If his place is in Denver, you go with him. You give me enough incentive, who knows, maybe I'll stick around long enough to see a grandbaby or two."

Nicki didn't know whether to laugh or cry. "That's blackmail, Dad."

"Yep."

"He didn't exactly ask me to go with him." But he had asked as a what-if scenario. She told herself it wasn't the same thing. He thought their relationship was based in the past.

Bernie frowned fiercely. Suddenly, his expression lightened. "No he wouldn't. Not now."

She wondered what he meant.

"Since when are you a coward, Nicholette? He's what you want. He's what you always wanted. In all these years, you've never looked at another man the way you looked at that boy."

"But—"

"That man loves you, Nicki girl."

"He never said so."

Her father grunted. "I saw the way he looks at you. I remember when your mother set her sights on me." A nostalgic gleam lit his face. "I bucked and carried on like a wild thing. She just ignored my antics until I finally had to cut her out of the herd and put my brand on her. You got a lot of your mother in you. Now get to work."

His lashes closed, but not before she saw the love shining in those tired old eyes.

"Go away and let me take a nap before your brothers

and sister descend on me for the evening. A man can't even be sick in peace around here.''

"I love you, Dad."

"I know. I love you too. Now get."

She kissed his cheek and stroked his wisps of white hair before stepping out into the hall. Alex was at the far end using the pay phone near the elevator.

He stood alertly, an unpredictable predator in this sterile environment. An incredibly sexy predator, who still had the power to send her pulses skittering at abnormal speed and her heart bumping with longing.

Alex continued speaking, but he watched her approach with dark, unfathomable eyes. She thought about what her father had said and wondered if the problem wasn't just that she'd become set in her ways. Maybe she didn't love Alex enough. Was he really asking too much of her?

He hung up as she reached him.

"How is he?" Alex asked.

"Cranky."

"That's a good sign, don't you think?"

"Yes. A very good sign." And she'd have to think about her father's words. "Who were you talking with?"

"My boss. I told him Matt isn't talking. He's going to talk with the aunt and uncle and see if they can suggest an approach."

"Do you think that's wise if they don't get along?"

"We're fresh out of ideas, Nicki. We need the information Matt has."

The elevator doors opened. The mysterious Jake Collins stepped out and started for the nurses' station.

"I think I just got a whole new idea, Alex. Mr. Collins?"

The man spun with the sinuous grace of a born hunter. She seemed to have predators and hunting on her brain, Nicki thought, as his gaze went from her to Alex and back again.

"Ms. Michaels, Mr. Coughlin. How's your father doing, Ms. Michaels?"

"Pretty well, all things considered. Thank you for asking. Are you here to see someone?"

"Chief Hepplewhite okayed a visit with Matt."

"Why?" Alex demanded.

Tension sparked between them as they sized one another up. Jake Collins finally nodded. "Matt's a troubled young man, but basically a good kid. I like him."

"He did odd jobs for you, didn't he?" Nicki asked.

"Yes."

"Do you think you could get him to talk to you?" she asked.

"Nicki…" Alex began warningly.

"About what, Ms. Michaels?" Jake said at the same time.

"He knows—"

Alex squeezed her arm. Under Jake Collins's watchful eye, he pulled out his badge and handed it to the man. "Matt has information we need. If you could convince him to cooperate, it might save his life."

Enigmatic eyes studied the badge before handing it back. "I'll see what I can do."

Ten minutes later he returned with a shake of his head.

"He won't speak with me either."

"He's scared," Nicki said sadly.

Jake Collins nodded.

"Thanks for trying," Alex said. "We need to go, Nicki."

"Thank you," she told Jake Collins. Despite his cool reserve, she liked him. The wild rumors that had circulated didn't fit with a man who'd visit an injured boy who simply did odd jobs for him. There was more to Jake Collins than anyone was apt to discover, unless he decided to disclose the information.

Collins inclined his head and walked to the elevator with them. They descended in silence, each lost in their own thoughts.

Nicki was totally aware of Alex standing beside her. Her father was right. No other man had ever so completely captivated her interest. But if he could walk away from what they had so easily, was he really worth pursuing?

Outside they parted company with Jake Collins. Nicki wondered if he saw Alex make a careful check of the car before letting her get inside. Would she ever be able to take getting in and out of a vehicle for granted again?

"Now what?"

"Now I take you back to the doctor's," Alex announced, putting the car in gear.

"Do you have a few minutes first?"

Alex tensed. "For what?"

"Don't worry. I wasn't planning to jump your incredible body." His gaze whipped toward her, but she kept her expression blankly innocent. "I just thought it would be worthwhile to go and check out that parcel of land Hope rented to Vic Unsdorf."

Alex was obviously off-balance. Her comment about his body had ruffled his usually steady composure. But he rebounded quickly, choosing to ignore her statement. "You aren't going anywhere near that place, Nicki."

"We need to see what he was doing out there."

"After I drop you off I plan to check it out."

"Aah."

"What does that mean?"

"You're in your hero mode again."

"This is an FBI investigation, Nicki. Believe it or not, I'm a trained professional."

"Oh, I believe it. But you don't have to tuck me safely back at the ranch, Tex. Now that Vic Unsdorf has been arrested, they certainly aren't using the site anymore so where's the danger?''

"Are you kidding? If they were using that property to strip identification from the cars before shipping them out, the place is probably booby-trapped out the yang.''

"But you're going out there,'' she pointed out.

"Only to glance around. Lemmer's going to send a team in the morning to do a thorough sweep.''

"Well, if you're going to just glance around, let me ride out there with you.''

"No.''

"I won't even get out of the car.''

"No.''

"I can act as your backup.''

"No. Positively not.''

"I CAN'T BELIEVE I let you talk me into this.'' Alex fumed to himself.

"You said you were just going to take a quick glance. I'll wait right here in the car.''

"You just bet you will.''

A heavy chain blocked the long driveway leading up to the ramshackle buildings Nicki told him were around the curve out of sight.

"Stay here.''

Alex got out of the car and examined the deep ruts in the gravel driveway. The imprint of a heavy truck tire had hardened in the dirt, leaving a clear impression. Forensics would probably be able to match the print to the truck Vic Unsdorf had been driving. But from the ruts and other marks, it was obvious a lot of vehicles had used the driveway recently.

He studied the gleaming chain and its lock without touching anything. Beyond the dense stand of pines, maples, and what had once been an apple orchard, judging by the number of large, aged trees, he could see that the ground opened up. An enormous old apple was the only tree anywhere near the buildings that stood a few yards up the driveway. A car coming up the driveway would be clearly visible long before it reached the dilapidated barn or the crumbling shell that had once been a house.

A decrepit silo leaned drunkenly to one side, doing a fair imitation of the Leaning Tower of Pisa. It looked as if a stiff wind would bring the structure right down on top of the unpainted barn.

Alex walked back to the car. "I'm going to have a look around. You stay right here. If anything happens, anything at all, you get out of here and go for help, got it?"

Nicki shifted looking suddenly nervous. "Maybe you should wait until tomorrow."

"It'll be fine, Nicki. I'm not going inside." He was pretty sure he knew what he'd find anyhow. This was obviously where they stripped the stolen cars of their VIN numbers and license plates and loaded them onto the car carriers for a drive to the Baltimore Harbor and a boat trip across the ocean.

"Alex?" He stopped and turned back toward her. "Be careful."

He relaxed at the concern so evident in her eyes. Maybe the situation between them wasn't hopeless after all. "Promise."

"See that you do."

She loved him. If he was being arrogant and foolish, so be it—he knew he was right. They'd work out the logistics somehow. The idea of walking away from her was becoming more and more unpalatable.

Since darkness was approaching fast, he skipped a survey of the house, circling the barn as quietly as possible. Up close he saw the main doors had been replaced with new, strong wood and a bright shiny lock. Remembering the last time he'd been inside a barn, he was in no hurry to repeat the process. Every gap on this one had been carefully covered except the loft opening, which hung at least twelve feet above his head.

He eyed the long, low branches of the apple tree. One thick branch extended toward the loft opening, but the idea of climbing the tree held no appeal whatsoever. Still, he really wanted a look inside the building. He started to scan the area around him for a convenient ladder and came to an abrupt halt. A late model dark blue four-door sedan sat parked beside an overgrown juniper bush in the shadow of the barn.

The car matched the description given to him by the two witnesses in the hospital parking lot that day.

Alex approached cautiously, gun drawn. Save for the call of birds, silence pervaded the scene. He laid a hand on the hood and found it cool to the touch. The interior had leather seats and lots of upgrades including an expensive stereo and CD system. A cell phone lay discarded on the passenger's seat. Was this a recently stolen car waiting to be stripped and loaded, or was someone inside the building?

Alex eyed the tree again. He estimated the distance between the tree and the loft opening. Makeable, but there was no telling what was on the other side of that opening.

No point being stupid. Alex headed for the main door. He examined it carefully and saw no sign of explosives. The hinges looked new and well oiled. If the door wasn't locked, it should open quietly. He decided to take a chance. Gun in hand, he inched open the heavy door enough to slip inside.

In the dark shadows that minimized visibility, Alex saw that most of the vast interior had been gutted and converted into a chop shop for cars. Thorton Biggs's work, unless he missed his guess. The man had been a good mechanic.

Three expensive cars lined one wall. Two still had their plates.

The barn was silent, so Alex moved further inside for a closer look. The expensive sports car was in mint condition, this year's model, a shiny silver gray. It had been cleaned and looked ready for transporting. The luxury car behind it was a top-of-the-line model whose interior had yet to be cleaned of personal effects. A woman's silk scarf lay on the backseat beside a tumble of books. He was about to open the door for a quick look inside when he heard heavy footsteps overhead.

Alex cursed. He wasn't alone in the barn. Someone was in the makeshift office in the loft overhead. The person was heading toward the newly constructed set of stairs he'd noticed.

Lights suddenly blazed overhead. Any second now the person would see him. Alex ducked between the two cars. He moved around the car as quietly as possible. The person started down the steps.

He crouched near the rear wheel and waited.

The person crossed quickly to the main door. Alex counted to five and raised his head to peer through the window of the car. The main door shut with a decisive slam. He heard the bolt click into place and knew he was in trouble. But why turn on the lights if you were leaving?

"Not good. Not good at all," he breathed.

He stood and surveyed the room, seeking another exit. There was none that hadn't been boarded over. There was also nowhere to hide in the big open room.

It suddenly occurred to him that if the person headed down the driveway for any reason he'd see Nicki's car.

And Nicki.

Alex slapped the roof of the nearest car in frustration and his gaze was drawn to the backseat. His heart slammed into the back of his throat as he came eye to eye with Thad Osher.

The man lay sprawled on the backseat of the car, still dressed in his police uniform. But it was his new accessories that caused Alex's heart to clench and roll. Several pipe bombs were taped to his shirt, connected to the man's own watch. His mouth had been taped shut with duct tape. In fact his entire body was taped into immobility. Only his eyes were alive with desperation.

Alex started to reach for the door and stopped. Carefully, he examined the car looking for any sign of more explosives. He didn't find any, but caution and the stark terror in the man's eyes made him hesitate to open the door.

"Look, I'm going to have to get help with this," he said. "I'll be back."

Rifle shots echoed in the distance.

Nicki!

Heedless of the possibility that someone else might still be in the loft, Alex sprinted for the stairs. The apple tree was his best hope for escape. He ignored the open invitation of the office door, desperate to reach Nicki.

Standing in the open loft, he realized he had a clear view of the top of her car between the trees. So had whoever just left. They'd gone after Nicki!

Alex eyed the distance between the loft and the tree. Taking a deep breath, he leaped for the branch, praying it would support his weight. It snapped and swayed precariously, but it held. He ignored the jolt to his arms and the stinging pain in his hands and clung.

He managed to wriggle his way toward the sturdier limb from which the branch sprouted. Bug-ridden, half-formed apples rained to the ground with audible thuds. If *he* fell, the splat would be much louder. No matter, he had to reach Nicki.

He shinnied toward the crotch of the tree when a movement near the silo caught his attention. Between the leaves and the rapidly encroaching darkness, he couldn't make out any features, but someone had just entered the silo.

Alex scrambled the rest of the way down, ignoring a multitude of new scratches and scrapes. He drew his gun. The silo would have to wait.

Or not.

The figure came flying back out as Alex reached the ground. The person raced toward the barn and the spot where he stood.

Alex dropped into a crouch, training the gun on the running figure. It took him a moment to recognize the dark hair streaming out behind her. Nicki ran toward him as if the devil was on her heels.

Alex rose. She gave a startled yelp and came to a jerky stop.

"Alex!"

"Nicki! Thank God! You were supposed to wait in the car."

"Never mind that. You have to come. There's a man in the silo with a bomb taped to his chest."

Chapter Twelve

"What man?" Alex demanded.

"I don't know who he is, but he was in that lineup with you at the police station."

"Go back to the car! Get to a phone and—"

"I can't, Alex. Someone shot the car to pieces. The tires are gone, the windshield, the—"

"Were you hurt?"

"I wasn't in it at the time. I had to use the facilities." She shrugged, but her lower lip quivered. "Since there weren't any I opted for a tree. I was just going back to the car when someone started shooting. I crept over here trying to find you."

Alex swore. There was probably a phone inside the barn, but he had no way of knowing how long before the place would blow up—taking Sergeant Thad Osher along with it.

"Osher's in the barn rigged to a bomb as well," he told Nicki. "We'll have to try to go across the fields to get to your dad's house." Then he remembered the car parked next to the barn. There had been a cell phone inside it on the seat.

"Come on."

The car was still there. Alex smashed through a side window with the butt of his gun and unlocked the door. "I'll hot-wire it and get you out of here."

"The gunman will hear the engine."

"I know. Get in the back of the car on the floor. Call for backup while I try to get us out of here. If anything goes wrong, I don't want him to know you're in the car. No matter what happens, don't show yourself, okay?"

"You aren't invincible," she protested.

"No, but I have a gun and I can fire back. Trust me, Nicki."

Despite the fear that had dilated her eyes, she nodded. "Always."

She climbed in the back and hunched down over the phone. The car finally caught with a roar of sound. Alex wasn't nearly as proficient at this as Matt Williams probably was. But before he could put it in gear, a bullet whizzed through the back window, exiting through the front windshield.

Since he couldn't go forward, Alex threw the sedan in reverse, but a shot passed through the broken window narrowly missing his head. Two more shots were directed into the engine, easily tearing through the metal frame. The next one might hit Nicki. The guy was standing right behind them by the corner of the barn. Alex stopped the car.

"Stay down," he warned Nicki without moving his lips.

"Get out of the car!" Pavel Toskov ordered.

Alex raised his hands and stepped to the ground, shutting the door behind him. If Ilona's brother didn't shoot him out of hand, Alex might be able to buy some time. Maybe enough for the cavalry to arrive.

"It's over, Pavel."

"Drop your gun."

Exaggerating every movement, Alex did as he was told. Pavel Toskov looked quite capable of shooting him without a qualm.

"And your backup weapon."

Alex slipped the knife from his ankle sheath.

"Your other gun," Pavel demanded.

"This is all I'm carrying."

Pavel didn't look like he believed Alex. "Where's your girlfriend?"

"In a safe house along with the Williams boy. He's talking, Pavel. So's Vic Unsdorf. It's all over. Why not take your chances with a jury?"

A sneer marred Pavel's otherwise handsome features. "Thanks just the same, but I have other plans."

"What? Blowing up Osher and your other mechanic over in the silo?" He took a stab at the man's identity.

Toskov looked momentarily startled. His gaze flitted to the silo, and immediately returned to Alex before he could take advantage of the momentary lapse.

"Loose ends," he said with a shrug. "Like you. This way."

He motioned with his head. The gun didn't waver, not even when the car engine suddenly revved to life. Steam billowed from under the hood as the vehicle suddenly careened wildly toward them in reverse.

Only the top of her hair showed as Nicki crouched low behind the steering wheel and backed the car right at them. Pavel swung the rifle toward her. Alex lunged forward in a low tackle. The gun discharged. Nicki lost control and the sedan plowed into the side of the barn with alarming force. There was an explosion of sound as the air bag deployed.

Pavel had retained his grip on the rifle despite their fall. Alex felt the heat across his back as the weapon discharged harmlessly. Though he outweighed Pavel by a good twenty pounds, Pavel was surprisingly strong.

The rifle discharged once more before Alex was able to wrest it from his grip. The scent of gasoline assaulted his nostrils. Alex landed a lucky blow, stunning some of the fight out of Pavel. He used that moment for a glance toward the barn and the car. Nicki was slumped against the deflated air bag.

His insides locked. Gasoline ran from beneath the damaged car. If the bombs taped to Osher went off now, Nicki would die in the resulting explosion. Alex jumped to his feet, rifle in hand, and sprinted for the car.

Pavel also scrambled up. He ran in the opposite direction toward the remains of the house. Nicki was stirring when Alex reached for the door handle. The door was wedged shut due to the impact of the crash. The sour stench of gasoline was overpowering. Any spark could set the whole thing off—and the car's engine was still running.

"Nicki, turn your face away!"

Alex smashed in the glass window beside her with the butt of the rifle. White powder from the airbag covered the interior. He cleared away the glass so he could pull Nicki free of the car. Deciding that turning off the engine might be as risky as letting it run, he led her away from the car.

"Are you hurt?"

"I'm fine. Just shaken."

"Let's go!"

"Wait! I left the cell phone in the car."

"You got through, didn't you?"

"Yes."

"Then leave it."

"What about Pavel?"

"He won't get far on foot. We need to get away from here before—"

The concussion from the sudden explosion shook the ground. They staggered as the remains of the house blew apart in a giant fireball that lit the night sky.

"The barn or silo will be next. Come on!" Alex grabbed Nicki and began to run down the driveway toward the sound of approaching sirens. Lee Garvey met them at the tree line. He'd driven his cruiser around Nicki's car and through the chain that blocked the driveway entrance. More sirens screamed in the distance.

Quickly, Alex outlined the situation to Lee. "I don't know what happened to Pavel. He may have been caught in the explosion or he might have triggered it and run elsewhere. He's armed."

Lee swore.

"Know anything about bombs?"

"I had some explosives training in the military, but that was a long time ago," Lee said with a worried frown.

"Let's hope it all comes back to you. We've got to try and do something for Osher and the other guy Nicki found if we can. I don't know how much time they have left."

"That much I can probably figure out. Let's go."

"No!" Nicki grabbed Alex by the arm. "You can't go back up there!"

"We have to, Nicki."

"You'll be killed!"

He understood her panic. Fear feasted on his insides too. Every instinct urged him to snatch her and run as far from this nightmare as he could.

"We won't be killed." He tried for a smile and inclined his head at Lee. "This twerp has to marry my sister, and I plan to marry you."

"Alex! No!"

"Not the reaction I'd like to my proposal."

She didn't smile. Her features were desperate. "Wait here for the bomb squad!"

He gripped her arms. "I can't, Nicki. This is my job." He thrust the rifle into her hands, kissed her mouth and raced after Lee.

Her voice chased after him. "If you get killed, I'll never forgive you!"

Alex kept running. She loved him. And if he survived

this, Denver or not, he was marrying Nicki just as soon as he could.

"GOOD MORNING. Or I guess technically I should say good afternoon." Dr. Leslie Martin greeted Nicki with a warm smile when Nicki stepped into her kitchen with Ginger in her arms.

"Hi." She set the cat down and Ginger promptly leaped onto the table to reach the kitchen window.

"Bad cat. You know to stay off the table."

"She's all right," Leslie said. "Is Alex still sleeping?"

Nicki blushed. "No, he's just finishing his shower."

Actually, it had started out as her shower, but Nicki wasn't going to explain that part to Leslie. The doctor hadn't bothered offering them separate bedrooms when they'd arrived on her doorstep early this morning, bedraggled and exhausted. Just as well, since Nicki had clung to Alex all night long. Her relief that he was alive and uninjured was so intense that she kept waking to be sure he was really there and not dead.

She was certain last night was the longest night she'd ever spent, waiting for the bomb experts to arrive and defuse the bombs taped to the two men. The whole time she waited, she kept expecting the barn or the silo to blow up, destroying her entire world.

When Alex woke this morning and joined her in the shower, he'd showed her how alive he really was. She was sure the evidence of their lovemaking was emblazoned across her face.

"You and Alex made the front page again," Leslie said with a smile. "Another nice shot."

Nicki stared at the grainy black-and-white photo prominently displayed on the front page of the paper. She'd launched herself into Alex's arms, just as the photographer snapped the picture. All the love and terror she'd felt were exposed for the world to see. But it was the welcoming joy in Alex's expression, that caused the hitch in her breathing now.

"To update you," Leslie said, distracting her. "Your father is doing remarkably well and sends his love. The oncologist was in to see him to discuss possible protocols. Your brothers want you to call them immediately if not sooner. Those are Brent's exact words. And Gavin said something about beating Alex to a pulp?"

"Oh."

"I hope he'll give me a day to recover first," Alex said coming up behind Nicki. "I think I've had all the beatings I can handle for some time to come."

Nicki leaned back against the hard wall of his chest and managed a wry smile. "Who you? Naw, you're a tough guy, you can take it. Where are they?" she asked Leslie.

The woman smiled at their foolishness. "They were at your father's place. Apparently, the authorities recovered enough of Pavel's body for a positive identification. The FBI doesn't believe there's any need for further protective custody."

"Do they know why the house blew up?" Alex asked.

"If they do, no one's told me. Speculation is that the basement of that house was where the bombs were being made."

"That would explain why the explosion was so big," Alex said thoughtfully.

"I understand you and Lee played hero," Leslie continued, "staying with Thad Osher until the bomb squad got there."

Alex shrugged. Nicki shuddered and headed for the coffeepot. "When Lee realized the bombs wouldn't go off until midnight, he decided not to tamper with anything," Alex explained. "We had plenty of time to wait for the experts, and we didn't know then that Pavel was dead. We didn't want him coming back in and setting them off ahead of schedule.''

"Who was the man in the silo?" Leslie asked.

"The other mechanic working on the stolen cars. He's catatonic from fear. Even if he recovers, I don't know how much help he's going to be. Neither he nor Osher will walk away from this incident without mental scars. Having explosives taped to your chest all that time, never sure they wouldn't explode at any minute, has to be a mind-altering incident.''

"I hope it alters Osher's attitude," Nicki said, handing Alex a cup of coffee and taking a sip from her own.

"Well, if you two will excuse me, I have patients to see," Leslie said. "Help yourself to food or whatever you need. My car keys are on the counter.''

"Thank you."

Alex nodded. "I don't know how we're going to repay you.''

Leslie waved that off and disappeared downstairs. Nicki turned to Alex. "Why are you frowning?"

"Was I frowning?"

"Either that or your face is pleating."

Alex offered her one of his slow, sexy smiles. How crazy that it only took one look from him to start that weak feeling in the pit of her stomach. She told her blood to stop racing in anticipation, but her body had its own ideas.

"Have I told you yet this morning how beautiful you are?" Alex asked.

"I think you mentioned it earlier, but feel free to mention it as often as you like."

His face grew serious. "How about every day for the rest of our lives?"

Her foolish heart skipped a beat, stuttered and went into overdrive. "I'd like that."

"Then we'll make it happen. I love you, Nicki."

"But—"

"No buts. A simple statement of fact."

Nicki smiled. "Okay. I love you too."

"Good. See how nicely that works out?" He jumped suddenly. Ginger parrumphed and began stropping his leg.

"Cat, you're going to scare me to death one of these days."

"She just doesn't want to be left out," Nicki explained.

He set his cup down and bent to stroke the cat. "Sorry, Ginger, but you have to learn to share her."

Nicki knew she was grinning like a fool but she couldn't seem to stop. "I'm sure Ginger will be willing. After all, she gets another human to bug."

"Good point. I have a question."

"Yes?"

"Do you have some sort of fetish for driving vehicles into barns? I mean, it's not a big problem or anything unless it escalates to other types of buildings in which case—"

Nicki made to hit him and he grabbed her arm, pulling her tightly against his body, a low chuckle rumbling from his throat.

"I love to hear you laugh," she told him.

"Then I'll do it more often. I do love you, Nic. More than anything. Even Denver."

"I don't want you to give up—"

His mouth silenced her so effectively she was weak all over when he finally let her go.

"If I didn't have to report in this morning, I'd drag you right back to that bedroom."

"We could race," she tempted him in a voice that sounded as breathless as she felt.

He stroked the side of her face. "How did I end up with such an insatiable woman?"

"Luck?"

"Definitely." He reached for his coffee cup and took a long swallow, but she was absurdly pleased to note that his hand was none too steady either.

"We have a lot to discuss," she warned him.

"I know. Like how you don't follow orders."

"Or how you take foolish risks?" Alex shook his head, but she saw the start of another smile at the corners of his eyes.

"How about we discuss this over dinner."

"You mean like a real date?"

"Yeah." His expression was somewhat abashed. "A date would be a novel approach in our relationship don't you think?"

"True, but our relationship has been pretty interesting, you have to admit."

"If you like guns and bombs going off."

Nicki shuddered. "I don't."

"Me either."

Not until they were in Leslie's car did Nicki get back to her original question. "So what were you frowning about?"

"Hmm? Oh." He gazed at her thoughtfully before pulling out onto Perry Road. "Something doesn't feel right. Like there's a piece missing."

"Ilona for one. Do you think her brother killed her? She could have been in that basement you know."

Alex shook his head. "They'd know by now, Nicki. No, I'm sure she'll surface somewhere now that her brother is dead."

"Then what's bothering you?"

"I keep thinking about Pavel's expression when I mentioned the man in the silo. He seemed surprised."

"Maybe because he didn't think you'd discovered the mechanic at that point."

"Maybe." Alex didn't look convinced. "Would you

mind if I drop you at your dad's house without coming inside?''

"Coward.''

"You betcha. You have two very large brothers.''

"Don't worry, they wouldn't dare beat up the man I plan to marry.''

"Hmm. I like the sound of that.''

"So do I. Do you think—that is, do you want a long engagement?'' She found she was holding her breath.

Alex smiled gently in immediate understanding. "How about tomorrow? City Hall? Say sixish?''

Nicki relaxed, content in the knowledge he was only partially teasing. "Maybe not quite that fast, and I'd rather have a church wedding.''

"So would I. Soon.'' He looked at her meaningfully. "I'd like to see your dad walk you up the aisle.''

Her eyes burned with unexpected tears. "Yes.''

"Let's make that part of the plan.''

As Alex turned the car up the drive leading to her father's house, Nicki asked the question that had been troubling her.

"Alex? Who was Ilona having the affair with? Darrin Lange or Thad Osher?''

"I'd guess both, maybe Unsdorf as well, but Lange for certain. I'll find out what Osher had to say when I check in.''

"But you think it was Pavel who beat Ilona up.''

"We're guessing right now, but Pavel did have a history of using his fists when he was angry.''

"So she lied about that too.''

Alex raised his eyebrows at her angry tone. "Remember, we're still piecing this together. I know she's your friend—''

"Is she? I'm starting to wonder. If she lied about who hurt her and who her lover was, what else might she have lied about? You're pretty sure she was helping her brother with this stolen car ring, aren't you?"

"Helping may be too strong a word, but I think it's safe to assume she at least fed information to him. He may have forced her, Nicki. She could still be a victim, at least in part."

"I want to give her the benefit of the doubt too, Alex. But I think I'd like to talk to Matt again. Alone this time."

Alex turned off the engine. He was silent for several seconds, obviously pondering her request.

"You think she shot Thorton Biggs don't you?" he asked abruptly.

Nicki nodded unhappily, not surprised he'd come to the same conclusion. "It always bothered me that she was so insistent that you were the one who shot him. I'm feeling pretty stupid and a little used right now, Alex, but it finally occurred to me that we only have her word there was a man in that alley that night. What if she lied? What if Ilona and Thorton Biggs were the only ones back there and Matt saw the whole thing?"

Alex tapped the steering wheel thoughtfully. "Matt would know who she was because essentially, he worked for her brother."

Nicki nodded. "Say Matt sees her kill Thorton Biggs. He knows she'll probably tell her brother."

"Which she does. Pavel decides to blow the kid up, or at least scare him into silence by blowing up his aunt's house." Alex nodded. "It fits, Nicki. But what's Ilona's motive for killing Biggs?"

"You said it yourself, a falling-out among thieves. Or in this case, maybe a spat between lovers. Someone did beat her. Maybe it was Biggs."

Alex nodded. "I like the way it fits."

"Unfortunately, so do I. Ilona must have seen you loitering across the street that night."

"Or she's the one who arranged for me to be there that night."

Nicki looked stunned, but began to nod. "She talked to my sister a few days before she arrived at my place. What if it wasn't Unsdorf, but Ilona who convinced Hope to call and pretend to be me? Ilona knew about our previous relationship."

"Two birds with one stone."

They shared an excited look of understanding.

"Ilona knew I was undercover because of her relationship with Darren Lange. If you had identified me as the murderer, I would have been pulled from the case, buying her brother additional time to finish the last shipment."

"And by setting me up to act as the witness to Biggs's murder, she created her own alibi," Nicki said sadly.

"This is still just conjecture, Nic. We don't have any proof," he reminded her.

"Sure we do. We have Matt."

"If we can get him to talk. I'm going to come inside with you after all. I need to use your telephone."

"Going to check on Matt?"

Alex nodded. "Until we pick Ilona up, I don't want them to relax the guard on him."

Chills chased themselves down her back. Matt was in considerable danger if they were right. She opened the front door and stepped inside.

The silence inside the house felt downright spooky. Nicki frowned. "Gavin? Brent? Hope?" She looked at Alex. "They must have gone on to the hospital."

Alex strode into the dining room. "There's a note on the table, Nic. Right next to our picture." She heard the smile in his voice. "They did go to the hospital."

"Okay. While you use the telephone, I want to run upstairs and get a pair of earrings my sister borrowed from me."

Nicki shivered as she ran lightly up the stairs. Her nerves were shot, no question about it, but she had to stop feeling so fanciful. The house was not strangely brooding. It was simply empty.

Yet something felt out of place.

She stepped into Hope's bedroom and sniffed the air, aware of a lingering scent of perfume. It smelled heavier than the sort of stuff Hope usually wore. Frowning, she rummaged through her sister's jewelry box until she located her favorite pair of crystal earrings. She paused to slip one in her ear.

A floorboard creaked behind her.

Nicki whirled so fast she knocked a bottle of bath oil to the floor. The bottle cracked, sending the contents oozing into the rug.

"Hello, Nicki," Ilona said. The gun in her hand was aimed at Nicki's chest. At this distance, she couldn't miss. "Get over there on the bed."

Ilona's face was a map of ugly dark bruises. The damage was much worse than the first time she'd come seeking Nicki's help. Her perfectly coiffed hair was now horribly tangled around her face. She had obviously stepped from Hope's closet where a knapsack lay on the floor beside a pile of clothing. Was that a length of pipe sticking out of the knapsack?

Ilona wore one of Hope's long-sleeved silk blouses and matching skirt. The blouse wasn't completely buttoned, as if Nicki's arrival had interrupted her while she was getting dressed. The fit was poor and the style definitely didn't suit Ilona's usual exacting sense of fashion.

But she continued to hold the gun rock-steady.

"Ilona, what happened?" Nicki couldn't stop the wash of sympathy that swept her. Ilona's left eye was mostly closed, her lip was split and swollen, and if Nicki wasn't mistaken, her nose was broken.

"Never mind. Just do what I say."

Nicki didn't move. "It was Pavel, wasn't it? Your brother did this to you."

"Get over on the bed."

"It's okay. You don't have to be afraid anymore, Ilona. Pavel can't hurt you ever again. He was killed in an explosion last night."

Ilona laughed. The hideous sound sent new chills racing up Nicki's arms. "I know that," Ilona said. "Who do you think triggered the explosion?"

Nicki gasped at the savage expression of satisfaction on Ilona's once pretty face.

"Don't look so appalled. He deserved to die. Or are you surprised because I don't fit your boyfriend's profile? You know, bombers—white male, middle-aged, reclusive, highly intelligent..." She laughed again.

"Are you saying you made those bombs?"

Ilona inclined her head toward the knapsack. "Every—single—one."

Nicki stared in horror at her former friend. "We thought Pavel—"

"Pavel only liked to use his fists on people who were weaker than he was." Ilona's features knotted in anger. "All those big brave men willing to screw me, but not one willing to go up against Pavel and his temper. But I showed them. I showed them all. Pavel has always been nervous of my interest in explosives. He was right to be nervous," she said in satisfaction. "Get that look off your face! You were always such an innocent," she sneered.

"But why—?"

"Because I hated him. Do you understand? I hate them all. Users, every one. But I knew how it was going to end this time. Pavel's rages were getting too frequent. He was filled with self-importance because of his ties to certain people. He was a fool."

Her eyes glazed with righteous indignation. "He had the contacts, true. But he forgot who put this all together time and again. All Pavel could do was run the shipping end of things. I took care of the recruitment. I supervised everything—even to finding that helpful little FBI agent who willingly looked up potential personnel for me so I wouldn't hire any criminals."

She laughed again, with a bitter edge. "I knew exactly who to trust thanks to that philandering fool. The female body is a wonderful weapon, Nicki. Too bad you never learned that lesson."

"You set Alex up for Biggs's murder, didn't you?"

"Of course. I had Unsdorf convince Hope that Alex was pining away for you. The hard part was arranging the romantic reunion at precisely the right time."

"I don't understand. Why did you kill Thorton Biggs?"

Ilona shoved at a dirty strand of hair. "He was a poor lover and he was getting too hard to control. He was afraid of Pavel. Once I had Unsdorf panting after me, I didn't need Biggs any longer. It would have worked perfectly if you'd done your part. I'm not at all happy with you, Nicki. You nearly ruined everything."

Nicki knew she had to continue to stall. Sooner or later, Alex would come looking for her. Obviously, Ilona didn't realize Nicki wasn't alone in the house.

"Why kill me?"

"You can testify I was at your place the night of Biggs's murder."

"But I told…"

"Your family. Yes, I know. I'm afraid when I finish here your family will suffer a string of terrible losses. I have a few more bombs, you see. Your father is going to survive all his children. Ironic, isn't it? Now get on the bed. I'd rather blow you up than blow you away, but I'm an excellent shot."

Nicki trembled, but she stood her ground. The overwhelming smell of the bath oil at her feet made her want to gag. And a flicker of motion at the door caught her eye. She kept her focus on Ilona. "Why should I make this easy for you? Either way, I'm dead."

"True. Have it your way."

THE CRASH OVERHEAD, brought Alex's eyes to the ceiling. "Hold on, John."

The hairs on the back of his neck prickled in a warning that kept him from calling out to Nicki. He carried the handset with him to the staircase. The faint sound of a woman's shrill laugh drifted down. It definitely hadn't come from Nicki.

"John? Get me some backup out here fast. No sirens. I think Ilona's upstairs with Nicki."

Alex disconnected. Hepplewhite could have someone here in a matter of minutes, but Nicki might not have minutes. Not if what Vic Unsdorf was saying was true. Vic had decided to turn state's evidence in exchange for a reduced sentence. And what he'd told Hepplewhite made Alex's blood run cold.

Alex crept up the stairs, silently, testing for loose boards that might give him away. As he neared the top, he knew he needn't have bothered. Ilona's strident voice carried plainly.

"Now get on the bed or I'll shoot you here and now."

Alex drew his gun. He heard Nicki give a soothing response. Good girl. She was stalling for time. But Ilona was a ruthless killer. Nicki had no idea the danger she was in. He had to force himself to move slowly down the hall toward the open door.

"Why should I make this easy for you? Either way, I'm dead," Nicki was saying.

Alex peered around the corner. The women stood sideways to the door. He was pretty sure Nicki spotted him as Ilona responded.

"True. Have it your way."

"Okay, I'm moving," Nicki said. She took a sideways step toward the bed. "But I don't want to die. What if I promise to lie for you?"

Ilona sneered. "Are you going to beg like that stupid cop when Pavel tied him up for me?"

Alex was relieved that Nicki didn't look at him. Instead, she smartly moved to the foot of the bed so she was facing him. Predictably, Ilona followed the movement with her entire body. That put her back to Alex—exactly what he needed.

Alex stuck his gun in his waistband and rushed forward. He grabbed Ilona from behind in a fierce grip designed to pin her arms into immobility. At the same time, Nicki threw herself on the bed. The gun discharged, the bullet tearing through the bedroom window.

Like her brother, Ilona was surprisingly strong. She struggled violently to free herself, still retaining her hold on the weapon. Nicki grabbed her sister's radio off the nightstand and brought it down across Ilona's gun hand with enough force to jar Alex's arm and make the woman scream in rage and pain. The gun fell harmlessly to the carpeting.

"My arm! You broke my arm!"

"Good!" Nicki bent and retrieved the gun, aiming it at the woman in a businesslike fashion. "If you don't stop struggling, I'm going to break something else," she promised.

Ilona stopped moving, but Alex didn't relax his hold. He found himself almost smiling in admiration of the steely determination in Nicki's eyes.

"Impressive."

"Hey, any idiot can shoot one of these. All you have to do is squeeze the trigger."

"Maybe so," he agreed, "but not many people are as proficient with a radio."

"Remember that," she warned.

"Yes ma'am."

"What took you so long? I was running out of conversation up here."

"I think I'm getting too old for fieldwork," Alex said wryly.

NICKI SAT BACK in the comfortable restaurant chair, staring at the man she loved.

"…so my boss in Denver understands and he's going to see what he can do about a transfer from that end. Lemmer is willing to keep me on at his office if we can work everything out with the powers that be," Alex said triumphantly.

"If you'd bothered to tell *me* your plans, I could have saved you all that work." Nicki stated.

"How?"

"I had a long talk with my family. As long as we can be married here and I can make periodic trips home, there's no reason we can't live in Denver. Brent's going to quit his job and come back to work with Hope and the horses. Gavin and I are going to help with the financial side, and all of them have wished us well."

"What about your shop?"

"The insurance will cover most of the damage, and I'm thinking that I'm really not too old to go back to school. What do you think?"

Alex leaned forward and took her hands in his. "Your happiness is all that matters to me, Nicki. I don't care where we live."

Her heart soared. "Me either. They have good schools in Denver, don't they?"

"I'm sure they do."

"Good. I love you, Alex."

"I love you, too."

"Good evening."

Nicki looked up to find Jake Collins standing beside their table.

"I trust everything is satisfactory this evening."

"We were working on it," Alex told him a bit gruffly.

Jake inclined his head. His lips curved slightly upward in acknowledgment of the rebuke. "Glad to hear it."

"Have you seen Matt?" Nicki asked.

Jake nodded. She was pretty sure she saw sadness in his dark eyes.

"He still won't talk?"

"No."

"Does he understand that no charges are pending against him?" Alex asked.

"Yes."

"Give him some time," Nicki said softly. "He's only a boy. I think he was badly scared. I wish he had someone he could trust."

"He does." Jake said enigmatically. "Enjoy your meal."

They watched him move to a table across the room.

"Strange man," Alex said with a frown.

"It's obvious that he cares about Matt." Nicki scolded. "He's just very deep."

Alex tipped his head to one side. "Are you implying that I'm shallow?"

She smiled willing to put aside the topic of Matt for now. She reached for his hand and squeezed gently. "No, you're perfect."

"I like the sounds of that."

"Did I mention that my father wants to be a grandfather?"

Alex raised his eyebrows. "Now?"

"Well, I think he'd like us to hurry."

"What about school? What do *you* want, Nic?"

"Besides you? I think I could handle more than a classroom assignment. We aren't getting any younger, you know. A boy and a girl would be nice, but I'll take whatever we're given, I'm not fussy."

Alex shoved aside his plate. "Do you want dessert?"

"Oh, yes." She grinned naughtily. "But I think we'd shock the inhabitants of Fools Point if I started on you here and now."

Alex motioned to their waiter. "Check, please."

"Does this mean our evening is over?"

"Our evening is just about to get started."

Looking For More Romance?

Visit Romance.net

Look us up on-line at: http://www.romance.net

Check in daily for these and other exciting features:

Hot off the press

View all current titles, and purchase them on-line.

What do the stars have in store for you?

Horoscope

Hot deals

Exclusive offers available only at Romance.net

Plus, don't miss our interactive quizzes, contests and bonus gifts.

PWEB

HARLEQUIN®

I N T R I G U E®

presents

LOVERS UNDER COVER

*Dangerous opponents, explosive lovers—
these men are a criminal's worst nightmare
and a woman's fiercest protector!*

A two-book miniseries
by RITA Award-nominated author

Carly Bishop

They're bad boys with badges, who've
infiltrated a clandestine operation. But to
successfully bring down the real offenders,
they must risk their lives to defend the
women they love.

In April 2000 look for:

NO BRIDE BUT HIS (#564)
and
NO ONE BUT YOU coming soon!

Available at your favorite retail outlet.

HARLEQUIN®
Makes any time special ™